MORE DARK THAN SHARK

: but one deadly fin

2 ⟶

MORE DARK THAN SHARK

- COMMENTARIES
  BY RICK POYNOR

- DESIGNED
  BY MALCOLM GARRETT
  AT (assorted iMaGes) Ⓐⁱ

- PHOTOGRAPHY
  BY MARTIN AXON

- ADDITIONAL PHOTOGRAPHY
  BY DAVID BUCKLAND

ff

faber and faber
AN ⟨OPAL⟩ PRODUCTION

ENO & MILLS

4 First published in 1986 by Faber and Faber Ltd., 3 Queen Square, London WC1N 3AU
In association with Opal Ltd., 330 Harrow Road, London W9 2HP

Designed by Malcolm Garrett,
with Steven Appleby and Damian Wayling
at Assorted iMaGes, London.

Photography of colour images by Martin Axon.
Cover photography by David Buckland.
Typesetting by The Printed Word, London.
Printed and bound by Conzett and Huber AG, Zurich.

Cover designed at Assorted iMaGes incorporating
images by Russell Mills

Background images are details from the painting:

SOUND – SHADOW
1985
670 × 920
Acrylic, nail varnish, interfacing, on plaster on board

Inset images are details from the following paintings
(left to right):
back cover
BABY'S ON FIRE, SOME OF THEM ARE OLD (a),
BIG DAY, GOLDEN HOURS (b), GOLDEN HOURS (a)
front cover
SEVEN DEADLY FINNS (b)

British Library Cataloguing in Publication Data.

Eno, Brian
More dark than shark.
1. Music, Popular (Songs, etc.)—Texts
I. Title   II. Mills, Russell
784.5'05   ML54.6

ISBN 0-571-13810-1
ISBN 0-571-13883-7 Pbk

CONTENTS

...BECAUSE...

In his critical and analytical writings T. S. Eliot has often suggested, in diverse permutations, the possibility that the poem a reader reads may appear to be better than the poem the poet has written. While an author may consciously attempt to imbue a piece of writing with specific meanings, a reader's interpretation of that writing cannot be predicted. Similarly, Eliot's 'auditory imagination' (and its potential for tangential associations) can be applied to visual images which can also generate a multitude of images beyond those that the artist has consciously embedded within a work.

I was interested in ideas – not merely in visual products. I wanted to put painting once again at the service of the mind. *Marcel Duchamp.*[1]

These observations and their inherent possibilities were the mental touchstones from which, unconsciously at first, this book evolved.

Prior to my entry into the Illustration Department of the Royal College of Art in London, in 1974, I had not been especially interested in illustration as a separate medium divorced from the other arts. I was as confused as most art students are when attempting to pinpoint a specific future or career; all I knew for certain was that I was not entirely sure of my ideas or talents and would benefit from a further period of experiment and study.

Having considered the options of several postgraduate courses in fine art and printmaking I eventually discovered that the illustration course at the RCA was exceptional in that it did not promote a dogma or philosophy of teaching, as did most others, but instead offered a sympathetic commitment to the development of students as individuals in a laboratory experiment environment in which diverse personal ideas and obsessions could be thoroughly explored. The department had also produced some individuals whose works were distinctly unique and stimulating; Sue Coe, Stewart MacKinnon and the Brothers Quay being those who I felt closest to in terms of historical references/preferences, sensibilities and possible future directions; I felt that their ideas echoed my own and their presence in the Illustration Department strongly suggested which course I should follow. Coe and MacKinnon, though employing very different stylistic methods were both committed to investigations of the strengths of 'social realism' through painting, collage, drawing and polemic; the Brothers Quay manipulated collage and film in their collaborative explorations of psychological 'inner worlds', and in doing so they produced some of the strongest and most inspired poetic personal images that I have seen.[2]

Following such a strong legacy, my three years spent at the RCA were made even more rewarding by the company of several more very talented, interesting and inquisitive fellow students,[3] for whom, like myself, curiosity was paramount. In such a lively environment, I quickly became aware of, and was reluctantly sympathetic to, the generally held view of contemporary illustration, which was and I believe still is prevalent; that it is overly reliant on and concerned with stylistic mediocrity and superficial techniques, and sadly almost totally devoid of intellectual content. I found that most illustration was ignored because, quite simply, it was wholly ignorable. Those producing, and similarly those who commission, illustration had not escaped from the obvious and literal definition of illustration: i.e. to elucidate by means of pictures; to clear up; to explain clearly, etc. Adherence to these comfortable and constraining definitions has generally resulted in images which merely imitate rather than complement in a manner likely to enlarge upon the already known or stated. Within the small world of illustration I believe this attitude to be redundant. I would prefer to look back to now obsolete definitions in an attempt to formulate new ways of perceiving the future possibilities of illustration; 'to illustrate' also used to mean to illuminate; to make lustrous, or bright; to beautify; to adorn; to set in a good light; to confer honour or distinction upon. Similarly, it also meant illumination (spiritual, intellectual or physical). The dilemma of illustration extends into all other areas of the arts, and I believe will continue to do so as long as those practising the arts and those responsible for their administration continue to live with and accept the compartmentalizing of the various disciplines. The limitations created by the increased promotion of specialization and the training of art students to fit into the nebulous so-called market place of industry is a complete and absurd contradiction of what I believe to be the essence and purpose of art, which is to probe and question, suggest and prompt ideas and issues in ways and means usually outside the scope of 'workaday' experiences.

However, to return to the question of illustration, and the stigma of subservience that it has acquired in relation to the other arts. Though initially disillusioning, this stigma also served to prompt me into analysing the situation in an attempt to find alternative ways of thinking and less literal modes of working which might extend the possibilities which I believed (and still believe) to be inherent in the marriage of image and text/idea.

One reason for illustration's apparent low standing in the arts is based on a snobbery which considers that because a work is commissioned then it cannot be valid or 'pure'. This is a view generally

1 *Interview by James Johnson Sweeney.* **The Bulletin of the Museum of Modern Art,** *Vol. XII No. 4 – 5 1946.*

2 *Sue Coe is based in New York and is still working in 'Social Realism' and related areas of concern. Stewart MacKinnon is now a film-maker and lecturer. The Brothers Quay are still producing films, predominantly a hybrid of puppet animation and various documentaries. See Sue Coe and Holly Metz,* **How to Commit Suicide in South Africa** *(Raw Books and Graphics, New York, 1983); and* **Paintings and Drawings: Sue Coe** *(Scarecrow Press, New York, 1985) with an introduction by Russell Mills.*

3 *Chlöe Cheese, Robert Ellis, Anne Howeson, Robert Mason, Muriel McKenzie, Ian Pollock, and Liz Pyle.*

held by 'fine artists' and art critics alike, most of whom seem to have a convenient mental block regarding their knowledge of art history when any discourse which touches on the subject of 'applied' or 'commercial' art ensues. In fact, it is only relatively recently in historical terms that this attitude has prevailed. Up until the 1940s and 1950s it was still considered respectable and valid for painters such as Sutherland and Nash to accept commissions to illustrate and design wine labels, transport posters, menus, etc. And if one looks back to those artists who are generally considered to be the most important of the past, such as da Vinci, Raphael, Caravaggio, Turner, Constable, Stubbs, *ad infinitum*, it will be discovered that a great number of their most important works were commissioned. Laslo Moholy-Nagy, another multi-talented artist was commissioned to produce typography, design, shop displays for Simpsons of Piccadilly, posters, textiles, advertisements, and he even designed the original, classic Parker 51 fountain pen in 1941. Kurt Schwitters is another, who while also producing innovative paintings, collages, sculpture and phonetic poetry was, in the mid-1920s responsible for all the design work for the municipalities of Hannover and Karlsruhe, and in 1924 after founding The Merz Werbezentraler Advertising Agency, Schwitters undertook a whole range of advertisements for Pelikan Inks. In 1927, he co-founded the 'ring neuer webegestralter' an association of leading European advertising agencies. To Schwitters nothing was 'mean'. Examples such as these abound throughout art history. So it seems that up until the relatively recent past, the role of the artist was wider in its application, implying that any means of expression and creativity was open to exploration and experiment. Artists didn't look upon commissions or the patronage system simply as a means of earning a living but also as an opportunity through which personal ideas and skills could be extended and seen more widely.

In attempting to redress this situation, for my own understanding, particularly focusing on illustration, the thoughts gleaned from the wide history of art led me to some of the sources which had, in varying degrees influenced and shaped my thinking.

A book which I had first read when I was about 14–15 years old, and whose possibilities had lain dormant in my brain since then, suddenly became of great importance; this was *The Life and Opinions of Tristram Shandy Gentleman* by Laurence Sterne.[4] On re-discovery, this episodic, comic novel struck me as being an apt reference for many of the directions I wished to pursue. In literary terms it anticipates the 'stream of consciousness' writing of Joyce and pre-empts the cyclical absurdities of writers such as Roussel, Jarry and Flann O'Brien. As an object it is distinctly interesting as it employs visual devices and an approach to type and design that was, at the time of its publication, revolutionary. For instance, a blank page to denote that a chapter has been torn out; another blank page which invites the reader to

provide his/her own description of a character; a black page that denotes a memorial to the death of a character; graphs that 'demonstrate the narrative line in earlier volumes'; chapters intentionally misplaced but which appear later; various near abstract typographic devices which complement and enliven the text; chapters deliberately censored in which characters are discussing censorship, etc. For me *Tristram Shandy* proves that illustration can be used in a more inventive and oblique way whilst remaining faithful to the text it accompanies. It contradicts the norms of illustration, which have generally assumed that the reader is only capable of or interested in recognizing that which s/he already knows; *Tristram Shandy* on the other hand, encourages the reader to exercise his/her own options in following his/her own imagination.

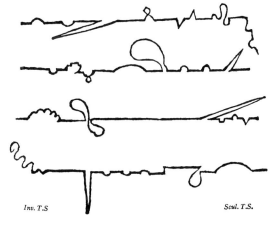

Inv. T.S   *Scul. T.S.*

In parallel with my thoughts on *Tristram Shandy* other influences were providing notions and pointers towards a wider formulation of alternative approaches to illustration. Marcel Duchamp,[5] whose work and the questions it poses has always been an encouraging and strengthening model for me, often provides confirmation of my own observations. In a television interview with James Johnson Sweeney in 1956[6] Duchamp said that, '.... painting should not be exclusively retinal or visual; it should have to do with the grey matter, with our urge for understanding'. I think that I have always intuitively felt this to be true and have consequently aspired to approach my work from this base. In doing so some avenues of work which initially seemed to be most unpromising have proved to be rewarding, mostly leading me into areas of work and thought which I had not originally foreseen. This detective's curiosity which Duchamp quietly excelled in utilizing, has always guided my work, whether it be commissioned or personal.

Another important touchstone is Samuel Beckett, whose investigations of language and perception I see as obliquely analogous to Duchamp's work; both artists having extended our perceptions of literature and vision by creating new means of expression, new languages with which to express their unique views of their perceived realities.

A common factor to Duchamp, Beckett and to Eno, apart from their individual visions, is their belief in their ideas and in their work, which they have chosen to expose publicly, thereby challenging critical and popular opinion and risking loss of

favour. They have all worked outside of conventionally recognized methods and means, in varying degrees, preferring the experiment to the comfortable, the possible failure to the expediency of financial or fashionable rewards.

Whilst digesting the ideas of *Tristram Shandy*, Duchamp and Beckett towards a less linear approach to illustration, I was also experimenting with the potential of forms of 'directed chance', i.e. a process or system that, once established, could be interrupted, reversed, abused, etc. in such a way that an end result is not predictable. While the process and its means of execution are established, their arrangement, evolution and final form cannot be guessed at beforehand. As with the Dadaists and surrealists who had employed collage as a tool to by-pass linear thought, to eradicate and/or subvert the rational in order to encourage the subconscious or the unknown, I too felt the techniques of collage were the most promising means through which a valid and exciting form of illustration could be achieved. I had soon reached a point in my work where I felt mentally and technically ready to test these ideas in a more rigorous manner. In order to do this I decided that I needed a subject or theme which was capable of fulfilling several conditions/constraints/rules, these being:

1 such a subject or theme should be capable of sustaining my close scrutiny and interest over a long period;
2 it should give me the opportunity to utilize and experiment with a wide range of both traditional and non-traditional materials in juxtaposition;
3 it should be a subject or theme that had not been approached visually before;
4 it should be broad enough in its range of subjects and topics so as to oblige me to research into areas of which I had no prior knowledge.

I also decided that whatever this project happened to be, it would also fulfil my obligation to produce a 'major project' as part of the essential requirements to attain a 'Master of Arts' Degree from the Royal College of Art.

This book and its contents are the results of that 'major project'. Beginning as an experiment using Eno's music and lyrics as a vehicle or springboard, it has expanded over the years to become what I believe to be a unique study of Brian Eno and his work and the influential contribution of that work during and beyond an exciting and inspiring era of recent musical history. While recording the diverse results of our collaboration and friendship, it also serves to document an important stepping-stone in my development as an artist during the crucial, formative years following my graduation from the RCA.

I hope that readers of this book will find the questions raised, the possibilities suggested and the solutions reached, through both the visual and textual contributions, to be of interest and use in a discovery and appreciation of the potential for individual creativity. I believe that those who approach this book with an open mind will accept it in the spirit in which it has been conceived and in which it is offered. Moreover, I hope that readers will experience as much enjoyment from their reading of it as I have had in my involvement in its evolution.

Russell Mills.

4 *Laurence Sterne,* The Life and Opinions of Tristram Shandy Gentleman *(published in nine volumes, 1759-1767).*
5 *see Michel Sanouillet and Elmer Peterson (eds.),* The Essential Writings of Marcel Duchamp *(Thames and Hudson, London, 1975).*
6 *'A Conversation with Marcel Duchamp', NBC, January 1956. Filmed at the Philadelphia Museum of Modern Art.*

THE PREPARED OBSERVER

The poet Baudelaire once suggested that the truest response to a work of art, the purest act of criticism, was to produce a second work of art in a different medium. Poetry, he argued, was much better equipped than rational analysis to interpret and convey the essential quality of a beautiful painting. In pursuing his obsession with the music and lyrics of Brian Eno to these extraordinary limits, illustrator and artist Russell Mills has undertaken just such a project. During the two years in which he worked on his mixed-media interpretations – collected together for the first time in this book – thirty-eight songs yielded up fifty-seven separate pieces, an even larger body of work. But far from being exhausted, reduced, or explained away by Mills's efforts, one set of enigmas was simply reformulated in the language of another. In the process of translation, the power of Eno's mysterious texts was both confirmed and strengthened.

This book documents and explores a particular phase in the work of both artists. It begins in 1973, when *Here Come the Warm Jets*, Eno's first solo album, was released, and it has two endings. The first came in 1978, when *After the Heat* came out; the second in 1980, when Mills put a match to the third and final version of *Third Uncle* under the gaze of the BBC television cameras.[1] (This, ironically, had also been the song with which he began the series.) *After the Heat*, which Eno recorded in Germany with Cluster, marked a natural end to Mills's unwieldy project. It contains the last lyrics that Eno has recorded to date, with the exception of two songs on *Remain in Light* by Talking Heads, which were co-written with David Byrne.

Russell Mills has often spoken of the 'disorientating' effect which *Here Come the Warm Jets* had on him when he first heard it in 1973. 'For me it had that same stunning effect that one acquires if one is hit on the bridge of one's nose by the edge of a brick,' he says.[2] The album came at a time when, in Mills's view, little of interest was happening on the music scene – a time of trivial, vacuous pop on the one hand, and overblown 'concept' albums on the other. Alone among the bands of the period, Mills admired the art-rock group Roxy Music, but it was Eno in particular, as the real catalyst of the group, who had riveted his attention. In the artist revealed by the random experimentation of *Here Come the Warm Jets* Mills was certain he had discovered a kindred spirit:

For me it seemed to illustrate clearly that a new viewpoint depends on one's capacity to risk. The willingness to accept risk as a part of one's working methods was very close to the way I was trying to work visually as well.[3]

After inconclusive visits to both Island Records and EG Management, to discuss the possibility of designing album covers for Eno, Mills wrote a carefully worded letter to Eno himself in 1974, enclosing examples of his work. The letter took a long time to reach Eno, but an arrangement was eventually made for Eno to visit Mills one afternoon at the Royal College of Art, where he was studying illustration. Mills remembers that they discussed approaches to illustration and that Eno admired the processes that lay behind his work. There was no talk, at that stage, of collaboration, although they did agree to meet again.

By the autumn term of 1976, and the third year of his course,

Mills had decided to illustrate Eno's songs for his final year project:

I'd been working for the last three years in mixed media, but very tentatively and very clumsily. I felt I was getting a lot looser with the processes I was working with, but I needed something quite strict – in the sense of being an endurance run – to test these things, to really stretch it all as much as possible. I don't think it was a case of even thinking of other alternatives. Brian's lyrics and music seemed to be the most obvious thing to work on, simply because they offered so many tangents, and the opportunity to work in the way that I thought illustration actually was, rather than in the dictionary definition of the term – which is to describe, or clarify, or decorate, or make pretty. With Brian's lyrics and music it seemed to me that there was room to manoeuvre, to be very flexible and bounce ideas all over the place.[4]

Some time during the term, Mills and Eno discussed the idea behind the project, and Mills restated his views on the limitations of traditional approaches to illustration. In December 1976, Eno sent Mills background material for four songs: 'The Paw Paw Negro Blowtorch', 'Driving Me Backwards', 'The Fat Lady of Limbourg', and 'The Great Pretender'. In the accompanying letter he comments:

I'm sorry that these interpretations aren't more specific, but most of my words are a bit like some of the devices in your drawings – they are there for the kind of odd mood they create (partly by incongruity, partly by apparent relevance) rather than for a particular 'meaning'.[5]

1 *Arena*, BBC2, 9 April 1980, directed by Nigel Finch.
2 Interview, Radio Station JJJ, Australian Broadcasting Commission, 1980.
3 Ibid.
4 Interview by the author, London, 26 November 1984.
5 Letter from Eno to Mills, 27 December 1976.

ESCAPE

Someone pointed out that most of my songs concerned escape. I started thinking about this; it lodged in my mind. A while later Russell Mills sent me a list of titles from the book about Houdini (Secrets of Houdini) that he was reading. I just realized why I found them so exciting. He was the great escapologist.

Mystifying Passengers in a Liner
Escape from Iron Boxes.
Walking Through a Brick Wall
Spirit writing on a Sealed Slate

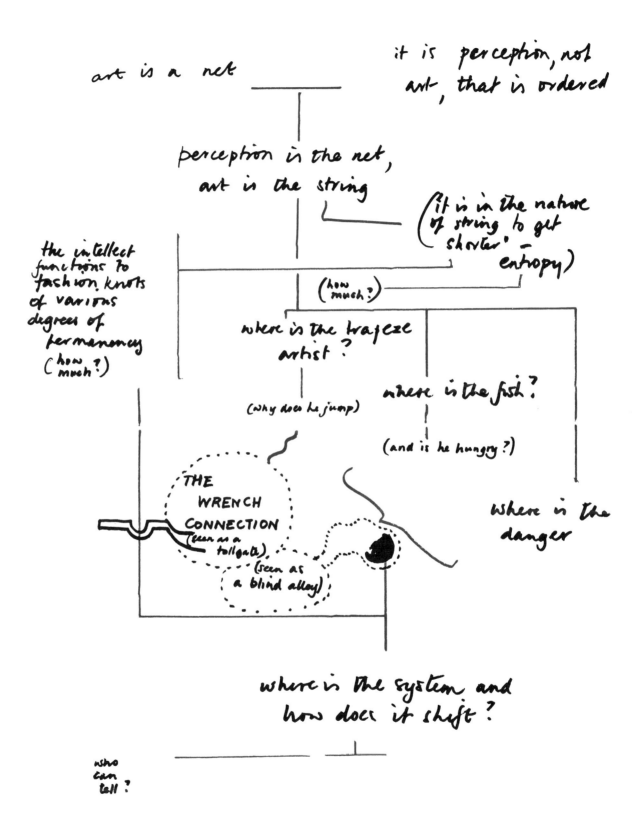

art is a net

it is perception, not
art, that is ordered

perception is the net,
art is the string

(it is in the nature
of string to get
shorter' —
entropy)

the intellect
functions to
fashion knots
of various
degrees of
permanency
(how
much?)

(how
much?)

where is the trapeze
artist?

where is the fish?

(why does he jump)

(and is he hungry?)

THE
WRENCH
CONNECTION
(seen as a
tollgate)

where is the
danger

(seen as
a blind alley)

where is the system and
how does it shift?

who
can
tell?

(Note: the bait must be on the other
side of the net
or the trapeze may be faulty.

Present studio kit :

1 Box Oblique Strategies
The 'Schwarzwald' (Coronoray) vox of words)
2 Backgammon dice
WEM Project Fuzz box
Gibson 335 guitar
Stanway Guitar
Antoria Fretless bass
Sony portable recorder
Medion negative ioniser
This notebook
This pen
Mini moog synthesizer
AKS synthesizer
A box of percussion instruments
1 spare sweatshirt
1 pair loose trousers
1 bottle of Shen-kue-lu-Jung pills
A jar of Essence of Chicken (or beef)
Two or three cigars (Rössli 7 or
King Edwards)
1 electric metronome
1 electric rhythm generator

Although Eno was aware of the progress of the project during the following months – mainly through letters and telephone calls – it was not until Mills's degree show at the RCA in the summer of 1977 that he saw the full scope of the endeavour. Alongside the other student work he had carried out in the past three years, Mills exhibited twelve of his Eno interpretations. Excited by what he saw at the show, Eno returned the following day, accompanied by David Enthoven, who was his manager at the time. Enthoven also liked the work, and together they proposed that Mills should continue the project with the idea of publishing a book. It was shortly after this that Mills received the first consignment of Eno's celebrated notebooks. The second batch, covering the period up to the summer of 1978, followed later, midway through the project.

Over the years, Eno's notebooks, which he carries with him wherever he goes, have been the source of considerable speculation – much of it misguided.[6] More than one reviewer, in a burst of journalistic hyperbole, has compared the notebooks to those of Leonardo da Vinci. The truth is that Eno's notebooks are sufficiently fascinating in their own right not to need this kind of exaggeration. Taken together they offer an extraordinary behind-the-scenes glimpse of a creative mind at work and at play. The pages of the journals jostle with diagrams, messages, jokes, drawings, exclamations, ideas, instructions, anagrams, aphorisms and Eno's 'amateur mathematics'. Song lyrics are endlessly transcribed, crossed out, and reworked. Studio kit is logged, dreams are recorded, shopping lists are compiled, and rainfall is mapped. Fragments of autobiographical confession merge with descriptions of landscapes. Ideal living and working environments are visualized and sketched. There are comments on people, places and events. There are lists of tasks to be done, books to be read, and songs to be recorded. In pages of quotation from admired writers – Beer, Peckham, Waddington, Trungpa – Eno explores ideas about art, music, genetics, and cybernetics that will surface in essays and lectures, and in his own working practice.

THE INTUITIVE ORIENTEER

From the outset of the project, Mills confined himself to illustrating the songs which had lyrics, rather than the instrumentals, although these had been a feature of Eno's work since *(No Pussyfooting)* – recorded with Robert Fripp – was released in 1973. One reason for Mills's decision was simply to keep the project within manageable bounds. The other had more to do with the status of the songs as both music and text – the bizarre imagery of Eno's lyrics offered obvious clues and pointers for visual interpretation. Mills's training as an illustrator, combined with his enthusiasm as a reader, made him especially receptive to the implications of Eno's texts:

Eno's lyrics intrigued me as they did not, on the whole, fall into any of the usual categories of popular music, but reflected his diverse interests, such as spontaneous human combustion, dream notation, random associations, and phenomena in general. His lyrics are not the normal throwaway lines… their randomness, nonsense and contradictory 'feel' are the appealing thing that never fails to excite, incite, amuse and confuse me.[7]

Nevertheless, Mills was determined that the works he produced should stand up in their own right, out of context. He would treat Eno's texts as maps and compasses with which to explore unknown territory, but the interpretations he produced would be his own, rather than Eno's. This was a point of view which Eno shared:

You function as an interpreter partially, or at least as someone who is using a perception of these pieces as the basis for making works which can then be seen independently of the pieces, and are successful in those terms. In my view, your work is most successful when it loses its reverence for the 'truth' about mine, and when it goes off on its own, asserting its independence. We both have to accept at the outset that there are implications in my pieces that won't appear in your drawings and that the reverse is also true.[8]

In the catalogue that accompanied the *Fine Lines* exhibition of his work in 1980, Mills describes his journey through alien territory, aided only by his intellect and intuition, as a process of 'intuitive orienteering':

My visual interpretations use (Eno's) lyrics and music as a springboard, from which the work develops at tangents and tangents again. I've treated each song with the attention and merit it deserves, in whatever medium/materials seem 'right'. This approach requires that I range widely through the accumulated experience of my life, selecting and discarding, adapting and manipulating at will and by whim, employing both the commonplace and the sophisticated; each piece is a result of a search for an economic unity from a sometimes chaotic multiplicity.[9]

In the same statement, Mills likens the psychological processes involved in his work to the practice of synectics, an American technique for developing creativity in small teams of individuals. The discovery of *Synectics* by William J.J. Gordon in 1977 was important to Mills because it helped him to formulate ideas about creativity which he felt instinctively to be true, but which he had, until then, been unable to express in intellectual terms. In an attempt to produce imaginative solutions to a wide range of problems in business and industry, synectics teaches students to sidestep rationality and convention in favour of more intuitive approaches. Its principal tool is a freewheeling use of four kinds of metaphor and analogy: personal, direct, symbolic and fantasy. In this way, problems are approached and addressed from unexpected directions. The familiar is made strange (or mysterious) and the strange is made familiar (or knowable). Synectics places particular emphasis on examining the processes by which such solutions are achieved, so that circumstances conducive to creative work can be provided in an organized way:

6 *Throughout the period 1967 to 1978 Eno experimented with a number of different notebook formats, most of them pocket-sized. His preferred format was the 6⅜in × 4in Alwych, with 80 feint-ruled leaves, and a black, textured, 'all-weather' cover. At least thirty-seven notebooks from this period are known to exist.*
7 *Russell Mills, private papers, 1980.*
8 *Letter from Eno to Mills, Penang, 27 December 1978.*
9 *Catalogue to the* **Fine Lines** *exhibition, held at the Thumb Gallery, London, from 1 April to 2 May 1980.*

Human beings are heir to a legacy of frozen words and ways of perceiving which wrap their world in comfortable familiarity. This protective legacy must be disowned. A new viewpoint depends on the capacity to risk and to understand the mechanisms by which the mind can make tolerable the temporary ambiguity implicit in risking.[10]

Even more important than synectics as a source of inspiration for Mills, was the work and example of anti-artist and Dada affiliate, Marcel Duchamp. Duchamp, along with Brian Eno and Samuel Beckett,[11] belongs to Mills's holy trinity of heroes:

Duchamp for me is a god. He covers all areas, all art movements. His pioneering work preceded and anticipated all recent art genres years before they evolved. His investigations and interpretations of metaphor, science, and language into a unique, personal work, and his refusal to pander to the so-called fashionable attitudes of the day, have been a constant source of strength for me.[12]

Though his output was small by some standards, and he withdrew from formal artistic production in 1923, Duchamp's work, and – more crucially, perhaps – his ideas, have exerted an enormous influence on later artists. Duchamp's use of chance as a factor in shaping a work of art – as, for example, in the 'standard stops' unit of measurement which he used in the composition of the *Large Glass* – anticipates such developments as indeterminate music, abstract expressionism in painting, and much of the 'conceptual' art of recent years. Another Duchampian use of chance, the 'dust breeding' experiments of the *Large Glass*, find a direct parallel in Mills's second interpretation of 'Some Of Them Are Old'. Here, the box and its contents were exposed to kitchen dust and cooking grease for a year.

Interestingly, Duchamp did not believe that the workings of chance were completely random. Chance, he thought, was always personal. 'Your chance is not the same as my chance, just as your throw of the dice will rarely be the same as mine,' he once explained.[13] The sentiment finds an echo in a personal maxim which Mills derived from the ideas of the French chemist and bacteriologist Louis Pasteur: 'Chance favours the prepared observer.'[14] In other words, unless you are ready to recognize and exploit the gifts of chance when they occur, chance will be of little use to you. Using techniques such as the *Oblique Strategies* cards, Eno made these gifts central to his working methods. Like both Eno and Duchamp, Mills has always been prepared to explore the unexpected avenues opened up by chance. On occasions during the course of the project Mills, too, made use of Eno's oracle cards. There are examples of visual solutions inspired by *Oblique Strategies* in his interpretations of 'Baby's on Fire', 'The True Wheel', and 'Tzima N'Arki'.

PROCESS AND PROCEDURE

In constructing his mixed-media interpretations, Mills has drawn on a prodigious variety of non-art materials. He was bored, he says, with everyday art materials – all they could offer were dull, easy solutions. As well as the more traditional media, such as pencil, pen, ink, graphite, watercolour, gouache, acrylic paint, and crayon, Mills employed enamel paints, aluminium paint, fluorescent paint, varnish, etching varnish, shoe dye, shoe polish, lacquer, blood (his own), metallic spray, and photo dyes. Heavier materials include adhesive labels, plasters and tapes, silver foil, aluminium foil, wood, balsa wood, cellophane, cardboard, graph paper, toilet paper, tracing paper, cigarette paper, stamp album paper, sewing patterns, fabric, gauze, netting, bandaging, perspex, slate, and xeroxes.

Mills's radical approach to materials was strongly influenced by his admiration – shared by Eno – for the work of the Dadaist Kurt Schwitters. Schwitters never officially belonged to either the Berlin or Cologne Dada groups, founding instead, in 1918, his own Hanover-based branch of Dada which he called Merz. His Merz collages and constructions are renowned for their aesthetic use of everyday detritus: tram tickets, cheese wrappers, playing cards, cigar bands, shoelaces, nail files, wire, and dish cloths. Schwitters also composed a number of nonsense and sound poems. An excerpt from the longest of these, the thirty-five minute *Ursonate*, was used by Eno in 'Kurt's Rejoinder' on *Before and After Science*. The song offered Mills an ideal opportunity to salute his hero. As a playful homage to the unknown adhesive used by Schwitters in his assemblages, Mills incorporated seven types of glue in the work.

Like literal readings of Lautréamont's surrealist dictum 'Beautiful as the chance encounter of a sewing machine and an umbrella on a dissecting table', many of Mills's images consist of poetic marriages of unlikely elements. Objects collaged into the works include computer punch cards, electric valves, fragments of a broken windscreen, sewing needles, scissors, mirrors and mirror tiles, nails, chain, a hook, a feather, a fluorescent light, artificial eyes, one of Eno's notebooks (sealed for ever in resin), an Emergency War Diary, wired security glass, the gloved hands of a mannequin, postcards, a magnet, and a map of

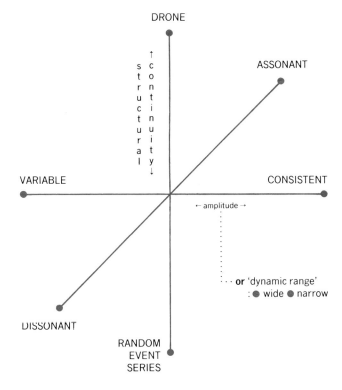

the world. Other textural effects are achieved by staples, wire, typing, matchbox strikes, burning, and the sewing of cotton and lurex threads. A wide variety of printed papers and photographs from magazines and other sources have been incorporated. Some of the works have been constructed directly on the prepared – or 'rectified'[15] – surfaces of found objects: wooden trays, a noticeboard, and a lacquered and enamelled wooden box.

The main problem for Mills, as he writes in his notes to 'Burning Airlines Give You So Much More', was organizing these disparate components, combined with the elements he had produced himself, into a satisfactory composition:

11

10 *William J. J. Gordon,* Synectics: The Development of Creative Capacity *(Collier Books, New York, 1968). Eno was also impressed by the book which he discovered, independently of Mills, in 1978.*

11 *The influence of Samuel Beckett on the work of Russell Mills falls outside the scope of this commentary, but Mills's notes to* Tzima N'Arki *show how a reading of Beckett directed his interpretation of the song. In 1979, Mills began work on a series of illustrations of the work of Beckett. He was particularly fascinated by the way in which the structural devices of later works –* Worstward Ho, Company, Ill Seen Ill Said *– seemed to exemplify Eno's Oblique Strategy, 'Repetition is a form of change'.*

12 *Russell Mills, private papers, 1980.*

13 *Quoted in Calvin Tomkins,* The Bride and the Bachelors: Five Masters of the Avant-Garde *(expanded edition, Viking Press, New York, 1968).*

14 *Pasteur's actual words were: 'In the field of experimentation, chance favours only the prepared mind'.*

15 *'Rectified' is a Duchampian term. See Michel Sanouillet and Elmer Peterson (eds.),* The Essential Writings of Marcel Duchamp *(Thames and Hudson, London, 1975).*

Whilst the imagery itself usually develops quite naturally, with the occasional asides suggesting successful alternatives, the composition is forced to be continually altered either by intuition or the random dictates of the various integral pieces. I consider both careful composition and chance to be more important than strong or complete colour.

Mills termed the process by which he cut out and manipulated the hand-drawn or painted elements – such as human figures and furniture – 'decisive incisions'. The sinister surgical implications of this phrase are characteristic of the black humour of many of these images. The phrase also acknowledges Eno's tendency to characterize his musical procedures in terms of their effects, as in the 'spasmodic percussion' and 'uncertain piano' which he played on 'Golden Hours'.

The unpredictable qualities and irregular shapes of the elements with which he worked prevented Mills becoming complacent about his compositional solutions. Nevertheless, certain stylistic traits do recur throughout the series. Many of the images feature backgrounds constructed out of grid-like elements, or even graph paper, which emphasize the feeling of movement caught against a static backdrop, and give a sense of scientific reportage to the bizarre events of the foreground. Mills's use of the grids in his backgrounds is very similar to the compositional processes of Eno's songs. Over and over again Eno

would set the melodic information of his music (the movement) against stable and unvarying rhythm tracks (the grid). In fact, many of Mills's images have been assembled by a procedure directly comparable with the way in which Eno composes his music by building up layers of sound on tape in the studio. These layers are then stripped away one by one – not necessarily in the order in which they were established – until the patterns of sound which remain suggest further treatments and modification. Once again, chance (the patterns can be guessed at in advance but not predicted) is guided by intuition (you have to recognize something successful when you hear or see it):

My pictures are usually built up in layers with drawings on one surface that are then covered with another surface. Therefore elements of that drawing are completely lost. I forget what's underneath most of them. But I usually also try to bring elements out from underneath. This means I either have to cut or rip to expose surfaces underneath. And usually, dependent on how deep the layers are, I can bring out several different formats underneath the actual image, the surface image.[16]

Again, the idea of hidden drawings, lost for ever beneath the surface of Mills's pictures, images the spectator can never know and which even the artist has forgotten, recalls Duchampian and Dadaist parallels. Duchamp's 'assisted' ready-made *With Hidden Noise*, a ball of twine compressed between two metal plates, contains a mysterious object only ever known by two people, and never by Duchamp himself. Man Ray's *The Enigma of Isidore Ducasse* of 1920, a homage to Lautréamont, is a sewing machine wrapped in cloth and bound by rope; it can be known but it cannot be seen. Some of Mills's works contain hidden information that is accessible only to those who know where to look for it. A hinged shelf in *Taking Tiger Mountain* drops down to reveal examples of military strategy useful in the taking of the mountain. *Sky Saw* is a photographic plate box that snaps shut, concealing the images inside. A series of dots and dashes, hidden in the pictures, spells out the title of the piece in morse code.

As a student at art school, Eno exhibited a number of 'hidden' pictures that were painted in the same colours and textures as the surfaces that they were hung against. The same playfulness marked his approach to 'Here Come the Warm Jets', Eno's lost song, on the album of the same name. Eno himself has no written record of the words, and on disc the vocals were deliberately mixed so quietly that the lyrics are virtually indecipherable. Short of locating the original master tape (if it still exists) there is no way of discovering what these lyrics are. 'Here Come the Warm Jets' is consequently the one song by Eno which Mills was unable to illustrate.

'Chance is always powerful. Let your hook be always cast; in the pool where you least expect it, there will be a fish' *Ovid.*

'The mines of knowledge are often laid bare by the hazel-wand of chance' *Tupper.*

If Mills's use of chance procedures and unorthodox materials borrows heavily from Dada, the unsettling imagery which he evolved in these works belongs to both the Dadaist and surrealist traditions of irrational picture and object making. Mills's highly suggestive combinations of objects within boxes and frames also recall the poetically charged found-object constructions of the American surrealist box-maker, Joseph Cornell. The songs, many of which are small surrealist scenarios that leave out much more than they reveal, seem to cry out for this kind of treatment. 'I like the idea of you as a listener entering a story after it's begun and leaving it before it's finished, so that you just hear a fragment of a story and you're left to conjecture the beginning and the end,' Eno says of 'The Fat Lady of Limbourg'.[17] Taking his stage directions from the songs, Mills gave many of the pictures a posed, theatrical quality that recalls the dark, brooding atmospheres of surrealist paintings by Giorgio de Chirico, René Magritte, and Max Ernst.[18]

16 *Interview, Radio Station JJJ, Australian Broadcasting Commission, 1980.*

17 *Interview by Tom Zelinka, Radio Station JJJ, Australian Broadcasting Commission, 1977.*

18 *Along with Duchamp and Schwitters, Ernst was one of the biggest influences on Mills's development as an artist. See* **Geek** *magazine (RCA, London, 1977). Mills's illustrations for the footnotes of* **The Third Policeman** *by Flann O'Brien draw on the same kind of Victorian imagery used by Ernst in his collages and collage novels.*

Most of Eno's lyrics felt as if they could be taking place within a defined area – a kind of expanded stage set. And I'm outside the stage set manipulating the objects, the characters, the action, the scene, from just outside the picture frame. But I could be in the picture frame at any minute, somehow.[19]

Like a puppet master toying with his creations, Mills presides over his arenas of surrealist menace. In three cases he is more than just metaphorically present in the action. *The Seven Deadly Finns*, *Spider and I*, and *Broken Head*, which is explicitly autobiographical, all include self-portraits. Many of the earlier images, particularly, appear to function as theatres for the expression of an extreme personal desire which cannot fail to implicate the viewer. Mills seems far more at ease exploring the dangerous implications of Eno's most violent images than he does with those of the gentler, more sentimental songs. Think of the voyeuristic burning of Baby, and the Third Uncle; the fiery breath of the Paw Paw Negro Blowtorch; the destructive beam of the Painted Sage in *Burning Airlines* (entirely a Mills invention); the clinical interior of the Limbourg asylum; the surgical/sexual furniture of *The Great Pretender*; the captive bodies in *Miss Shapiro*. *Luana – Chemical Choices* is a disturbing visual re-enactment of one of Eno's dreams (see 'The Words I Receive') that refers only obliquely to the lyrics of 'Driving Me Backwards'. A dark wit operates even in Mills's interpretations of the quieter songs. In *Put a Straw under Baby* the immanence of God is rendered literally; there really is a brain in the table and a heart in the chair.

Divorced from their potentially reassuring context as illustrations for the songs, and removed from the explanations provided here by Mills, images like these defy rational analysis. Viewers are left to discover meanings of their own in the pictures, just as Mills, and many other listeners, have found private kinds of significance in the act of interpreting Eno's enigmatic lyrics.

THE CONDITION OF MUSIC

Over a hundred years ago the aesthete and essayist Walter Pater wrote that, 'All art constantly aspires towards the condition of music.' Within fifty years developments in painting had made his insight explicit, as pioneering artists like Kupka, Kandinsky, Malevich, and Mondrian purged their work of representational imagery, producing instead completely abstract pictures that explored the (musical) resonances of colour, shape, line and form. Five years after finishing work on his Eno interpretations, the art of Russell Mills, too, seems to aspire increasingly towards the condition of music. 'I know that if I wasn't doing this, if I wasn't making images, statements in vision, then I would be involved in music more than I am,' he says.[20]

In 1980, Mills formed an alliance with Graham Lewis and Bruce Gilbert, members of the group Wire and subsequently of Dome. A mutual exchange of ideas led to the recording of 'Kluba Cupol', a twenty-minute record on which Mills provided percussion and effects. This music was used as the key to a live performance at the Notre Dame Hall, London, for which Mills designed an evolving stage set-cum-visual score which was constructed during the performance by the Japanese artist Shinro Ohtake. Mills also played synthesizer in this performance. As a floating group, Lewis, Gilbert and Mills have collaborated on a number of experimental projects. These include a one-month recording installation under the name of *MZUI* at the Waterloo Gallery, London, in 1981 (released on an album of the same name in 1982); and a two-month sound and vision installation called *MU:ZE:UM/Traces* at the Museum of Modern Art, Oxford. As in all his undertakings, what attracts Mills to these recordings, installations, and performances is the element of risk they involve, and the chance they offer to explore unknown territory.

In his work as an artist and an illustrator Mills has also tended more and more towards the, for him, ideal abstraction of music. Many recent works, such as the *Hushes* and *Drifts* series exhibited at the Curwen Gallery in 1983, are entirely devoid of representational imagery.[21] A selection of miniature xerox works from the *Drifts* was used by Mills in his cover design for Eno's *Music for Films Volume 2*. *Fanfare Score* from the *Hushes* series, a much larger work in acrylic and plaster, which incorporates invented forms of musical notation, was used on the cover of both the Skids' *Fanfare* compilation album, and *The Fifth Generation*, a book about artificial intelligence. Other work has included a cover design for *The Pearl*, an album by Harold Budd and Brian Eno, and *Still Point* (1984), a mixed media abstract, with atmospheric effects inspired by the colour studies of J.M.W. Turner, which was commissioned by David Sylvian for the cover of Japan's compilation double album *Exorcising Ghosts*.

Meanwhile, by a curious paradox, the art of Brian Eno, who has established an international reputation as a musician, aspires increasingly towards the condition of painting. 'I want to be a painter again,' Eno wrote in a notebook towards the end of 1976, and in his recent video paintings and sculptures he has achieved that aim, as a painter not just of sound but of light.

19 Arena, *BBC2, 9 April 1980.*
20 *Interview by the author, London, 26 November 1984.*
21 *...returns an echo, exhibition held at the Curwen Gallery, London, from 10 August to 3 September 1983.*

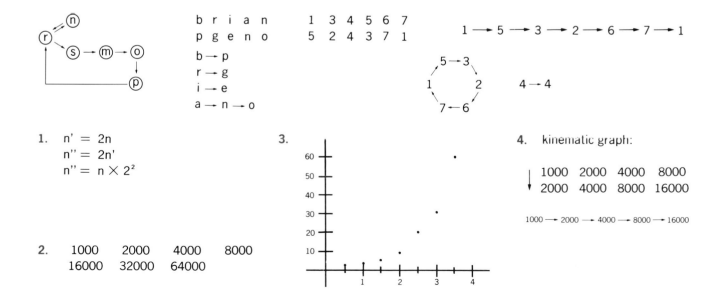

Those who know
They don't let it show
They just give you one long glance
And you'll go oh, oh, oh, oh.

Goes to show
How winds blow
The weather's fine
And I feel so, so, so, so, so.

Birds of Prey
With too much to say
Oh what could be my destiny
Another rainy day.

Why ask why
For by the by and by,
All mysteries are just more
Needles in the camel's eye.

14 Needles In The Camel's Eye

What can I tell you about this inexplicable lyric? It was written in less time than it takes to sing. The word 'Needles' was picked up from the guitar sound which to me is reminiscent of a cloud of metal needles.

Phil Manzanera played and I beat his tremolo-arm rhythmically with my hand.

BIBLICAL : ——————— the camel passing through the eye of a needle
SURREAL : ——————— a needle in an eye (like in *Un Chien Andalou*)
SPORTING : ——————— as in hitting a bullseye.

I've never really understood this song. I regard it as an instrumental with singing on it.

B.E.

illusion of art.
cezanne – cube, triangle, sphere
& cylinder.
when viewed from
different angles take
on new forms/shapes
reality / secret life
truth & deception

All mysteries are just.... beyond human knowledge to explain: ...anything artfully made difficult. As the lyrics combined with the music seemed to evoke life continuing despite problems, setbacks, etc., I decided to concentrate on a catalogue of types of mysteries that interest me. This included illusionistic devices, visual paradoxes, apparent depth, and the ever mysterious assassination of President John F. Kennedy on 22 November 1963 (my eleventh birthday).

Whilst considering these ideas, I talked with Eno about the 'assassination'. He had been reading about the subsequent investigations and the constantly accumulating theories being published in pursuit of the truth. One of these theories concerns a character dubbed 'The Umbrella Man', who appears on a film of the motorcade and shooting; (not the Zapruder film). The film shows an extremely out of focus figure, dressed in a dark raincoat; and despite it being a hot, sunny day, he has an umbrella which he opens up a split second before the fatal shots were fired. The possible significance of his actions were, like all the theories,

investigated exhaustively, and, like all the others has proved inconclusive. The figure of 'The Umbrella Man' is the central figure in my picture. Half of his head is based on a 'still' of Ray Milland from *The Man With X-Ray Eyes.*

The window, (top left, beneath cloud of needles) represents the Dallas Book Depository window from which Oswald supposedly fired. The splotches of blood at the base are the shots making contact. The silver/blue background sky, was made as a conscious experiment utilizing unfamiliar 'non-art' materials, namely shoe dyes and aluminium foil. The foil was stretched and burnished flat, matt side up, score lines were then made. Several shoe dyes were mixed and speedily applied with cotton wool. Torn strips of undyed foil were then glued horizontally across the sky, and sewing needles were then glued to these 'clouds', parallel to the score lines.

Most of the other elements within the picture deal with illusion, i.e. the partially scraped silvering of the mirrors, the gauze and the impossible box.

R.M.

True as the needle to the pole,
Or as the dial to the sun.

Song—Barton Booth 1681-1733

My, my, my, we're treating each other just like strangers
I can't ignore the significance of these changes
But you can't treat it lightly, and you have to face the consequences
All my worst fears are grounded
You have to make the choice between the Paw Paw Negro Blowtorch and me (no, no, no).

By this time I got to looking for a kind of substitute
I can't tell you who I found, except that it rhymes with dissolute
But my baby's so lazy, she is almost unable, and it's driving me crazy
And her loving's just a fable that we sometimes try, with passion, to recall.

Send for an ambulance or an accident investigator
He's breathing like a furnace
So I'll see you later, alligator
He'll set the sheets on fire
Mmm, quite a burning lover
Now he'll barbecue your kitten
He is just another learner lover
You have to make the choice between the Paw Paw Negro Blowtorch and me.

16   The Paw Paw Negro Blowtorch

'The Paw Paw Negro Blowtorch' is based on something I read about a
24-year-old negro called – – – – who emerged from the forests around
Paw Paw, Michigan with a strange ailment – his breath caused things to
ignite. He was investigated by numerous scientists of the day, but they
failed to identify the cause of the malady. It was said that he could set a
newspaper on fire by breathing on it. The song celebrates the possibility
of a love affair with the man.

    B.E.

Hello boyfriend, coming my way?

(Issued by the Ministry of Health in its campaign against V.D.)

'There is the celebrated case of A.W. Underwood, of Paw Paw,
Michigan, about whom Dr. L.L. Woodman wrote in the 'New York
Sun' 1 December, 1882: "He will take anybody's handkerchief, hold
it to his mouth, rub it vigorously, while breathing on it, and
immediately it bursts into flames and burns until consumed!"
Underwood would strip, rinse his mouth out and set any cloth or
paper alight by his breath. It was most useful, he said, when he was
out hunting, he could have his camp fire going in seconds.' *

The picture depicts the imaginary consequences after a particularly
passionate bout of love-making, albeit very brief. The attached
polythene bags, which are suspended from the base, betray my
interest in forensics and the images of court evidence; one being a
startled, barbecued cat, the other containing fragments of burnt
sheets.

The wooden panel that serves as the 'ground' for this picture, has
been left almost as I found it. The composition was stripped down
to its minimum components, as dictated by the lyrics.

    R.M.

* John Michell and Robert J.M.
  Rickard, **Phenomena** *(Thames
  and Hudson, London, 1977).*

Baby's on fire
Better throw her in the water
Look at her laughing
Like a heifer to the slaughter
Baby's on fire
And all the laughing boys are bitching
Waiting for photos
Oh the plot is so bewitching.

Rescuers row row
Do your best to change the subject
Blow the wind blow blow
Lend some assistance to the object
Photographers snip snap
Take your time she's only burning
This kind of experience
Is necessary for her learning
If you'll be my flotsam
I could be half the man I used to
They said you were hot stuff
And that's what baby's been reduced to.

Juanita and Juan
Very clever with maracas
Making their fortunes
Selling second-hand tobaccos
Juan dances at Chico's
And when the clients are evicted
He empties the ashtrays
And pockets all that he's collected
But baby's on fire!
And all the instruments agree that
Her temperature's rising
But any idiot would know that.

18   Baby's On Fire

These lyrics are so self-explanatory, because at the time of approaching this piece I was reading about spontaneous human combustion – my mind was already alive to the possible imagery.

The 'Baby' of the song appears not as a young child, but as a young woman in a chiffon skirt, because I was fascinated by the number of incidents of spontaneous human combustion that had inexplicably claimed the lives of young female ballroom dancers in the 1920s and 1930s. All attempts to find rational causes of these deaths proved inconclusive…

On her face is an expression of both sustained pain and forced glee, this is because, (a) she is burning to death!
      (b) the photographers have asked her to pose…

The absence of the photographers indicates that their cameras are set for a delayed exposure or for long exposures and corresponds with the lines from the lyrics – 'Take your time she's slowly burning…' Presumably they are taking a tea break or phoning in their reports. At one stage, near the completion of this piece, progress ground to a halt; the left-hand section lacked something. Eventually I consulted the *Oblique Strategies* cards ✱ and found the card with the word 'Cascades' printed on it. Having submitted myself to the experiment, I began thinking about 'Cascades' in relation to the dilemma I was facing. Nothing for a few days. I

considered cheating but I felt that a genuine result (whether aesthetically good or bad) was more important than a predictable and safe solution. Eventually, I came to thoughts of substitute (transient) entrances and exits; this led to the various types of doors seen in places of constant movement, such as those in restaurant kitchens through which waiters/waitresses have to carry trays, etc. without being able to use their hands/arms. The thought of doorways hung with plastic strips of bright primary colours reaching the floor, soon presented itself. As well as equating to a form of 'Cascades', this image also solved the purely compositional problem which had been nagging me.

The line: 'And all the instruments agree that', is derived from the poem 'In Memory of W.B. Yeats' † by W.H. Auden:

He disappeared in the dead of winter:
The brooks were frozen, the airports almost deserted;
And snow disfigured the public statues;
The mercury sank in the mouth of the dying day.
What instruments we have agree
The day of his death was a dark cold day.

> *The inclusion of a thermometer and a measure of distance as border devices were documentary afterthoughts to add to the voyeuristic/reportage style of the lyrics.*

R.M.

✱ *Brian Eno and Peter Schmidt,* Oblique Strategies (Over one hundred worthwhile dilemmas), *(London, 1975; 2nd edition slightly revised, 1978; 3rd edition slightly revised, 1979).*

† *W.H. Auden,* Collected Shorter Poems 1927-57 *(Faber and Faber, London, 1975).*

(i) Girl On Fire
8.5 × 7
reproduction from the *Strand* magazine, 1890's. The photograph illustrates an article on developer distortion in photography.

(ii) Baby's On Fire
9 × 5.75
Etching, soft ground and aquatint,

Both the reproduction and the etching were found in an old portfolio of mine, dating back to 1974, suggesting that this project has been developing since 1974 at least.

R.M.

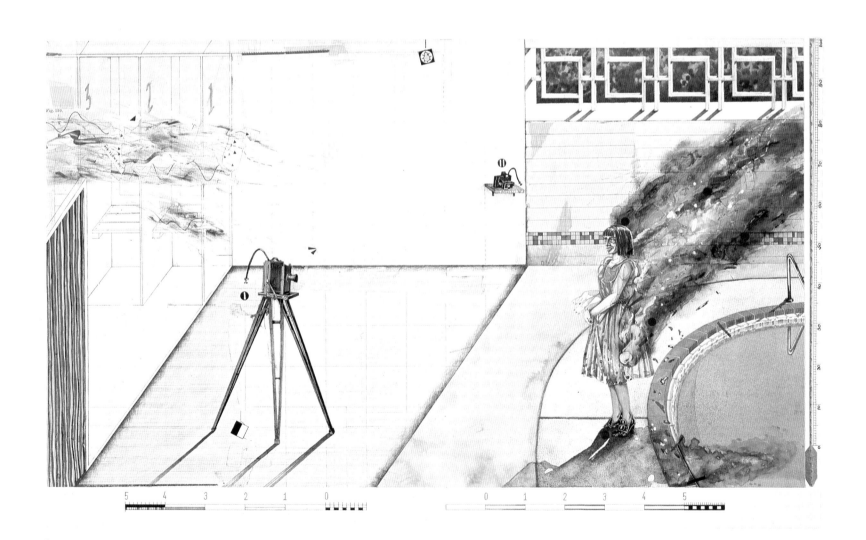

Cindy tells me, the rich girls are weeping
Cindy tells me, they've given up sleeping alone
And now they're so confused by their new freedoms
And she tells me they're selling up their maisonettes
Left the Hotpoints to rust in the kitchenettes
And they're saving their labour for insane reading.

Some of them lose – and some of them lose
But that's what they want – and that's what they choose
It's a burden – such a burden
Oh what a burden to be so relied on.

Cindy tell me, what will they do with their lives
Living quietly like labourers' wives
Perhaps they'll re-acquire those things they've all disposed of.

20 Cindy Tells Me

This evolved by chance. Having sewn two pieces of stamp album paper together, primarily to discover how the sewing machine could be utilized, the resulting 'union' suggested a clinical, aseptic room. When thinking about this piece a similar room evolved out of the lyrics, and consequently I searched out the sewn papers.

I like the line: 'Left the Hotpoints to rust in the kitchenettes' and its suggestion of a facile, empty existence coloured only by the acquisition of time-saving gadgets. It seemed like a sad state, synonymous with the deceptively insidious advertising methods that have proved so powerful. Bored, wealthy housewives, losing former interests missing former friends, with too much time on their hands, falling into the 'agony column' syndrome.

The picture represents the point of departure.

R.M.

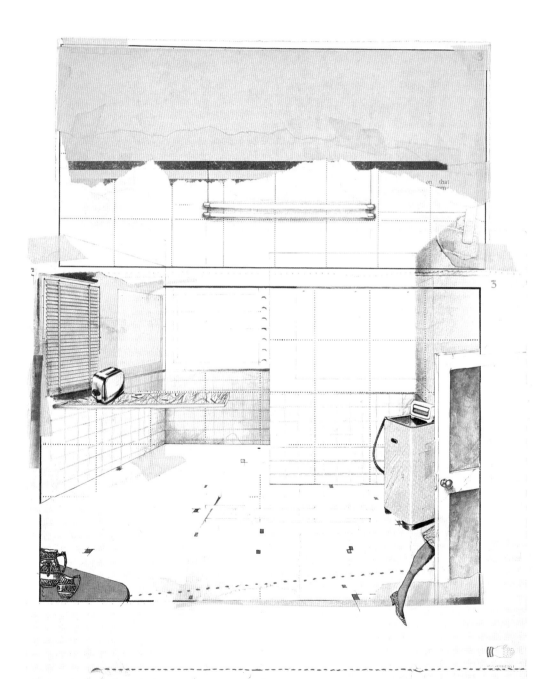

...*the rich girls are weeping*

Ohohohohohohoh oh
Doo doo doo doo doo doo dah
I'll be there.

Oh driving me backwards
Kids like me
Gotta be crazy
Moving me forwards
You must think that I'm lazy
Meet my relations
All of them
Grinning like facepacks
Such sweet inspirations
Curl me up
A flag in an icecap
Now I've found a sweetheart
Treats me good just like an armchair.

I try to think about nothing
Difficult
I'm most temperamental
I gave up my good living
Typical
I'm most sentimental
Ah Luana's black reptiles
Sliding round
Make chemical choices
And she responds as expected
To the only sound
Hysterical voices
And you – you're driving me backwards
Kids like me have gotta be crazzzzzy i-i-i-i-i-i-i
doo doo doo dodoo dodah I'll be there.

22   Driving Me Backwards

… a mixture of a series of thoughts about controlled existence – the desirability of being stripped of choice if you like. 'Chemical choices' indicates choice without volition. It is based on another song I wrote (but didn't record) played backwards. It's hard to explain – when I saw the film *Taxi Driver*, I felt it struck a chord with this song.

… has a combination of qualities that would not have been arrived at by anyone else, since it is the product of my musical naïveté on one hand, and my ability to manipulate extant ideas on the other. In this track as in most of the others, the musical idea is very simple – there are only three chords each different from the other by only one note, there are no tempo changes and the tempo is simply 4/4. I enjoy working with simple structures such as these for they are transparent – comparable to a piece of graph paper and its grids. The grid serves as the reference point for the important information – the graph line itself.

B.E.

The hysterical drive of this music appealed to my penchant for randomness. Every couple of lines are different in imagery from the rest and yet they all express a similar feeling of idiot glee or confusion. Confronted with the kaleidoscope of images, I felt that the best way to tackle this song was to concentrate on the lines that, after repeated listening would stick in my mind. These happened to be:

Meet my relations
All of them
Grinning like facepacks

This struck me as being very personal to my own relations as well as having universal recognition. The simile reminds me of the constant grins exchanged with one's own relations on meeting after a long separation.

All five pictures were done in the same period, because I couldn't stop doing them; I liked inventing relations! With hindsight I can't recall that any oblique references crept into the pictures; they seemed to evolve intuitively, only changing in scale and materials. They're all fictional portraits.

R.M.

Meet my relations
All of them
Grinning like facepacks

(c)

meet my relations
all of them
grinning like face packs.

(b)

(d)

(e)

Given the chance
I'll die like a baby
On some far away beach
When the season's over.

Unlikely
I'll be remembered
As the tide brushes sand in my eyes
I'll drift away.

Cast up on a plateau
With only one memory
A single syllable
Oh lie low lie low.

26   On Some Faraway Beach

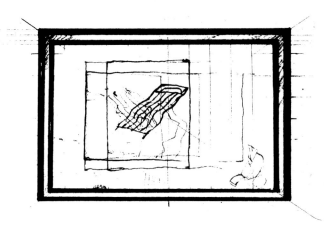

The whole picture is based (compositionally) on a funeral memorial card, in particular an Irish design. These cards usually have black and silver borders, a quote from the Bible, and a photograph of the deceased, all in a stock composition.

The washed up li·lo replaced the photograph of the deceased; an obvious pun.

The tea tray was bought for 50p in a junk shop in Kentish Town. Even under years of grease and varnish, there was enough wood grain visible to suggest water to me.

R.M.

kids bricks in bright colours

Before (17th in music

C + F sharp was called the Devil's interval & was
felt to be particularly disturbing, even
dangerous, a kind of quasi-forbidden interval

Blank Frank is the messenger of your doom and your destruction
Yes, he is the one who will set you up as nothing
And he is one who will look at you sideways
His particular skill is leaving bombs in people's driveways.

Blank Frank has a memory that's as cold as an iceberg
The only time he speaks is in incomprehensible proverbs
Blank Frank is the siren, he's the air-raid, he's the crater
He's on the menu, on the table, he's the knife and he's the waiter.

28   Blank Frank

Blank Frank was a small-time Ipswich gangster (his name was really just Frank; I added the rest). He was a hired hand and would duff up anyone for a relatively small sum. There used to be a café called The Gondolier where all the Mods used to go and where he could occasionally be found. He had a remarkable resistance to pain – his 'conversation piece' consisted of burning himself quite badly with a lighter. His friend was a guy called Georgie W—, who was a blonde-haired gypsy of circus origins, and who used to eat sandwiches of bread with razor blades inside for bets. He had a brother whose name was George "Rebel" W— (their father's name was also George) and for a brief period I shared a flat in Cemetery Road, Ipswich, with these three characters, an abortionist named Pete, and a hooker called Angie. Anyway, Frank himself was a benzedrine head, most of what he said, in origin no doubt commonplace, became fascinatingly garbled and obscure.

He was a born victim and he ended up getting six years for a number of offences including GBH and receiving.

.... was recorded in reverse. The conventional method of recording is to lay down rhythm tracks of bass, drums and rhythm guitar, then add melodic instruments later. Fripp and I found ourselves alone in the studio so we decided to write a song there and then, supplying a basic rhythm with an electronic rhythm generator. The effect of this is that the normally melodic instruments – the lead guitar and the voice – both attempted to fill-in the missing rhythm element. The bass and drums were added last – so everything is rhythmic rather than melodic. The organ at the end is played by four people simultaneously, none of them keyboard players, on a four manual organ.

B.E.

Blank Frank, as main character in my picture, is based on a photograph of a friend who tended to dress in bizarre clothes and suffered for his habit. Although he looked visually strange and threatening he was a very quiet and gentle person. The trousers he wears in my picture are or were apparently used by US pilots, they are called 'G-Suits'. The idea being that if forced to ditch the plane in the sea, the pilot activates a pocket-sized bellows which inflates the suit, thus providing the buoyancy to remain afloat until rescued.

He is standing in the garage doorway of Cemetery Road, Ipswich, with a parcel bomb wrapped in string and brown paper. There is a minor explosion to his right.

In this picture I attempted to flatten the perspective, compensating for the loss of depth by employing varying scales, hence the placing of the café interior, the pavement, etc. in false perspective against the flatness of the figure and garage.

The use of colour is minimal, only employed to emphasize certain elements that I considered to be important in the picture.

The cream coloured paper used in this and others in the set was acquired whilst I was in Berlin on a scholarship in 1976. An old stationery shop in the Moabit district was closing down, and I found some packs of the paper covered in dust at the back of some shelves. Apart from it being very cheap, it's surface, colour and faded grid appealed to me.

R.M.

blank frank

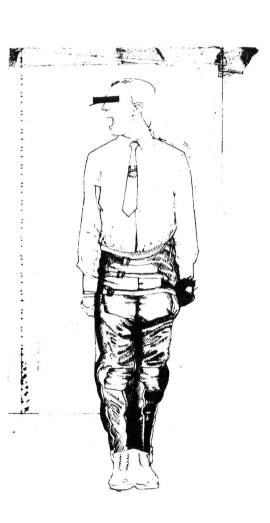

. . . is the siren, he's the air-raid, he's the crater
He's on the menu , on the table, he's the knife and he's the waiter.

Oh cheeky cheeky
Oh naughty sneaky
You're so perceptive and I wonder how you knew.

But these finks don't walk too well
A bad sense of direction
And so they stumble round in threes
Such a strange collection.

Oh you headless chicken
Can those poor teeth take so much kicking?
You're always so charming
As you peck your way up there.

And these finks don't dress too well
No discrimination
To be a zombie all the time
Requires such dedication.

Oh please, sir will you let it go by
'Cos I failed both tests with my legs both tied
In my place the stuff is all there
I've been ever so sad for a very long time
My my they wanted the works can you this and that
I never got a letter back
More fool me bless my soul
More fool me bless my soul.

Oh perfect masters
They thrive on disasters
They all look so harmless
Till they find their way up here.

But dead finks don't talk too well
They've got a shaky sense of diction
It's not so much a living hell
It's just a dying fiction.

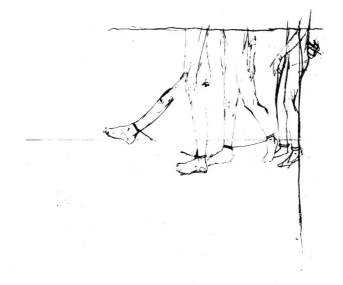

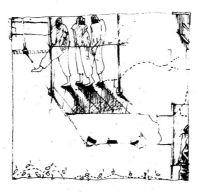

chairs Knocked over.

30   Dead Finks Don't Talk

It is about being ambitious and smarmy at the same time. The spoken bit in the middle refers to an undefined kind of aptitude test where the victim of the test is prepared to humilate himself before the tester if that will achieve a favourable result. The personality is niggardly and fauning. The various characters who appear are all ranked in particular places on various social ladders. 'Perfect master' is obviously a reference to the spiritual materialists (who were a bit more prominent when I wrote that song) and cosmic floaters, and 'dead finks' is a generic reference to a bunch of people who are still current and evident in the world of things; the fashion world; the world of people we look up to. Now the fashion world does not connote only a world to do with clothes – it is any kind of fashion, material, mental or spiritual. Thus Maharaj Ji is as much a part of the fashion world as Yves St Laurent, and their functions are socially indistinguishable; they offer a prescription by which you can feel that you are at the real centre of things. The singer of this song wants to feel at the centre of things, but is also poking fun. The 'headless chicken' is another way of saying 'dead fink' – it refers to the capacity of chickens to stay mobile after their brains are removed, a capacity that many members of the human race also seem capable of. The title comes from *Dead Fingers Talk* by William Burroughs.

B.E.

At the time of constructing this picture (construction is more truthful of the way I work, rather than painting or drawing) for this song I didn't know any of the above and worked only with the lyrics and music.

I made a wall of weaved paper (top left, behind figures) that in its comparative complexity confuses the 'dead finks' – who prefer to walk close to a semi-transparent screen. They remain close together to ensure safety. The attendant crutches (bottom left) are available if they need support during their mindless ramblings.

Again, colour has been kept to a minimum. ●

On finishing this picture I realized that I had dressed the 'dead finks' in contemporary clothes and looking around at other illustrative work at the time found that the clothes portrayed were either very ambiguous or from the 1930s – 40s at the latest. It was the first time that I'd become really aware of the use of clothes as depicted in pictures.

R.M.

They thrive on disasters
They all look so harmless

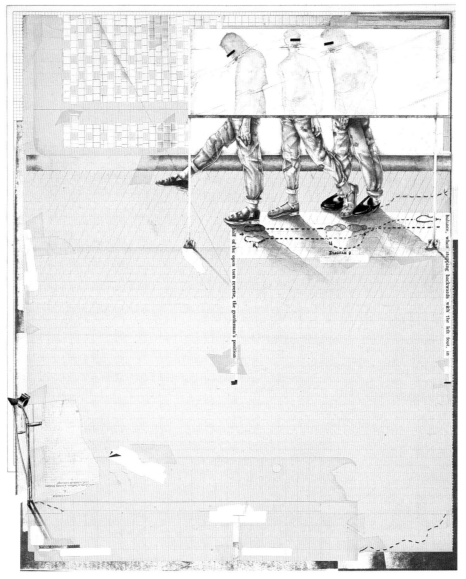

People come and go and forget to close the door
And they leave their stains and cigarette butts trampled on the floor
And when they do, remember me, remember me.

Some of them are old, some of them are new
Some of them will turn up when you least expect them to
And when they do, remember me, remember me.

Lucy you're my girl, Lucy you're a star
Lucy please be still and hide your madness in a jar
But do beware, it will follow you, it will follow you.

Some of them are old but it would help if you could smile
To earn a crooked sixpence you'll walk many crooked miles
And as you do, remember me, remember me.

32   Some Of Them Are Old

This song, like 'Golden Hours', suggests to me a need and a respect for the singer's privacy. Also it seems to regret the fact that most of one's visitors, (usually unconsciously) play on or abuse one's hospitality, and sometimes forget to employ a little common courtesy. For this reason the illustration I did became five separate images, three of which deal with the above problem; one breaking off on a slightly sexual tangent and the other dealing with an interpretation of the lines:

Lucy you're my girl, Lucy you're a star
Lucy please be still and hide your madness in a jar
But do beware, it will follow you, it will follow you.

These lines inspired the small old box piece. It led me to the story of St Lucy, a Sicilian virgin, who, after suffering denouncement as a Christian by her rejected suitor, was miraculously saved from exposure in a brothel, and from death by fire, was eventually killed by a sword in the throat (c.AD340). Legend has it that she felt obliged to gouge out her own eyes so as to discourage the advances of an admirer; hence her status as patron saint of oculists and the use of her name as insurance against ocular diseases. In art she is often represented holding her eyes on a dish.

I intended the box and its contents (which had been exposed to

dust and cooking grease in my kitchen for a year or so) to represent a collection of discarded objects found at the back of a cluttered kitchen shelf, implying that some intrusions and memories do not disappear as quickly as one might wish.

The image that utilizes the cut-away armchair and a woman's high-heeled shoe is a clue of some sexual encounter which has been and gone. I don't really understand this picture, it simply seemed right.

The three rectified magazine photographs of interiors are a more literal translation of my understanding of the song and are self-explanatory. That is apart from the floating numerals which catalogue the types of stain or damage left after a visit. I remember when I was young (very), seeing in cigarette coupon catalogues, pictures of arranged rooms or collections of articles that one could acquire for a certain stated amount of coupons; all items had a floating numeral next to them for identification. In my youthful naïveté I imagined that when one had traded the coupons for, say, a wrought iron side table (wrought iron furniture seemed to be quite abundant then!) one would also get a floating numeral to accompany it magically.

I was very disappointed and confused when the numerals never materialized. ↑

R.M.

within a very unexciting frame/box/shelf unit. plain wood
tie the jar with fine thread   + dust.

possibly bookbinders thread — strong yet fine
            & slightly buff coloured.

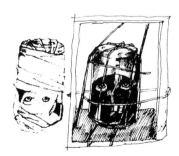

Lucy you're my girl, Lucy you're my star,
Lucy please be still and hide your magic in a jar
But do beware, it will follow you, it will follow you.

(b)

(ci)

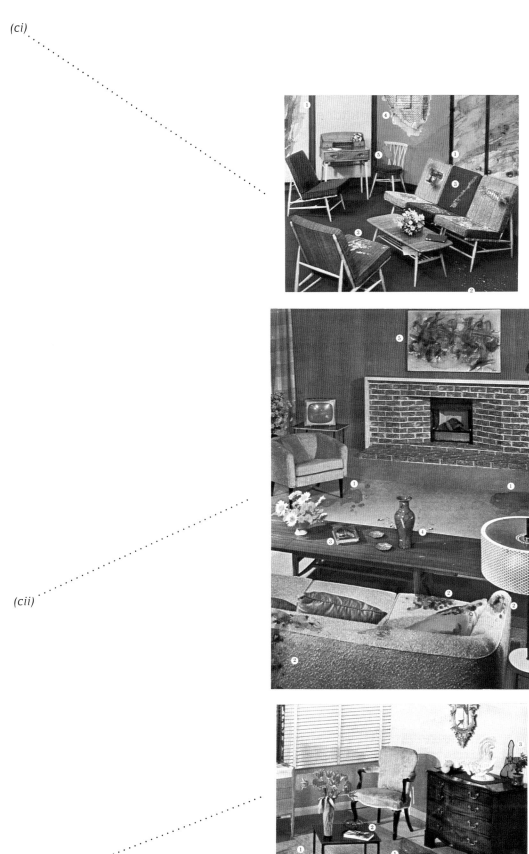

(cii)

(ciii)

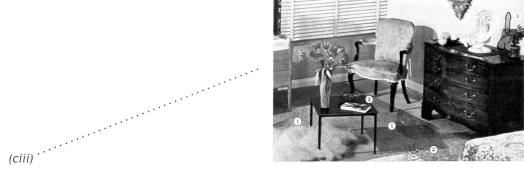

Oh oh the French girls with the strings of pearls
Think it's such a burning shame
That the local boys with their country joys
Never make them daisy chains
They're swopping disappointing incidents
While at the docks another ship pulls in
And suddenly the door breaks down (ooh la la)
It's the Seven Deadly Finns.

Oh oh oh soldiers and sailors
Have all been here before
Gigolos and governments
Have tumbled through that door
Because they need those French girls with all their kiss curls
And powder in their guns
And the Seven Finns with the deadly grins
Tend to measure beauty in tons.

The first is a freak with a masochistic streak
And the second is a kitten up a tree
The third is a flirt with an awful print skirt
And the fourth is pretending to be me
The fifth wears a mac and never turns his back
And the sixth never shows his eyes
But the seventh Deadly Finn is so tall and slim
'He shoulda never been with those guys'.

Although variety's the spice of life
A steady rhythm is the source
Simplicity's the crucial thing
Systemically of course (work it all out like Norbert Wiener)
So when those French girls say to you
'Would you like your ashes raked?'
You'll have to take their word for it
It's the only thing to take...

36 Seven Deadly Finns

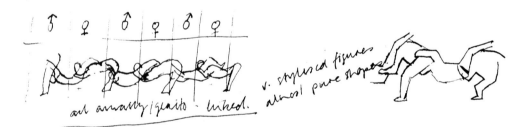

Before I could begin this piece I learnt from Eno the American
hooker's slang which is used as follows:

The French girls with their *strings of pearls*, (semen on the neck) ●

Think it's such a *burning shame*, (golden shower or piss on the head) ●

That the local boys with their *country joys* (joys of the cunt) ●

Never make them *daisy chains*... (genitally linked series of adult humans) ●

And so on. And the last lines of the song:

'Would you like your ashes raked?'
You'll have to take their word for it
It's the only thing to take...

constitute a pick-up language.

Provided with these translations, the obvious images are stimulated;
the archetypal B-movie brothel – dimly-lit, sleazy hotel rooms,
peeling wallpaper, faded elegance or cheap tat, inhabited by ladies
in varying stages of undress, static or moving aimlessly/lazily
awaiting potential clients. Whilst behind worn doors animal grunts
and bizarre fantasies are sometimes realized.

I felt that this atmosphere/scene would be too predictable and
might prove to be so cluttered as to become self-indulgent pattern
making. I decided to strip away all the superfluous elements to be
left with the barest essentials, hence the simplicity and flatness of
'The French Girls'. Despite this sparseness all references to the
hooker's slang is present in the picture.

Once this picture was complete I decided to pursue the effective
simplicity into the making of 'The Seven Deadly Finns', which
became imaginary portraits of the Finns.

R.M.

(a)   *The French Girls*

38

Each Finn has been appointed to a position in the Merchant Navy, his trade represented by various, relevant objects or environments. Also each Finn corresponds to a relevant Deadly Sin.

1: **Ship's Cook** — Gluttony

2: **Ship's Purser** — Avarice

3: **Officer's Bar Steward** (off duty) — Lust

4: **2nd in Command** — Envy

5: **Ship's Doctor** — Sloth

6: **Stoker** — Anger

7: **Captain** — Pride .... (this portrait is a homage to Marcel Duchamp)

(b)   *The Seven Deadly Finns*

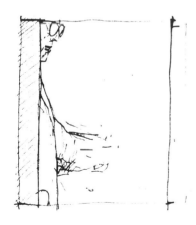

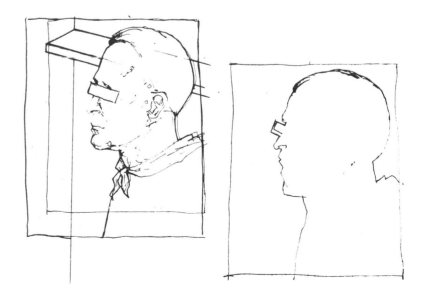

THE PAINTED SCORE

Like many other rock musicians of the 1960s and 1970s – John Lennon, Pete Townshend, Bryan Ferry – Brian Eno enjoyed the benefits of an art school education. He studied, first at Ipswich then at Winchester, at a time when the art colleges were peculiarly liberal institutions, much further from the academic mainstream than they are today. If you were non-conformist, creative, a square peg in the round hole of formal education, the English art school appeared to offer you a haven. In reality, though, not all of these institutions were as free and easy as they might at first have seemed. Some of those who taught in the art schools undertook their calling with near missionary intensity. Educators like Roy Ascott, whose tenure at Ipswich Art School coincided exactly with Eno's time there, brought a steely intellectual rigour to the teaching of art, as Eno himself recalls:

I guess that we were all united by one idea – that art school was the place where you would be able to express yourself, where the passionate and intuitive nature that you felt raged inside you would be set free and turned into art. As it happened, we couldn't have been more wrong. The first term at Ipswich was devoted entirely to getting rid of these silly ideas about the nobility of the artist by a process of complete and relentless disorientation. We were set projects that we could not understand, criticized on bases that we did not even recognize as relevant.[1]

Such an education was bound to leave its mark. In Eno's case the effects of this training were deep and lasting. Without the influences, both theoretical and practical, that he experienced at art school, it is doubtful that Eno's ideas and music could have developed in the way that they did. Where some of Eno's rock world colleagues paid mere lip service to the aims of fine art, plundering styles and stances for effect rather than meaning, Eno made many of the assumptions of his education central to his later work. The degree to which he was able to import these ideas and approaches makes him unique in Seventies rock music. But it is well to remember that ideas which look positively iconoclastic in the parochial world of rock were often common currency on the contemporary art scene. Eno's originality derives at least as much from the context in which he chose to apply his ideas as from the ideas themselves.

THE QUADRANGLE DILEMMA

Eno began his pre-diploma course at Ipswich Art School in 1964 and stayed there for two years. At that time, Ipswich was under the direction of Roy Ascott, a visionary teacher whose unorthodox methods earned him the disapproval of many of his less adventurous art world colleagues. In the early Sixties Ascott had been head tutor at Ealing Art College, where he taught Pete Townshend. There, his approach was interdisciplinary, owing as much to the new field of cybernetics, the science of organization and control, as it did to conventional art theory. Assisted at Ipswich by colleagues like Anthony Benjamin, Noel Forster and Tom Phillips,[2] Ascott was far more concerned to explore the nature of creative behaviour than to teach students how to mix their oil paints. He wanted his students to react to new situations with a broader, less predictable range of responses; to learn to discover art in unfamiliar places.

One procedure employed by Ascott and his staff was the 'mindmap'. In this project each student had to invent a game that would test and evaluate the responses of the people who played it. All of the students then played all of the games, and the results for each student were compiled in the form of a chart – or mindmap. The mindmap showed how a student tended to behave in the company of other students and how he reacted to novel situations. In the next project each student produced another mindmap for himself that was the exact opposite of the original. For the remainder of the term he had to behave according to this alternative vision of himself. 'For everybody concerned this was an extraordinary experience,' recalls Eno, 'and it was instrumental in modifying and expanding the range of interaction each student was capable of.'[3]

The disorientation provoked in Eno by this and other exercises was confirmed by an incident which took place towards the end of the first term. Later, Eno dubbed this incident 'the Quadrangle Dilemma'. Returning one day from lunch, the students discovered a notice instructing them to assemble in the school's courtyard, a quadrangle surrounded on all sides by studio buildings. Once all the students were inside the courtyard the door was locked from the outside by one of the teachers. There was no other exit. Then members of staff began to appear on the roofs above, watching the students from the comfort of chairs:

They said nothing and would not answer our questions. Furthermore, they continued to say nothing for more than an hour. During this time, our mild amusement at this situation changed to uneasiness and then complete perplexity. We all had an idea that we were expected to do something, but none of us knew what. I think we were all frightened of doing the wrong thing, frightened to look foolish. All kinds of odd things began to happen – guys tried to scale

1 Eno, text for a lecture to Trent Polytechnic, 1974.
2 Tom Phillips and Eno remain friends to this day. The cover of **Another Green World** features a detail from Phillips' painting **After Raphael**. In 1977, Eno's Obscure Records label released a recording of Phillips' opera, **Irma**, based on his treated Victorian novel **A Humument**.
3 Eno, text for a lecture to Trent Polytechnic, 1974.

the walls, others banded together into ad hoc revolutionary committees, some said this was the last straw, others cried or formed conga-chains and walked round chanting abuse at the staff.[4]

A tape came on: a recording of the voice of their teacher, Tom Phillips. The voice said:

You are worse than chickens. A chicken is afraid to step outside of a chalk circle drawn around her, but at least she can say in her justification that the circle was drawn by a strange hand. But you have drawn with your own hands the formula, and now you look at it instead of reality.[5]

For Eno, the shock of this experience was compounded by the refusal of the staff to discuss its meaning. Only later did he decide that the Quadrangle Dilemma embodied a mental condition that he knew from his own work, and that Ascott and his colleagues had used the incident as an object lesson in 'the tension that arises from being plunged into a novel situation'. During the mid-1970s, this idea would come to assume increasing importance in Eno's ideas about the function of art.

BEHAVIOURAL MAPS

Eno's first experiments with the musical potential of tape recorders date from his time at Ipswich. Encouraged by Tom Phillips, he began to turn away from painting towards musical composition. A large metal lampshade was the sound source for the first piece that Eno recorded. When struck it sounded like the clang of a very deep bell. By recording the sound of the lampshade at different speeds, Eno produced the effect of a cluster of bells, very close in pitch, chiming together. Eno's earliest experiments were carried out on the art school tape recorder, but by the time he was twenty he owned thirty tape recorders of his own in various states of disrepair. Only one or two of the machines worked properly. Each of the others generated its own characteristic sound – an unstable motor, for instance, might cause the noise to oscillate – and Eno would combine these different sonic elements together in musical ways.

Eno was not alone in making the transition from painting to music. Other students at Ipswich were moving in the same direction, for reasons which Eno himself explains:

In the mid-1960s, music was definitely the happening art. Painting seemed extremely cumbersome, bunged up with old ideas and incapable as a medium of responding to a new feeling that was moving through the arts. This new feeling was expressed by the motto 'process not product'. The movement represented a sense many people felt that the orientation towards producing objects was no longer exciting, and, instead, processes were becoming the interesting point of focus. Most of the country's art teachers found this orientation very difficult to stomach, because they had been educated in a climate that talked in terms of 'balance', 'harmony', 'spatial relationships', and 'colour values' – all of which are formal qualities of the object. And they were faced with a group of students who were effectively saying, 'I don't care what the painting looks like; it's simply a residue of this procedure that I am interested in.' But music seemed to avoid this dilemma completely – music was process, and any attempt to define a single performance of a piece as its raison d'être seemed automatically doomed. A music score is by definition a map of a set of behaviour patterns which will produce a result – but on another day that result might be entirely different.[6]

Eno did not mean by this the music which results from conventional musical notation. He meant the deliberately open, frequently verbal scores employed by many experimental composers

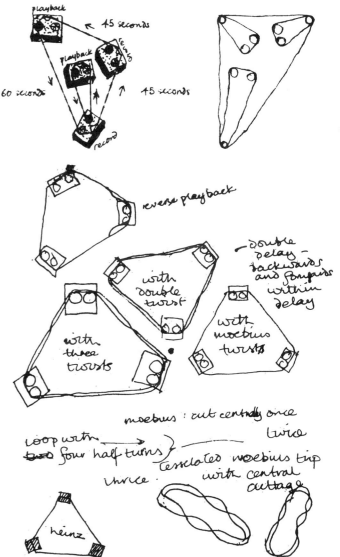

of the period. In *Experimental Music: Cage and Beyond*, Michael Nyman offers this definition of such a composer's concerns:

Experimental composers are by and large not concerned with prescribing a defined time-object *whose materials, structuring and relationships are calculated and arranged in advance, but are more excited by the prospect of outlining a* situation *in which sounds may occur, a process of generating action (sounding or otherwise), a* field *delineated by certain compositional 'rules'.*[7]

John Cage had been one of the first composers to signal this shift of emphasis from the purity and repeatability of the work as a predetermined pattern of sounds, to the idea or process used to generate it. The score of *4' 33"*, Cage's famous 'silent' piece of 1952, instructed the performer to do nothing at all for each of the work's three numbered movements. The musical content of the work then became whatever sounds could be heard in the background – cars in the street outside, birds in the trees, the creak of a chair, a cough in the audience. Clearly, sound phenomena like these were completely beyond the control of both composer and performer. The important thing was that the work

4 *Ibid.*
5 *Ibid.*
6 *Ibid.*
7 Michael Nyman, Experimental Music: Cage and Beyond (Studio Vista, London, 1974).

had created a setting in which the sounds could be considered as music; just as Marcel Duchamp, by selecting and signing a urinal, had designated it art. At the same time, as Michael Nyman has pointed out, *4' 33"* underlined the nature of the music performance (or in this case non-performance) as theatre, as something not just to listen to, but to look at.

To Eno, the heady blend of zen philosophy and musical iconoclasm proposed by Cage's seminal book *Silence*,[8] which he read many times during this period, seemed to vindicate the apparently 'goalless' activity that was a characteristic of his own musical experiments. By concentrating on behaviour rather than results, and process rather than product, Cage had helped to create a basis for dialogue between all the arts, a recognition that ideas held in common were more important than purely local differences of media.[9]

This dialogue had immediate consequences on Eno's work as a diploma student at Winchester Art School, where he started in 1966. As he delved deeper into the textual processes that could be used to generate music, so Eno's approach to painting and sculpture became increasingly conceptual. If two performances of the same piece of music could differ in such interesting ways, then why shouldn't the same thing apply to two 'performances' of the same picture? To test this idea, Eno produced, in 1967, two 'scores for painting' that were directly comparable with many of the musical scores written by experimental composers like Christian Wolff, LaMonte Young, Cornelius Cardew and George Brecht. Both of Eno's scores took the

form of written instructions. In the first, two or more painters, working in isolation from each other, attempt to paint the same picture. Geometrical references indicate where marks should be placed in the picture space, and British Standard Colour codings specify the colours. When the paintings are completed they are exhibited side by side. In the second score, one painter has to reconstruct the missing painting of another. He is allowed to examine the first painter's rags, brushes and paint splashes for 'evidence' and, acting as 'detective', he can question eye-witnesses about the appearance of the missing picture. Once again the paintings which result are exhibited together.

During this period Eno also constructed a number of 'sound sculptures', in which the distinction between the sculpture's function as an art object, and its potential as a music generator, became ever more blurred. One of these pieces consisted of a large column with a speaker at the top. The sound of voices and other ambient noise, relayed from elsewhere in the installation, caused a ping-pong ball to tremble and vibrate in the mouth of the speaker.

Pursuing his investigations of the area where art, music and performance overlapped, Eno formed Merchant Taylor's Simultaneous Cabinet, an avant-garde performance group, with a floating student membership. The group performed works by Eno, Christian Wolff, Tom Phillips and George Brecht. Among these were two versions of Brecht's *Drip Music (Drip Event)*:

> For single or multiple performance.
> A source of dripping water and an empty vessel are arranged so that the water falls into the vessel.
> Second version: Dripping.[10]

The four-line score for this piece allows the performer the maximum possible scope; both the scale of the *Drip Event* and the components used to effect it are entirely at the performer's discretion. A tabletop version performed by Brecht himself, for example, consisted only of a laboratory clamp, a pipette and a bottle. Eno's first version of the *Drip Event* was constructed at Wolverhampton College of Art, where Brecht himself was teaching, in the summer of 1968. The second version of the event, built towards the end of Eno's time at Winchester, was much larger – an enormous cube, with a capacity of 1000 cubic feet, through which rainwater passed by various routes.

Instructions:

Stage 1

1 As source material for this project, you will need to refer to two paintings either 1) in postcard or reproduction form or 2) in the flesh.

2 Having chosen two paintings, you are required to assume that they are both the result of the same set of instructions, the product that is, of a set of rules that the artist(s) did not break during making the paintings.

3 Deduce from observation of the paintings only, as many of the rules as possible.

4 Notate these rules as a set of instructions for making a painting.

Stage 2

1 From any sample of text, read until you find the word 'object'.

2 Rewrite the whole of the sentence in which the word occurs, but replacing it by the word "art-object".

3 You now have a fairly specific context that in some way describes the art-object in question.

4 Using the limitation of the instructions derived in stage 1, create the art-object that satisfies the context above.

REPETITION IS A FORM OF CHANGE

Eno's interest in sets of instructions (scores) that generated different 'mutations' reached its peak with his performance of *X for Henry Flynt* (1960) by LaMonte Young. Though his work is little heard today, the importance of Young in the development of both experimental 'art' music and the rock avant-garde should not be underestimated. As an early exponent of the ultra-rigorous style that came to be known as minimalism (in reaction to the indeterminacy of composers like Cage) Young was a key influence on such well-known American minimalists as Steve Reich, Terry Riley and Philip Glass. His impact on John Cale, shortly to form the Velvet Underground with Lou Reed, was equally powerful. 'LaMonte was perhaps the best part of my education and my introduction to musical discipline,' Cale said later.[11] In 1964, as a member of Young's Theatre of Eternal Music, Cale learned to produce sustained drones with his viola that would be used to devastating effect with the Velvet Underground, one of the most important bands in the history of rock, and a major influence on Eno's early albums. Much impressed by the part Cale played in shaping the Velvets' sound, Eno has himself made extensive use of both harsh and gentle drones.[12]

Gruelling repetition is the essence of *X for Henry Flynt*. The piece requires its performer to reproduce a single unspecified sound, or cluster of sounds, with as little variation as possible, for as long as he

8 *John Cage,* Silence *(Calder & Boyars, London, 1968).*

9 *In 1968, inspired by Cage's writings, Eno published twenty-five copies of a pamphlet entitled* **Music for Non-Musicians**. *Although the pamphlet is occasionally mentioned in articles about Eno in the press, Eno himself does not have a copy and no other copies are known to exist. According to Eno, writing in a letter to the author in 1984, 'It was a little manifesto written in the light of current developments in avant-garde music'.*

10 *One of the events from George Brecht's* Water Yam *(1960 – 63), a series of instructions for music and performance printed on rectangular cards of different sizes and presented as a boxed set. Eno's interest in these cards points forward to his own use of boxed instructions in* **Oblique Strategies** *(1975).*

11 *Quoted in Victor Bockris and Gerard Malanga,* Up-tight: The Velvet Underground Story *(Omnibus Press, London, 1983).*

12 *The musical debt Eno owes to John Cale – and through him to LaMonte Young – has been repaid in Eno's contributions to solo albums by Cale throughout the 1970s. In addition, the two performed together live on* **June 1, 1974**, *and Cale contributed viola to 'Sky Saw' and 'Golden Hours' on* **Another Green World**.

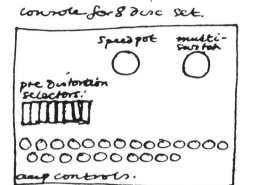

chooses. The length of the piece is determined by the arbitrary value the performer has assigned to X. In one of his own performances, Young beat a frying pan, without pause, as many as 600 times. For his rendition, Eno chose to perform *X for Henry Flynt* on a piano, and to let X equal 3,600 (the number of seconds in an hour). Linking his hands together, he smashed his forearms down on the keyboard at one second intervals. On each successive impact he tried to strike exactly the same cluster of notes:

Now, until one became accustomed to this fifty-odd note cluster, the resultant sound was fairly boring. But after that first ten minutes, it became progressively more absorbing. This was reflected in the rate at which people left the room – those who didn't leave within ten minutes stayed for the whole performance. One began to notice the most minute variations from one crash to the next. The subtraction of one note by the right elbow missing its top key was immediately and dramatically obvious. The slight variations of timing became major compositional changes, and the constant changes within the odd beat frequencies being formed by all the discords began to develop into melodic lines. This was, for me, a new use of the error principle and led me to codify a little law that has since informed much of my work – 'Repetition is a form of change'.[13]

The idea that true repetition is impossible for a human performer to achieve is one that Eno returned to over and over again. Speaking of *X for Henry Flynt* in 1981, he reiterated its importance: 'It really is a cornerstone of everything I've done since'.[14] The dictum 'Repetition is a form of change', which Eno's performance of the piece helped to inspire, became one of the most famous of his *Oblique Strategies*. Eno was fascinated by the slight differences that result between one performance of an action and the next, and by the mind's ability to ignore the information that is common to both occurrences in favour of the information that is new:

...the minute differences generated within a repeated motif fascinate me (since they are not arbitrary but reflect on the performer) partly because the very process of repetition perceptually alters a motif. That is to say something heard twice is different the second time because of an increase in familiarity with it. One analogue of the listening brain is the eye of a frog. The frog's eye, unlike ours, is absolutely static, so that its retina rapidly becomes saturated from looking at a static situation and ceases to distinguish detail. However, the most minute change (movement) in the environment is thus considerably highlighted. So the frog disregards the common (unvarying, continuous) information and becomes more intensely aware of any changing (new) information.

These musical qualities are fairly new to Western music – we

13 *Eno, text for a lecture to Trent Polytechnic, 1974.*
14 *Interview by Jim Aiken,* Keyboard, *July 1981.*

have tended to stress a teleological concept of progress within a piece of music, where climaxes are achieved by fulfilling or disappointing expectations generated by the previous progress of the music. An interesting thing happens to one's perception of music if this concept of pace and direction is removed, for example by repetition.[15]

In Eno's view, *It's Gonna Rain* by Steve Reich, an experiment with tape loops recorded in 1965, exemplified the kind of perceptual errors that could result from repetition. Playing loops of a phrase spoken by a black preacher 'it's gonna rain' simultaneously on two supposedly identical tape recorders, Reich had discovered that they were gradually slipping out of sync with each other. Intrigued by the musical implications of this discrepancy, he set about manipulating the spool on one of the recorders deliberately. In the course of the finished piece, the loops move gradually out of phase with each other and then back into unison. The effect of these subtle shifts and gentle repetitions over a period of time is to beguile the listener's ear into false perception. 'After a while you start hearing all sorts of things in there – a pigeon in the background, a truck going past and even things that aren't there at all – the sound of trumpets and bells,' Eno told an interviewer in 1982.[16]

Eno took the lesson of *It's Gonna Rain* very much to heart: 'A very simple illustration of effective technology, and a record which had a great influence on me.'[17] In this and other pieces from the period, Reich used found material as the basis of musical systems that are largely self-generating and self-regulating. 'Once the process is set up and loaded it runs by itself,' he explained.[18] For Eno, *It's Gonna Rain* demonstrated that captivating musical effects could be produced using the most basic of means, and with very little intervention on the part of the 'composer'. At the same time, it eliminated the traditional element of surprise by replacing crescendo and climax with a slowly unfolding process that was fascinating in its own right. On the two records he recorded with Robert Fripp – *(No Pussyfooting)* and *Evening Star* – and especially in his own *Discreet Music*, Eno would explore similar concerns, using tape delay techniques as generators of self-regulating music.

THE COLOUR OF SOUND

Although Eno's years of rock star glamour with Roxy Music took him into a different musical universe, he did not lose contact with the world of experimental music. For a short time after leaving Winchester in 1969, he was a member of the Scratch Orchestra founded by Cornelius Cardew, Michael Parsons and Howard Skempton, and he participated in a number of performances of Cardew's seven paragraph opus, *The Great Learning*, that were to have a decisive influence on his ideas. In 1969, Eno also joined the Portsmouth Sinfonia established by Gavin Bryars with staff and art students from Portsmouth Polytechnic. The Sinfonia, which numbered in its ranks both inspired amateurs and accomplished performers, was dedicated to musical misreadings of the popular classics. After he joined Roxy Music in 1971, Eno continued to perform with the Sinfonia occasionally – on one notorious occasion on the same bill. Later, in 1973 and 1974, he produced two albums by the ensemble.

Eno first approached Island Records (Roxy Music's record label) with the idea of releasing work by an experimental composer in 1973. Eno believed that *Jesus' Blood Never Failed Me Yet*, by Gavin Bryars, had commercial potential as well as being musically interesting. Unimpressed by the proposal, Island turned the project down. In 1975, Eno made a second attempt to float the idea of an experimental record label. On this occasion, he appealed to Island's commercial instincts by arguing the need for a research and development programme, comparable to those found in industry, to discover 'what people need

and how patterns of need change'. This time Island was persuaded. A trial budget was offered and in late 1975 Obscure Records was born.

In his first releases Eno planned to cover a wide range of material that existed in what he described as the 'borderline area' between experimental music and rock. He was interested, he said, in music from outside the mainstream which had the potential to be absorbed into, modify, and enrich the mainstream. In practice, Obscure Records developed a recognizable house style, entirely consistent with Eno's growing taste for less intrusive, more 'ambient' music. Drawing a direct analogy with the visual arts, Eno explained:

I believe that we are moving towards a position of using music and recorded sound with the variety of options that we presently use colour – we might simply use it to 'tint' the environment, we might use it 'diagrammatically', we might use it to modify our moods in almost subliminal ways. I predict that the concept of 'muzak', once it sheds its connotations of aural garbage, might enjoy a new (and very fruitful) lease of life. Muzak, you see, has one great asset: you don't have to pay attention to it. This strikes me as a generous humility with which to imbue a piece of music, though it is also nice to ensure that music can offer rewards to those who do give it their attention.[19]

Appropriately, Obscure Records was inaugurated by two pieces by Gavin Bryars: *The Sinking of the Titanic* and *Jesus' Blood Never Failed Me Yet*. Later releases included ensemble pieces by Christopher Hobbs, John Adams and Bryars; music for new and rediscovered instruments by David Toop and Max Eastley; songs and instrumental pieces by Jan Steele and Eno's mentor, John Cage; two delicate pieces for piano and bells by Michael Nyman; an opera by Eno's former teacher and friend, Tom Phillips; a quirky first album by Simon Jeffe's Penguin Cafe Orchestra; and four meditative works by Harold Budd (who would later collaborate with Eno on two further albums). It was indicative of the label's seriousness that many of the sleeves featured notes about the music and brief biographical details of the composers. From 1975 to 1978, Obscure Records released a total of ten albums, before Eno's move from Island to Polydor brought a natural end to the project. By that time the label had served its original purpose in attracting the attention of a wider public to accessible experimental music.

The third album in the Obscure series was Eno's own *Discreet Music*, in which he played one of his favourite roles: that of programmer and planner. If the music had a score, he said, it was the operational diagram, printed on the cover, that was the basis of the piece:

The key configuration here is the long delay and echo system with which I have experimented since I became aware of the musical possibilities of tape recorders in 1964. Having set up this apparatus, my degree of participation in what it subsequently did was limited to (a) providing an input (in this case, two simple and mutually compatible melodic lines of different duration stored on a digital recall system) and (b) occasionally altering the timbre of the synthesizer's output by means of a graphic equalizer.[20]

Therapeutically calming in its effect on the listener, and leagues away from the hyperactive frenzy of 'Baby's on Fire' and 'Third Uncle', *Discreet Music* was a turning point for Eno. It suggested for the first time the possibility of an unassuming environmental music, an intelligent Muzak 'as ignorable as it is interesting', that was to prove surprisingly controversial in the manic world of rock. Eno refined this approach with *Music for Airports* and the other records in the Ambient series, culminating in the masterly *On Land* in 1982. The earlier *Discreet Music*, however, continues to be one of Eno's most popular records, as well as being one of his personal favourites; a fitting tribute, in its conceptual simplicity and quiet beauty, to the experimental musicians who inspired him as a student.

15 *Eno, review of* Here Come the Warm Jets, *requested by* Spare Rib, *1973.*

16 *Interview by Mick Brown,* Sunday Times Magazine, *31 October 1982.*

17 *Ibid.*

18 *Quoted in Michael Nyman,* Experimental Music: Cage and Beyond.

19 *Eno, 'Shedding Light on Obscure Records',* Street Life, *15-28 November 1975.*

20 *Eno, cover notes for* Discreet Music, *1975.*

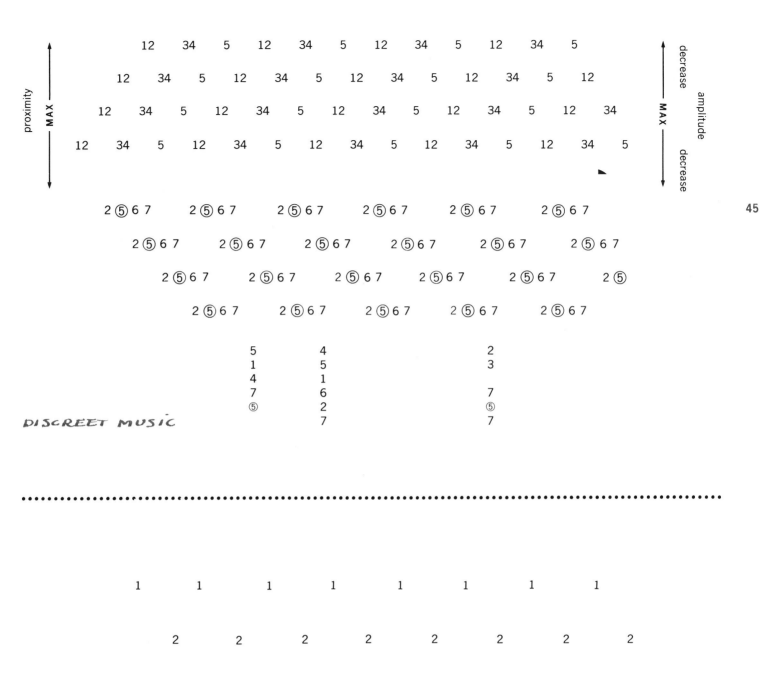

DISCREET MUSIC

MUSIC FOR AIRPORTS

etc.

The frequency of individual notes is decided by their 'relatedness' to the root note of the chord. Thus the root is most frequent.

Another system might entail using a large series of notes (say 8 or 10) and censoring whichever ones made a 'too-mutant' chord.

Invent a self censoring system.

When I got back home I found a message on the door
Sweet Regina's gone to China crosslegged on the floor
Of a burning jet that's smoothly flying
Burning airlines give you so much more.

How does she intend to live when she's in far Cathay
I somehow can't imagine her just planting rice all day
Maybe she will do a bit of spying
With microcameras hidden in her hair.

I guess Regina's on the plane a *Newsweek* on her knees
While miles below the curlews call from strangely stunted trees
The painted sage sits just as though he's flying
Regina's jet disturbs his wispy beard.

When you reach Kyoto send a postcard if you can
And please convey my fond regards to Chih-Hao's girl Yu-Lan
I heard a rumour they were getting married
But someone left the papers in Japan.

Left them in Japan.

46   ## Burning Airlines Give You So Much More

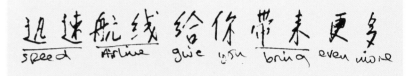

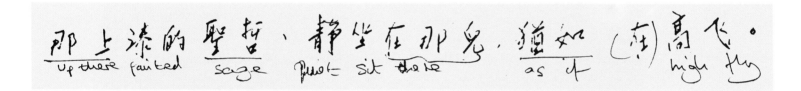

This song was originally called 'Turkish Airlines', based on what
was, up until then, about 1974, the worst air disaster ever known
– a Turkish DC-10 exploded at Orly Airport, Paris, killing all the
passengers.

I preferred to play upon the possibility/impossibility, that, as 'the
Painted Sage' was sitting in his aeroplane seat, meditating on the
mountain; (possibly posing for a portrait being painted in a
technique as specified in 'The Mustard Seed Garden Manual of
Painting'), he was so disturbed by both the noise and draught
caused by the jets, that he temporarily forgot his tolerant, generous
and sagely manner, to direct his powers against the intrusive jet. So
without disturbing his 'still' pose, he concentrates his gaze upon a
conveniently positioned mirror which reflects his destructive will
skywards, into the path of the jet, consequently causing a massive
explosion.

The main problem with this picture, as I find with most of my
pictures, is in finding/achieving a satisfactory composition. Whilst
the imagery itself usually develops quite naturally, with the
occasional asides suggesting successful alternatives, the
composition is forced to be continually altered either by intuition or
the random dictates of the various integral pieces.

I consider both careful composition and chance to be more
important than strong or complete colour.

R.M.

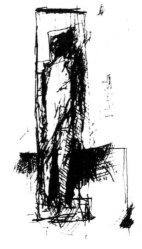

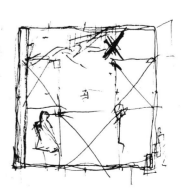

The cry of a curlew at night foretells disaster – old superstition.

The painted sage sits just as though he's flying

These are your orders, seems like it's do it or die
So please read them closely
When you've learnt them be sure that you eat them up
They're specially flavoured with burgundy, Tizer and rye
Twelve sheets of foolscap, don't ask me why.

We hit the jungle just as it starts to monsoon
Our maps showed no rainfall
All the boys were depressed by this circumstance
Trust in the weather to bless agricultural man
Who gives birth to more farmhands, don't ask me why.

Fifteen was chosen because he was dumb
Seven because he was blind
I got the job because I was so mean
While somehow appearing so kind
Drifting about through the cauliflower trees
With a cauliflower ear for the birds
The Squadron assembled what senses they had
And this is the sound that they heard

Back at headquarters khaki decisions are made
File under 'Futile', that should give you its main point of reference
It's all so confusing, what with pythons and then deadly flies
But to them it's a picnic, don't ask me why.

Thirteen was chosen because of his luck
Eleven because of his feet
One got signed up for exceptional pluck
Another because he was mute
Roaming about through the gelatin swamps
With a gelatin eye on the stripes
The Squadron assembled what senses they had
And this is the sound that they heard.

Back in Blighty there was you
There were milkmen every morning
$\frac{But}{Fuck}$ these endless shiny trees

Never used to be that way.

48   Back In Judy's Jungle

One of the recurrent themes of rock music is a preoccupation with new dances. And it's taken by intellectuals as the lowest form of rock music, the most base and crude. So I was interested in combining that very naïve and crude form of basic expression with an extremely complex concept like 'Taking Tiger Mountain', which would be a sort of double joke. First of all the joke of me doing a dance number and secondly the fact that it also has a complete symbology that discusses another question.

The idea is paraphrasing the dance as a dance between two technologies. One of McLuhan's contentions is that conflict, international conflict, is always conflict between two technologies, not two moralities. Moralities are dictated by those technologies. I've taken the conflict between the regular-type soldiers and guerrilla-type activities. I've called the regular soldier-type ones, since they're mechanically orientated, clockwork ones. The guerrilla-tactic ones are electronic...I'm not subscribing to any political point of view. It's to do with this technological rift. Technological rifts have always produced hybrid art forms. I mean the reason that England is such an interesting place artistically is because it's an incredibly diverse place with opportunities for several kinds of rifts. There's an electronical society, a mechanical society and a rural society. ✳

For the soldiers it's a set of emergencies,
For the guerrillas it's a set of opportunities.

B.E.

✳ *Interview by Cynthia Dagnal,* **Rolling Stone**, *12 September 1974.*

As a union of lyrics and music I like this song, and I am interested in Eno's theories related to regular and guerrilla fighters, but despite this I did not relish the thought of producing an accompanying image. I find the numerous vignettes of exaggerated war themes annoying. I would feel the same if I watched a collage of all the 'memorable/recognizable clichéd extracts from war films slightly out of focus – (*Bridge Over The River Kwai, The Longest Day*, etc.). Once my reluctance had been recognized and resolvedly overcome, I perversely enjoyed the experiment of attempting to create something that I like from something I don't like...

As the whole scenario is a sham, I provided a fake jungle backcloth and props. The figures **(seven again)**, are painted flatly – a reference to 'Paint by Numbers' kits which are equally fake. Only the Squadron's selected senses exist outside the netting that 'traps' the picture.

The guerrillas are represented by a few glinting rifle barrels poking through the jungle foliage in a rough circling ambush.

The jungle backdrop was built up with washes of watercolour from pale yellow through to very dark, dense green on a Japanese rag paper.

R.M.

number figures – next to heads of each in red against green

15 . 7 , I , 13 , 11 | , ANO.

dumb | blind | mean | lock | feet | pluck | mute
             Kind | ballet | head | bandaged.
        optics   ?

The Squadron assembled what senses they had

Well I rang up Pantucci spoke to Lucia
Gave them all they needed to know
If affairs are proceeding as we're expecting
Soon enough the weak spots will show
I assume you understand that we have options on your time
And will ditch you in the harbour if we must
But if it all works out nicely, you'll get the bonus you deserve
From doctors we trust.

The Fat Lady of Limbourg
Looked at the samples that we sent
And furrowed her brow
You would never believe that
She'd tasted Royalty and Fame
If you saw her now
But her sense of taste is such that she'll distinguish with her tongue
The subtleties a spectrograph would miss
And announce her decision while demanding her reward
A jelly fish kiss.

Now we checked out this duck quack
Who laid a big egg oh so black it shone just like gold.
And the kids from the city finding it pretty
Took it home and there it was sold
It was changing hands for weeks
Till someone left it by their fire
And it melted to a puddle on the floor
For it was only a candle a Roman scandal
Oh oh and now it's a pool.

That's what we're paid for
That's what we're paid for
That's what we're paid for here.

50   The Fat Lady Of Limbourg

...a fantasy about low-life. The speaker represents an unidentified
undercover organization (we) hiring someone for a job, the Fat Lady of
Limbourg is an expert on something – some unspecified substance.
Limbourg is a town in Belgium famed for its very large asylum. The inmates
outnumber the townsfolk. The Fat Lady is one of the inmates, and her past
may or may not be real. *'That's what we're paid for'* – we're just doing a
job – we have no feelings about it! A Burroughs-type song.

B.E.

I like the synthesis of the disorientating music and the ambigious,
mysterious lyrics in this song. This reminds me of my days at
Canterbury Art College where I was a Foundation Student for a year.
I was financially lacking, and was forced to take a weekend job as a
general porter at a mental hospital just outside the city.

(People huddled in corners, conspiratorial gestures, secret languages
just out of earshot. Patients, who shuffled so silently, creeping up
behind me in their thick slippers. Dingy uniform institution colours.
Factory high and wide corridors, with distant fanlights.)

The only clues to the Fat Lady's status is her veiled beany hat and
red socks, which have either been offered to her by frightened
fellow patients in exchange for favours, or have been extracted by
cunning from slow-witted members of the staff. The Doctor is one
who is trusted by the Fat Lady, he acts as an intermediary,
accepting the 'samples' from ? and passing them on to the Fat Lady.

R.M.

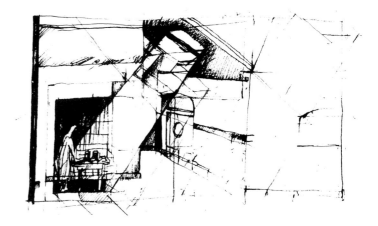

The examination is taking place whilst the hospital sleeps . . . .

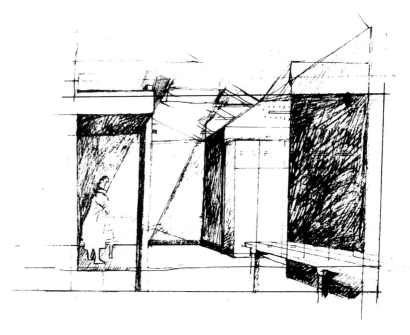

Looked at the samples that we sent

I can think of nowhere
I would rather be
Reading morning papers
Drinking morning tea.

She clutches the tray
And then we talk just like a kitchen sink play
Nothing ventured nothing gained
Living so close to danger
Even your friends are strangers
Don't count upon their company.

Places for the fingers
Places for the nails
Hidden in the kitchen
Right behind the scales.

What do I care
I'm wasting fingers like I had them to spare
Plugging holes in the Zuider Zee
Punishing Paul for Peter
Don't ever trust those meters
What you believe is what you see.

In my town, there is a raincoat under a tree
In the sky there is a cloud containing the sea
In the sea there is a whale without any eyes
In the whale there is a man without his raincoat.

In another country
With another name
Maybe things are different
Maybe they're the same.

Back on the train
The seven soldiers read the papers again
But the news it doesn't change
Swinging about through creepers
Parachutes caught on steeples
Heroes are born
But heroes die.

Just a few days
A little practice and some holiday pay
We're all sure
You'll make the grade
Mother of God if you care
We're on a train to nowhere
Please put a cross upon our eyes
Take me I'm nearly ready you can take me
To the raincoat in the sky
Take me my little pastry mother take me
There's a pie shop in the sky.

Walls have ears—war propaganda—home front

Wait! Count 15 slowly before moving in the blackout

Think before you speak

For vitality eat greens

Grow your own food, supply your own cookhouse

A clear plate means a clear conscience

Don't take more than you can eat

Lend a hand on the land

52   Mother Whale Eyeless

Like 'Back In Judy's Jungle', this song contains numerous exaggerated war movie clichés, and as with 'Back In Judy's Jungle', I was reluctant to tackle it. And again there are seven characters… the Magnificent Seven?

Blind patriotism, bravery, cowardice, pacifism, etc. I decided to concentrate on the various scenes in this song as almost separate units with the intention of juxtaposing and linking the fragments in a way that they themselves dictated. The 'Raincoat' is attached to the cover of the War Diary. The dead soldiers at the bottom of a trench are painted on the inside cover of a Bible. The Poppy equals dead heroes, the white feather equals living cowards.

•   •   •   •   •   •   Symbolism runs rife…

R.M.

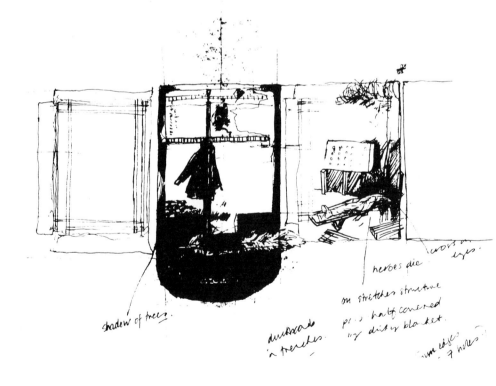

shadow of trees.

heroes die   cross on eyes.

on stretchers structure
pro. half covered
ny dirty blanket.

ambroads
in trenches.

men close.
7 nurses

sweet—fresh—heaven—higher	(esoteric knowledge)—1 sea
salt—bitter—earth—lower	(exoteric knowledge)—2 sea

PS The pies in the sky were taken from the *Beano* comic.

Heroes are born
But heroes die.

Monica sighed
Rolled on to her side
She was so impressed that she just surrendered

She was moved by his wheels
She was just up from Wales
He was fuelled by her coals and he was coming to catch her

Lose the sense of time
Nail down the blinds
And in the succulent dark there's a sense of ending

Joking aside
The mechanical bride
Has fallen prey to the Great Pretender.

Let me just point out discreetly
Though you never learn
All those tawdry late night weepies
I could make you weep more cheaply

As the empty moon enamels
Monica with spoons and candles
Bangs around without the light on
Furniture to get it right on

Settled in a homely fishpool
Hung with little eels
Often thinks that travel widens
'Stay at home, the trout obliges'

Monica sighed
Rolled on to her side
She was so impressed that she just surrendered.

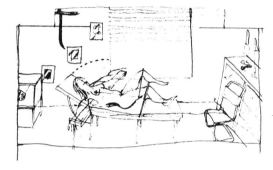

54 The Great Pretender

(a)

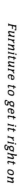

55

This is like the rape of a suburban housewife by a crazed machine. I like the verses:

As the empty moon enamels
Monica with spoons and candles
Bangs around without the light on
Furniture to get it right on

and

Settled in a homely fishpool
Hung with little eels
Often thinks that travel widens
'Stay at home, the trout obliges'

because I like the vision of confusion in it. On the other hand it could be this way round: Monica is machine-like, accurate and proper, and the Great Pretender (also the Trout) disturbs her balance.

B.E.

A longtime pet idea of mine has been that of completely furnishing a house with surgical equipment and appliances. With this interest in mind, the theme of rape in the song and the line 'Furniture to get it right on', I used the opportunity to visualize a couple of pieces of furniture, slightly re-styled so as to function for sexual play. I am pleased with the incongruity of the surgical/sexual furniture placed within the outlines of a suggested, archetypal semi-detached in the suburbs *(behind net curtains)*.

R.M.

(C)

She was moved by his wheels
She was just up from Wales

There are tins
There was pork
There are legs
There are sharks
There was John
There are cliffs
There was mother
There's a poker
There was you
Then there was you.

There are scenes
There are blues
There are boots
There are shoes
There are Turks
There are fools
They're in lockers
They're in schools
There in you
Then there was you.

Burn my fingers
Burn my toes
Burn my uncle
Burn his books
Burn his shoes
Cook the leather
Put it on me
Does it fit me
Or you?
It looks tight on you.

56   Third Uncle

Being a collection of arbitrary sentences which are full of conflicting and incongruous images, this proved to be a difficult piece to visualize as a single solution. One section that evoked for me, a sense of the whole, was the last:

Cook the leather
Put it on me
Does it fit me
Or you?
It looks tight on you.

The two images that I produced are, in effect, impressions sparked off by these lines within the random context of the whole song. Again colour is of little importance, with composition being more crucial. Both pieces owe thanks to the paintings of Francis Bacon. The dark, shaped board was originally a noticeboard which I salvaged from a burnt out timber merchant's office in Maidstone, whilst I was a student there. It required a lot of cleaning and preparation before I could work on it. I wanted to keep it as near to its original state as possible, yet manageable.

The image on the wood highlights the Uncle's fate, whilst the second image, on paper, is concerned with the exchange and fitting of the Uncle's burnt skin.

This is one of my favourite Eno songs; its disorientating mode appealing to my own approach/methods/accidents. It is also interesting to note how this piece anticipates the spirit of 'Punk' or 'New Wave' music by two or three years...

R.M.

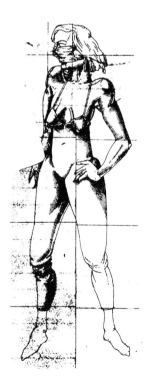

Does it fit me
Or you?
It looks tight on you.

(b)

Third Uncle (Arena Version)

This piece was produced for and during the filming of a BBC2 *Arena* programme, which deals with my work on this set of pictures, and my collaboration with Brian Eno. See 'Third Uncle', on page 56, for lyrics and further information.

As I find the ideal mode of producing/executing work is in total privacy, the intrusion of a film crew (eight people) and their camera and recording equipment, from 10.30 a.m. until about 9.30 – 10.00 p.m. every day for three successive days, severely curtailed my work. It also proved to be a strangely artificial situation in which to tackle a piece of work. Despite the obvious restrictions, I was pleased to be able to make what I consider to be successful solution to complement the song.

The previous two pictures for this song dealt respectively with,
(a) the burning of the 'Uncle',
(b) the fitting of the 'Uncle's skin';
so this third interpretation needed to be a new angle, even further removed from a reverence to the 'familiar', the truth of the lyrics. Therefore this picture deals with the scene after the burning of the 'Uncle', and immediately before the fitting of his skin. The 'Uncle' has been burnt in the chair, whilst the girl at the right wears a handkerchief covering her mouth and nose to avoid the smell; she is the 'You' of the song. The picture evolved after the chair was made and had been burnt. Up until this point I had no clear, focused idea of a finished piece, I couldn't envisage a final result, but this, and the unreal circumstances pushed the work into areas that I don't think I would've ventured into otherwise. The disorientation helped create the image, and it is reflected in the flat space of the picture.

The colours are either muted to suit the mood of the lyrics, or blues to realize the line 'There are blues', or signal red to symbolize the heat, violence and inherent danger that permeates the whole.

R.M.

There are scenes
There are blues

(skin/leather) Xipe, the Aztec God of Spring, wears skin of a sacrificed victim as his own symbolising the promise of re-birth, renovation in the annual return of spring.

Blues—the devil—evil demon   Apparitions seen in D.T.'s therefore deep despondency   blue funk—(slang) great terror   blue murder—extreme activity, commotion

burn blue—with blue flames—presence of sulphur   Blue/Black=*chaos*—passive sky sea   absorbs light—terrestrial or infernal.   cold, retreating, intellect,

Put a straw under baby
Your good deed for the day
Put a straw under baby
Keep the splinters away.

Let the corridors echo
As the dark places grow
Hear Superior's footsteps
On the landing below.

There's a place in the orchard
Where no one dare go
The last nun who went there
Turned into a crow.

Turned into a crow-crow
Turned into a crow
The last nun who went there
Turned into a crow.

There's a brain in the table
There's a heart in the chair
And they all live in Jesus
It's a family affair.

60   **Put A Straw Under Baby**

Following the experiment and discovery of the potential uses of the sewing machine as an alternative 'mark maker', in 'Cindy Tells Me', I went back to learn from the results. With two pieces of black stamp album paper with a subtle blue/grey grid as the two elements to be sewn the result became the background/set for this picture.

'Put a straw under baby' refers to the practice of placing a piece of straw under an altarpiece image of the Infant Jesus as a sign of reverence/homage. Variations on this theme have been made in Flemish paintings of the fifteenth century.

The song is gentle, mysterious and suggestive of the belief of God's omnipresent omnipotence. The last verse in particular reminds of the schooldays adage: '**God is everywhere. Therefore God is in my inkwell. If I put my hand over my inkwell I have caught God.**' The picture takes the last verse as its basis, using its unlikely juxtapositions as parallels to the unlikely proposition that God actually is in MY INKWELL!

There's a brain in the table
There's a heart in the chair
And they all live in Jesus
It's a family affair.

R.M.

. . . they all live in Jesus
It's a family affair.

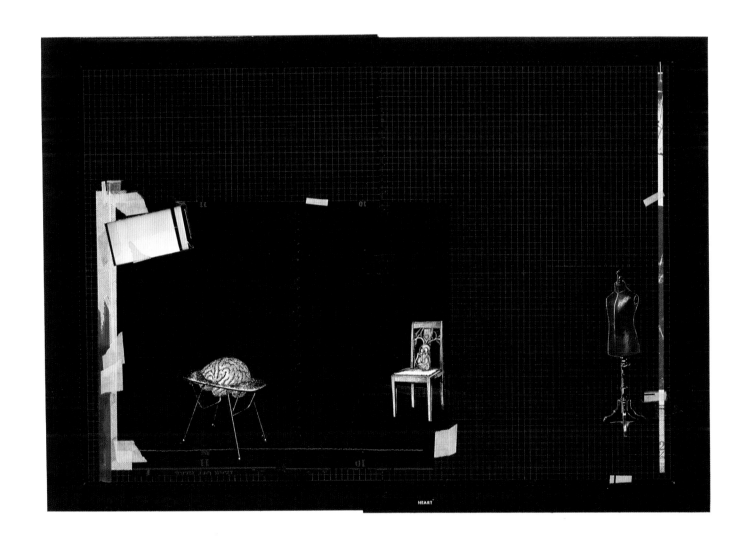

We are the 801
We are the central shaft

And we are here to let you take advantage
Of our lack of craft
Certain streets have certain corners
Sooner or later we'll turn yours.

We are the 801
We are the central shaft

And thus throughout two years we've crossed the ocean
In our little craft *(row, row, row)*
Now we're on the telephone
Making final arrangements *(ding, ding).*

We are the 801
We are the central shaft

Looking for a certain ratio
        Someone must have left it underneath the carpet
Looking up and down the radio
        Oh, oh, nothing there this time
Looking for a certain ratio
        Someone said they saw it parking in a car lot
Looking up and down the radio
        Oh, oh, nothing there this time
Going back down to the rodeo
        Oh, oh, oh, oh, oh, oh, oh, oh, here we go!

We are the table the captain's table let's get it understood
        Let's get it understood
We are the losers we are the cruisers let's get it understood
        Let's get it understood
We are the diners the final diners let's get it understood
        Let's get it understood
Most of us tinkers, some of us tailors
And we've got candlesticks and lots of cocktail sticks
We saw the lovers the modern lovers and they looked very good
        They looked as if they could
We are the neighbours the nosy neighbours we think just like you would
        We think just like you should.

62   The True Wheel

8—strength—Lion, King of Kings   *Randi/the head*
                Leo: represents all powerful subhuman forces. May also stand for
                Mars: War   *the pyramids*
                wreath: represents forces of nature kingdom of growing things   ↓

0—the fool— *zero:* symbol of absence of quality, quantity and mass. Denotes absolute   ⎡ *Final Diners*
                freedom from every limitation   *candlesticks*
                Sign of infinite and eternal conscious energy   *cocktailsticks*
                Superconsciousness   ⎣
                rose: white rose—freedom from lower forms of desire and passion
                        red rose—Venus—nature, desire
                dog: friend, helper and companion to man. Indicates that all non-
                human forms of life are elevated and improved by the advance of human
                consciousness
                sun: source of light, dynamo of radiant energy whence all creatures
                derive their personal force
                mountains: snow-capped peaks—indicate cold abstract principle of   *mountains*
                mathematics behind and above all warm colourful and vital activities of
                cosmic manifestation— *heights of abstract thought*
                        wisdom and understanding

1—the magician— *serpent:* symbol of wisdom for it tempts man to knowledge.   ⎡ *mathematical*
                Secrecy. Subtlety. Serpent biting tail represents law of endless   *starsigns*
                transformation.   *type marks*
                Also represents radiant energy descending into manifestation.   *abbreviations*
                lily: abstract thought untinged by desire.   ⎣ *magic symbols*

                                                                                    lily
                                                                                    radio

This track started from a dream. I was staying in the Drake Hotel in New York with a girl called Randi N—. I had a dream about her and a group of other girls (Randi and the Pyramids) and guys singing the song...they were sort of astronauts, but with all the psychological aspects of sailors.

There are two interesting things about this song. The first is that it is constructed in a circular fashion: the main section of the song is a three-chord sequence moving round within a four bar pattern like so; *1231 2312 3123 1231 2312 3123* etc. This means that the song is always being pushed in a peculiar fashion. There are two hidden treated guitar phrases at the beginning of the piece that give the game away. And the guitar solo at the end is also circular, but in another sense also: there is a special treatment on the guitar which makes it rotate in and out of phase. If you hear it on mono, you'll find that the guitar keeps disappearing. The circular effect is strongest on headphones.

The other strange thing about this song is its inadvertent links with the Cabala. I found out, long after I'd written the song, that the number 801

means 'Alpha and Omega' or 'The first and the last' in the Cabala and that this entity is a circular concept (i.e. the beginning and the ending being identical). It also means 'The Dove', which I like. The number 801 (which, with all of the rest of the chorus refrain, was plucked unaltered from my dream) has another meaning which I find interesting. In the Cabala, the twenty-two Tarot cards are arranged such that they rest on the paths between the Tree of Life. Each of the paths has a number, and each of the numbers corresponds to one of the cards in the Major Arcana of the Tarot. The paths 801 describe a pyramid whose individual sides are STRENGTH, THE FOOL, and THE MAGICIAN.

I offer all the above with no special interpretations – only with a certain curiosity. Make of it what you will, although I think a veiled reference to The Tree of Life would not go amiss.

Apparently, rumour has it in America that 801 derives from Eight Nought One. the initials of which spell...very ingenious, I thought, although it had never occurred to me.

B.E.

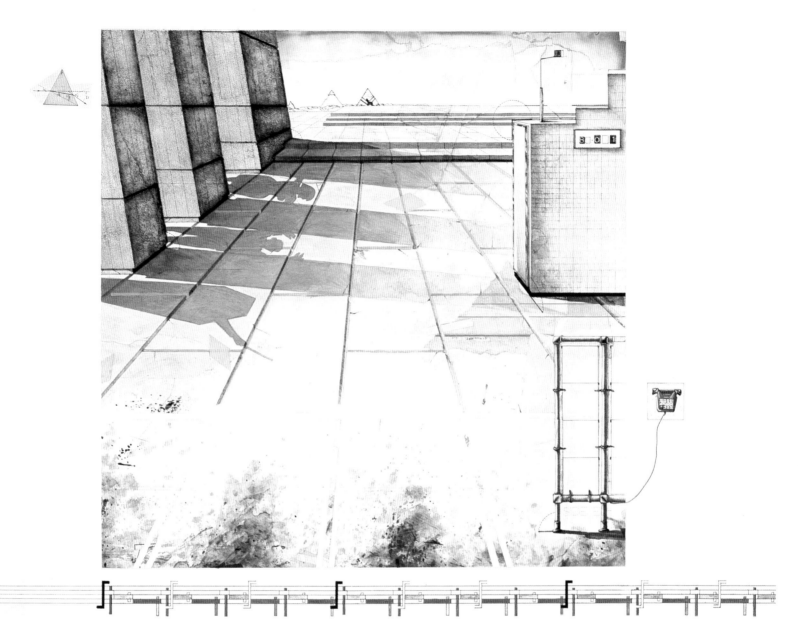

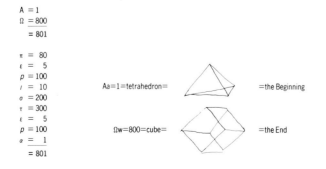

A $= 1$
Ω $= 800$
$= 801$

$\pi = 80$
$\varepsilon = 5$
$p = 100$
$\iota = 10$
$o = 200$
$\tau = 300$
$\varepsilon = 5$
$p = 100$
$a = 1$
$= 801$

Aa=1=tetrahedron=   =the Beginning

Ωw=800=cube=   =the End

Soror Mystica

androgyny and incest between siblings
headless bodies/decapitated → symbol for castration and
concept of order in the
creation of the cosmos.

pink for female garments—at Cos, husband wears a fake beard to first night of marriage.

the exchange of garments—an exploit—conquering a woman's heart.

Bosch: hooded crow pouring out from a little phial in it's beak a glimmering fluid that flows down into the
ovary—celebrating an alchemical marriage.

Duchamp: upper half—female, bride, sky   } *Large Glass*
lower half—male, batchelor, ground } *the Bride stripped bare by her Bachelors, even.*

The original androgyne—Home Major
Rebis (double thing)

brother in love with *sister* in the spring of life
↕ ↕
hero virgin

The letter 'Y'—symbol of $\dfrac{\text{immortality}}{\text{androgyne}}$

The immortal Hermetic/androgyne—Rebis—fruit of
'chemical nuptials' between:
mercury *(female lunar)* and sulphur *(male solar)*
anima *(female principle in man)* and animus *(male principle in women)*

Bisexuality has always been an attribute of divinity: the brother-sister incest pair
stands allegorically for the whole conception of opposites.

$\dfrac{\text{Brother}}{\text{Sun}} + \dfrac{\text{Sister}}{\text{Moon}}$

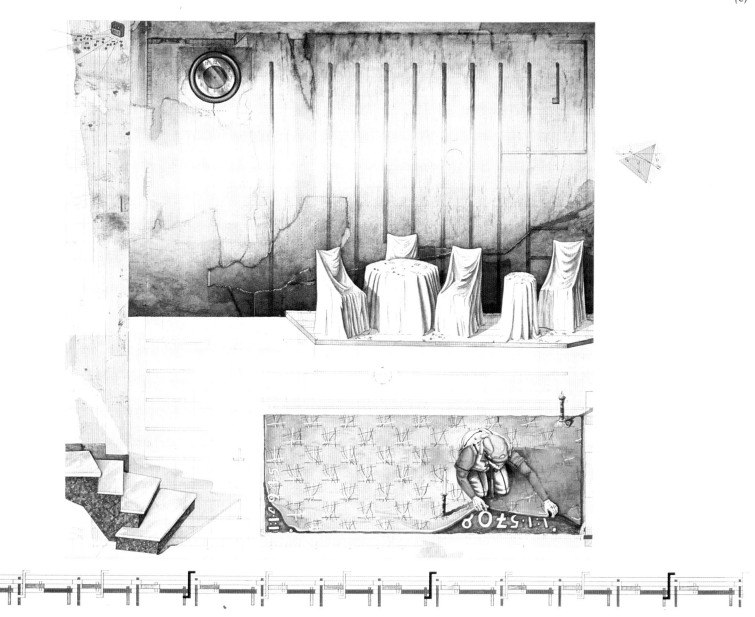

the flat mirror/symmetry — guarantees similitude of 2 objects but also affects them with incongruity: thus the right hand may appear to be similar and symmetrical to the left — but it is impossible to move a right hand glove to a left hand.
The same applies to two halves of the body.

(Kant)

Wheel: symbol of the whole cycle of cosmic expression. The centre or pivot is the archetypal or thought world; the inner cycle — creative; the middle circle — formative; the other circle — the material world.

The 8 spokes, like the 8 pointed star, represent the channels of universal radiant energy. (cards 7 and 10)

10 — Wheel of Fortune

The three pictures evolved out of the research based on the symbolism of and the translation of the Cabala, specifically the number(s) 801. [*]

The first describes the arrival of the '801' in a semi-desert-cum-technological environment; a car lot is suggested in the foreground. I don't particularly like pictures of cars and didn't want to include one of my own in this picture; the oil-stained divisions on the ground are an alternative solution.

The second and middle section portrays the '801' searching in an alien landscape. The 'landscape' came about one day when my wife, Ann, was cutting dress patterns which she spread over the floor. I thought of the line:

Most of us tinkers, some of us tailors

and stole some discarded pieces of pattern paper. These I glued down in six layers on card. The lines in their transparency created suggested planes and depths, that with a little manipulation became an environment in which the figures search. The '801' have been composed following the symbolism and the images of the Cabala.

66

strength—8—a woman, over whose head is the cosmic lemniscate/symbol of eternal life/infinity/∞ is shown confidently closing lion's mouth. Around her waist is shown a chain of roses—the union of desires which creates such strength that wild, unconscious force bows before it.   *Randi*

For a consciousness that is aware of the sign of Eternity above, there are no obstacles, nor can there be any resistance.
Spiritual power over material/love over hate/higher nature over carnal desires

the fool—0—a youth stepping (lightly/on toes) to edge of a precipice surrounded by lofty mountains. Looks out to distance—the abyss holds no terrors for him. A dog barks at his heels. A wand over his shoulder symbolises the will, a wallet slung over the end of the wand contains all knowledge of universal memory.   *the drummer / lower rating*
The rose he carries is white → freedom from lower forms of desire.

the magician—I—above his head again ∞   *snake belt/blue and gold/+ radio*
above his waist serpent devouring its own tail=∞
In right hand a wand towards sky. Left hand points to earth, therefore drawing power from above and directing it into manifestation.
On table before, are symbols of the four suits of Minor Arcara: *air, fire, water, earth.*
Roses and Lillies in the garden about him show the cultivation of desires.
He represents personal will in its union with the Divine.
Will, mastery, skill, occult wisdom, power, diplomacy.

The Dove: is a symbol of purity and the Holy Ghost—for this reason no witch or evil demon had power to assume its form. It also represents the soul, and if one circled over a particular person or perched on the roof it was taken as a sign of death. Miners would refuse to go down the shaft if a dove had flown over the pithead.

Despite this connection with death it was often said that the dying could not depart this life if their pillow or mattress contained dove feathers, and sometimes a live bird might be placed inside the sick room to prolong the dying person's life until relatives could be brought to say their farewells.

In Scotland the heart, liver and lungs ripped from a living dove were held to be an effective laxative for cattle.

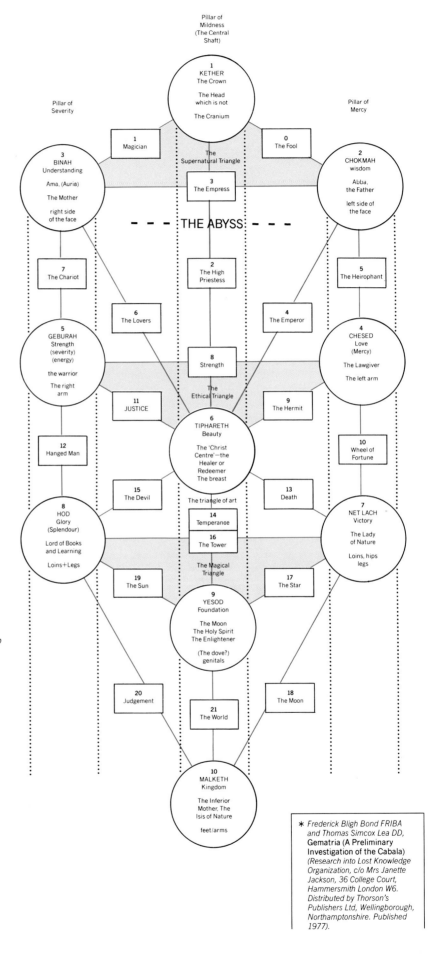

* *Frederick Bligh Bond FRIBA and Thomas Simcox Lea DD,* **Gematria (A Preliminary Investigation of the Cabala)** *(Research into Lost Knowledge Organization, c/o Mrs Janette Jackson, 36 College Court, Hammersmith London W6. Distributed by Thorson's Publishers Ltd, Wellingborough, Northamptonshire. Published 1977).*

8, being STRENGTH, in the form of Randi (leader of the Pyramids) is at the base and in the foreground.

0, being THE FOOL, accompanied by his dog, a Bull Terrier, is blindly approaching a sharp drop from the ledge at top right.

1, being the MAGICIAN, inhabits a coffin, his right hand pointing skywards, his left towards the earth.

The attitudes of the three correspond to their positions on the Tarot cards; only their dress and various attendent symbols have been changed (updated). For instance, in the Tarot, The Magician is portrayed with a serpent biting its own tail circling his waist, representing the law of endless transformation. I have used a contemporary parallel, an elastic snake belt, worn by schoolboys. The Fool and his dog appear with cracked white skin. This treatment was inspired by a particularly strange and wonderful world which sometimes featured in the *Superman* comics I used to collect when i was a kid. The planet Bizarro embodied pure Dadaist fantasies; i.e. everything is reversed, so that Bizarro best architecture is structurally unsound, bent, crooked, etc., the world is square, carpets are on ceilings, wallpaper on the floors, in sports the winner is the loser and is booed accordingly, diamonds are worthless ugly/ pretty, and coal (paradoxically today) is their currency. The lunacy was endless.

The third section shows the 'Captain's Table' left by the 'Final Diners'; the Fool serches for the 'Certain ratio' underneath the carpet. The 'Certain ratio' is painted on the underfelt, but as the Fool doesn't know what he's looking for, he fails to recognize the numbers as being significant.

The graphic notation that spans the base of all three sections is an interpretation of the circular guitar chord that drones within the song from start to finish. it is based on the simplified chart below:

R.M.

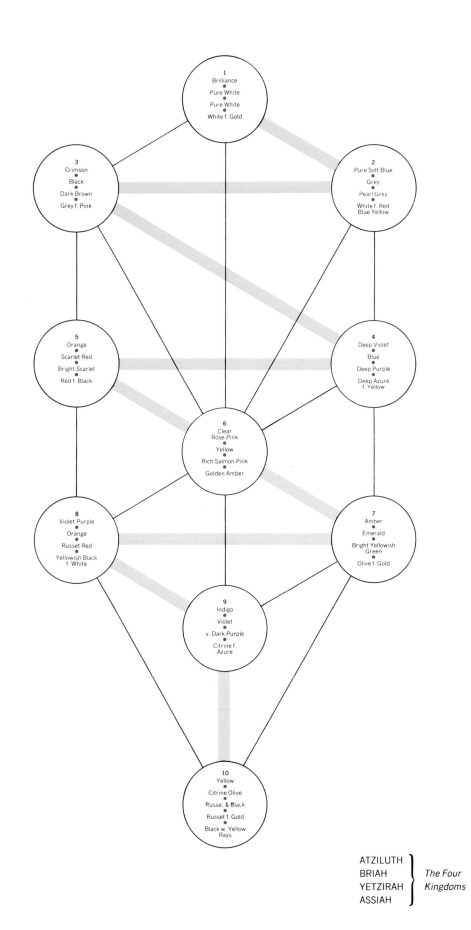

67

ATZILUTH
BRIAH
YETZIRAH
ASSIAH
} *The Four Kingdoms*

In the haze of the morning, China sits on Eternity
And the opium farmers sell dreams to obscure fraternities
On the horizon the curtains are closing

Down in the orchard the aunties and uncles play their games
(like it seems they always have done)
In the blue distance the vertical offices bear their names
(like it seems they always have done)
Clocks ticking slowly, dividing the day up

These poor girls are such fun they know what God gave them their fingers for
(to make percussion over solos)

China my China, I've wandered around and you're still here
(which I guess you should be proud of)
Your walls have enclosed you, have kept you at home for thousands of years
(but there's something I should tell you)
All the young boys they are dressing like sailors

I remember a man who jumped out from a window over the bay
(there was hardly a raised eyebrow)
The coroner told me 'This kind of thing happens every day'
You see, from a pagoda, the world is so tidy.

These poor girls are such fun
They know what God gave them their fingers for

68 **China My China**

The first scene takes place within a red square. The sky elements are
made of toilet paper – three slightly differing tones of blue; utilized
because of its poor quality through which specks of the red rag
paper are still visible. 'Vertical offices' are made from computer
print-out cards, rectified with watercolour; the windows are the
existing holes in the cards. The girls/typists are enjoying a well
earned break by the 'Democracy Wall' in Peking. Their fingers and
hands are bandaged due to their fanatical following of the guiding
motto on the large posters that dominate and run the length of the
wall; 'Defend Chairman Mao with your blood and your life.' Also
they have been 'making percussion over solos'. The vertical offices
bear, not the company names, but selected lines from the song,
in Chinese.

The second image, the box, expands the theme of the first picture. It
is a magnification of the poor girls' sad existence typing out
triplicate orders, proposals, manifestos and proclamations. It is an
elaborately conceived construction which illustrates a simple idea.

R.M.

(b)

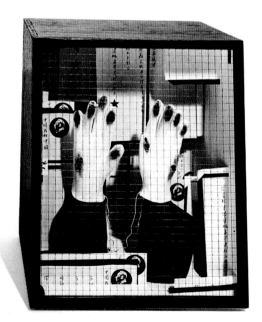

(a)

We climbed and we climbed

Oh how we climbed

Over the stars to top Tiger Mountain

Forcing the lines to the snow.

70 Taking Tiger Mountain

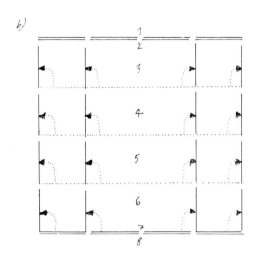

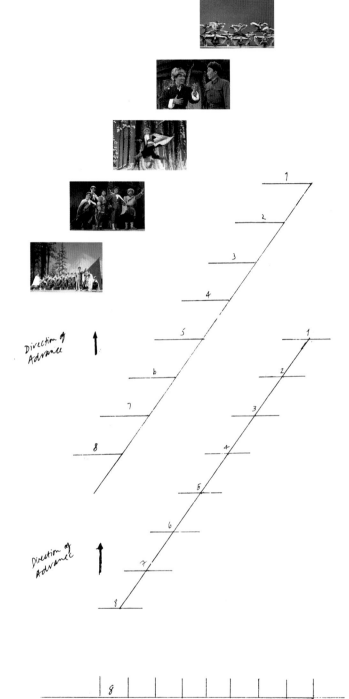

I nearly always work from ideas rather than sounds. Titles. It's that title that just fascinates me. It's fabulous. I mean, I'm interested in strategy, and the idea of it. I'm not Maoist or any of that; if anything I'm anti-Maoist. Strategy interests me because it deals with the interaction of systems, which is what my interest in music is really, and not so much the interaction of sounds. *

B.E.

The outlines of the small coloured rectangles already existed on the architectural dieline prints that form the basis of the picture. The colours graduate up from the green earth through the grey of rock to the blue sky; each line of rectangles representing the 'lines' of 'Forcing the lines to the snow'.

The hinged shelf unit shows on the front a collage of mountaineering equipment and activity, and on the back luminous stars against a deep blue/black sky.

The hidden area behind the shelf shows various examples and symbols of military strategy, some factual, some fictional, all directed towards the range of mountains above. War games.

This song and the album it is featured on were inspired by the title *Taking Tiger Mountain by Strategy* † a then 'modern' revolutionary Peking opera eulogizing Chairman Mao Tse Tung's thoughts on people's war, which Eno lifted from a set of twelve colour postcards depicting scenes from the opera.

R.M.

* *Interview by Cynthia Dagnal,* Rolling Stone, *12 September 1974.*

† Taking Tiger Mountain by Strategy (A Modern Revolutionary Peking Opera) *(Foreign Languages Press, Peking, 1970).*

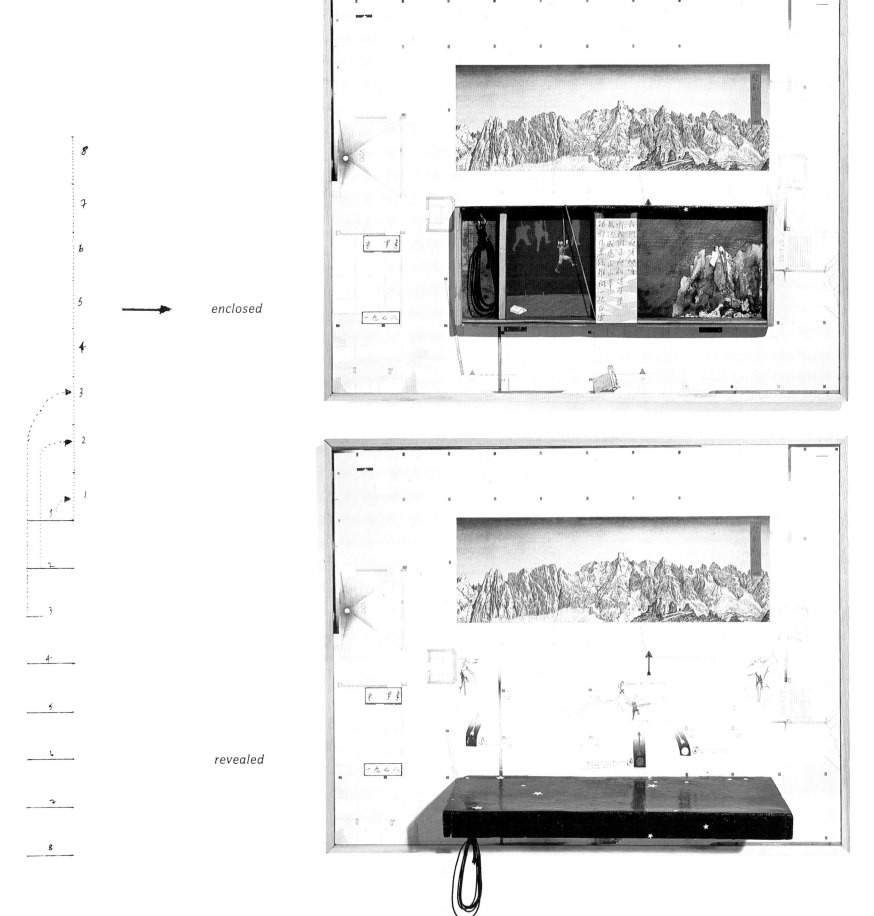

enclosed

revealed

THE DYNAMICS OF THE SYSTEM

From his earliest days at art college Eno was as interested in thinking and talking about his work as he was in producing it. So much was this the case, that tutors who doubted his natural ability as a painter assumed he would find his niche as a theorist and a teacher. In the event, like many of the most gifted creative personalities in the fields of art, music and literature, Eno became both artist and thinker. In Eno's work, theory and practice are twin components, indivisibly linked, of the same creative intelligence.

More than any other rock musician of the early 1970s, Eno was driven by the urge to explain and to justify the paths he had taken. 'I think that if you can argue yourself out of doing something, you should,' he told an interviewer in 1977. 'Anything that's strong enough will stand up to any amount of analysis.'[1] From the beginning, Eno regarded the press interview as a useful platform, a chance to articulate his ideas about music, art, cybernetics and society. 'The only rationale I have for doing interviews,' he insists, 'is that I want to think about certain things – and I find the most convenient way to think about them is to put myself into a position where I have to be articulate.'[2] The same impulse to explain his ideas and work led Eno to undertake lecture tours of universities and polytechnics, and to write two articles summarizing his ideas about the musical applications of cybernetics. With Eno's encouragement, *Enovations,* the journal of his official fan club, became a forum for the discussion of sophisticated musical ideas. By the end of the 1970s, Eno had established himself, in the words of one US magazine, as 'the prime theoretician of rock'.

Of course, Eno was not alone in his demand for explication. In the early 1970s, analysis was in vogue. The importance accorded to rock by the critics of the day – in the music press and Sunday papers alike – encouraged many artists, as well as journalists, to launch into theory. Sometimes, though by no means often, the results were valuable. Musicians such as Eno's friend Robert Wyatt, of Soft Machine and Matching Mole, and members of the avant-garde ensemble Henry Cow, provided penetrating insights into contemporary rock practice – both from a socialist perspective. But this type of self-reflection required an historical awareness and a capacity for detachment foreign to the training of most rock musicians. If anything, too much theory was a threat, as Eno himself understood. 'There's a real bogey among rock musicians about talking about music – they seem to think that if you discuss it, the magic dies or something.'[3] By contrast, Eno's knowledge of art history, and his experience of experimental music, gave him the critical and conceptual tools he needed to undertake an analysis of the still-young medium of rock.

Despite these intellectual concerns, Eno is not as coldly cerebral as his critics have sometimes painted him. Rarely, in fact, has he cut the cloth of his music to fit the pattern of his ideas. Like most musicians at work, Eno prefers to let his intuition guide him through the maze of creative possibilities. 'There has to be a period where you surrender your rational controls, where you become a servant of the work rather than a master of it. If that doesn't happen – well, with very rare exceptions, the work hasn't taken off.'[4] For Eno, analysis is a retrospective activity, a way of coming to terms with the work he has done:

But it is important to remember that all my ideas are generated by the music. The music is the practice that creates the ideas that generate the discourse. If there wasn't that practice, however simplistic it seems, there wouldn't be any discussion. I'm not a thinker in the sense of someone who does so in the abstract. My thinking is always related to my own behaviour.[5]

The insights that Eno gains from this discourse become the assumptions that underpin later projects. He believes that codifying his understanding in this way allows him to take short cuts and avoid many of the dead ends encountered by other, less rational musicians. Ideas, or 'intentions' as Eno has sometimes called them, create a frame in which the work can take place. If the work then proceeds at a tangent from the original intention, as it is almost bound to do when intuition takes over, it hardly matters. The idea has acted as a motor to the music.

intellect follows **action**

action follows *emotion*

emotion follows **intention**

intention follows *absorption*

absorption follows necessity

There is always a danger, though, that too much theoretical reflection too early in the musical process will paralyse creative action – that intuition will be thwarted. When this happened to Eno, as it did most notably with *Before and After Science,* the results were not happy on either a personal or an artistic level. The album took almost two years of agonizing indecision to complete. 'At one point I nearly argued myself out of doing it all,' Eno recalls.

ENDURING ERROR

Throughout the period covered by this book Eno was exploring questions that had preoccupied him, in one form or another, since his time at art school. What is the function of contemporary art? What are the psychological and cultural origins of this kind of work? What does the audience gain from exposure to it?

The touchstone of Eno's enquiry was the difficult new field of experimental music. But the conclusions he reached applied just as

1 *Interview by Ian MacDonald,* New Musical Express, *26 November 1977.*
2 *Interview by Steven Grant,* Trouser Press, *August 1982.*
3 *Interview by Ian MacDonald,* New Musical Express, *26 November 1977.*
4 *Interview by Caroline Coon,* Ritz, *No. 16, April 1978.*
5 *Ibid.*

forcefully to his practice as a member of the rock avant-garde. For answers to his questions, Eno looked partly to cybernetics, the science of organization and control fathered by the American mathematician Norbert Wiener,[6] and partly to biological theories of evolution and adaptation. Over the years he has drawn inspiration from the work of a number of writers and thinkers;[7] but two theorists were particularly important in the development of his ideas during the early to mid-1970s. The first was Stafford Beer, an internationally respected authority on the cybernetics of management, who remains a close friend of Eno to this day. The second was Morse Peckham, a professor of English at the University of Pennsylvania.

As a student, Eno had consulted the standard works on aesthetics, but found them wanting. The platitudes of the liberal humanist art establishment were completely out of key with his own experiences of art and music:

Like the standard issue art teachers of the day, their interest was in seeing the object as the fruition of the artistic process. And because twentieth century art frequently does not observe this premise, they were floundering – trying to graft a redundant philosophy onto a set of events that it had not been designed for. Their way out of this dilemma was never to say anything specific, but to allow all kinds of strange creatures to breed in what Stafford Beer calls 'the muck of language'. Aesthetics truly thrived on that muck, with grand and meaningless sentiments like, 'Art is the highest achievement of the human spirit', or 'Art is the embodiment of the most profound hopes and dreams of us all'.[8]

The most useful analogy with what Eno was doing at college – exploiting 'error' to produce works of art – came from an unexpected direction. Reading one of the monthly scientific magazines, Eno learned how sophisticated computers are programmed to generate a controlled flow of deviant (or erroneous) behaviour. These mutations are then checked by the computer against the quality of output produced by its existing procedures. If the new outcome is superior to the old, in the sense of being cheaper, or more profitable, or according to any other yardstick which the programmer has specified, the 'mutant' procedure is automatically adopted instead. In effect, the computer is learning as it goes along.

There was a close parallel here, Eno realized, with the biological process of mutation. A species periodically throws up random mutations of itself, but only those best suited to dealing with the changing conditions of its local environment survive. Survival, in turn, reinforces the new characteristic within the species as a whole; if the characteristic is more effective than the one it replaces it will eventually come to dominate. 'This was an exciting realization to me,' Eno recalls, 'for it seemed to indicate that there was some logic in setting up artistic processes that worked in the same fashion.'[9] Like computers and the animal kingdom, human beings also learn by mutation. But the behavioural innovations that new ways of doing things require are often resisted because they lead to unacceptable increases in the rate of error. In his book *Brain of the Firm: The Managerial Cybernetics of Organization*, which Eno cited on many occasions, Stafford Beer writes:

The observed tendency is normally to concentrate wholly on correcting the fault. Thus the organism's errors are wasted as progenitors of change, and change itself is rarely recognized as required. All the emphasis is bestowed on error correction rather than error exploitation. In turn, errors themselves are reiterated as being essentially bad. Thus it follows that when change is really understood (for some extraneous reason) to be necessary, people resist the need, because to attempt to change is automatically to increase the error rate for a time, while the new mutations are under test.[10]

To gain the full benefits of change, Eno was beginning to think, people would have to learn to accept and endure the temporary increase in error that arose from the natural process of mutation.

6 See Norbert Wiener, Cybernetics: or Control and Communication in the Animal and the Machine *(Wiley, New York, 1948).*
'Seven Deadly Finns' *includes a playful reference to Wiener.*

7 *In 1977, in addition to the books by Stafford Beer and Morse Peckham discussed in this commentary, Eno listed the following among books that he reread: H. G. Barnett,* Innovation: The Basis of Cultural Change; *Gregory Bateson,* Steps to an Ecology of Mind; *Stafford Beer,* Decision and Control *and* Platform for Change; *Chogyam Trungpa,* Cutting through Spiritual Materialism *and* The Myth of Freedom; *C.H. Waddington,* Towards a Theoretical Biology.

8 *Eno, text for a lecture to Trent Polytechnic, 1974.*

9 *Ibid.*

10 *Stafford Beer,* Brain of the Firm: The Managerial Cybernetics of Organization *(Allen Lane, London, 1972).*

11 *Morse Peckham,* Man's Rage for Chaos: Biology, Behaviour and the Arts *(Schocken, New York, 1967).*

THE FALSE WORLD

By now Eno was convinced that contemporary art must have something to do with biological process, and with the modification of behaviour patterns. Exactly where this link might lie continued to perplex him until, in 1970, he discovered *Man's Rage for Chaos: Biology, Behaviour and the Arts* by Morse Peckham.[11] He spent the next four years coming to terms with its contents.

In his brilliant and complex book Peckham attempts to establish a relationship between art forms that many scholars have been content to classify as quite different phenomena: poetry, painting, architecture and music. He does this by challenging the widespread assumption that the social and psychological function of the arts is to transform the chaos of human experience into a reassuring vision of order and unity. The opposite, he argues, is the case. Day-to-day human experience is not chaotic. Our perceptions are continually engaged in imposing order on the flux of information that reaches us through our senses. If this did not happen we would be powerless to act. In Peckham's view, what art really offers the perceiver is an escape from the orderliness of life. The arts, far from being characterized by order, exhibit a profound disorderliness: art creates expectations in its audience precisely in order to violate them. 'The distinguishing mark of the perceiver's transaction with the work of art is discontinuity of experience, not continuity; disorder, not order; emotional disturbance, not emotional catharsis...' All of the arts, whatever their formal dissimilarites, expose the perceiver to this kind of disorientation.

Two terms used by Peckham in the course of his discussion were especially important to Eno. The first of these is Peckham's concept of 'cognitive tension'. This is the feeling of deep unease that results when we realize that our mental models of how the world works – the unquestioned assumptions by which we live – are not adequate to describe the world as it really is. Cognitive tension was what Eno and his fellow students had experienced when their teachers locked them in the college quadrangle and watched them from the roofs: by all the rules teachers were not supposed to act in this way. In *Man's Rage for Chaos*, Peckham argues that high degrees of cognitive tension can only be endured in conditions of what he terms 'psychic insulation'. By this he means settings which are sufficiently cut off from the rest of life to allow the individual to lower his defences and expose himself to disorientation. A psychiatrist's office is one example of a psychically insulated setting; games and sports of all kinds are another. 'Only in protected situations, characterized by high walls of psychic insulation', Peckham writes, 'can [man] afford to let himself be aware of the disparity between his interests, that is, his expectancy or set or orientation, and the data his interaction with the environment actually produces.'

To Morse Peckham – and to Eno – the arts provide their audience with a safe area of precisely this kind. There is no physical risk, and little real psychic risk, in the creation and perception of most art (psychic discomfort is another matter). In the insulated settings in which works of art are created and perceived, artists and their audiences can experiment with ideas, attitudes, and behaviour that might, in real life, have disastrous consequences. No lasting damage will be done. In a phrase of Peckham's that became Eno's credo during this period: 'Art is the exposure to the tensions and problems of a false world so that man may endure exposing himself to the tensions and problems of the real world.' The idea that art has a biological function, that it is an 'adaptational mechanism' necessary for our survival as a species, went a long way towards resolving the uncertainty that Eno

felt about the relevance of the arts. It also reinforced, in Eno's mind, Stafford Beer's notion of the need to endure error:

The reason we invent procedures that expose us to the error and disorientation arising from unpredictability is because we need to be well rehearsed in enduring this disorientation. It is vital to our survival. To innovate successfully, we must be able to avoid panicking in situations where we are not in full control – and art offers us a rehearsal space for this very process.[12]

As Peckham puts it: 'Art is a rehearsal for the orientation that makes innovation possible.'

THE GREAT LEARNING

In 1971, Eno, along with seventy other musicians, participated in the recording of *Paragraph 2* and *Paragraph 7* of *The Great Learning* by the experimental composer Cornelius Cardew. The experience was to prove crucial to the development of Eno's thinking about contemporary art. Altogether he took part in four performances of *Paragraph 7*, and he used the close understanding of the piece that this gave him as the basis for two theoretical essays.[13] In *Paragraph 7*, a haunting work for voices, Cardew repudiates most of the controls that composers normally exercise over their music. As Eno points out in 'Generating and Organizing Variety in the Arts', the score appears, at first sight, to supply few constraints on the nature of each performer's behaviour, while the performers themselves can be of very mixed ability. Yet performances of the piece do not differ as dramatically as these factors might lead us to expect. Nor do they degenerate into

12 *Eno, text for a lecture to Trent Polytechnic, 1974.*
13 *'Generating and Organizing Variety in the Arts' appeared in* Studio International, *November/December 1976. 'Self-Regulation and Autopoiesis in Contemporary Music' was commissioned by Stafford Beer for a volume of essays on the application of cybernetics to various disciplines, which John Wiley planned to publish under the title* Challenge to Paradigm. *Eno completed his essay in 1978, but work by other contributors was not completed and the book has never appeared.*

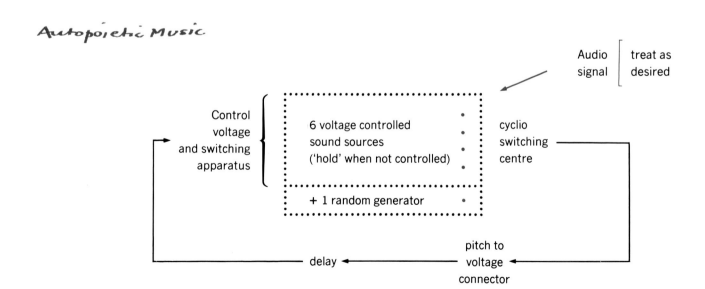

Autopoietic Music

Try '*1-2, 1-2-3-4*' with interesting sound input.

UNFREE JAZZ !   CONSTRAINED MUSIC

14 See W. Ross Ashby, An Introduction to Cybernetics (University Paperbacks, London, 1964).

15 In Brain of the Firm, Beer defines an heuristic as: 'a set of instructions for searching out an unknown goal by exploration, which continuously or repeatedly evaluates progress according to some known criterion'. Telling someone who wants to know the way to the top of a mountain with its peak lost in cloud to 'keep on going up' is an example of an heuristic. Compare this with Beer's definition of its opposite, an algorithm, as: 'a comprehensive set of instructions for reaching a known goal'. An algorithm for reaching the top of the same mountain would be much more specific: 'walk up the path 400 yards, turn right at the fallen boulder, proceed a further 150 yards', etc. 'Backwater' on Before and After Science includes a playful reference to heuristics.

16 Letter from Eno to Stafford Beer, 1975.

chaos. 'The fact that this does not happen', writes Eno. 'is of considerable interest, because it suggests that *somehow a set of controls which are not stipulated in the score arise in performance*, and that these "automatic" controls are the real determinants of the nature of the piece' (Eno's italics).

Using the concept of 'variety' – which he borrowed from cybernetics – Eno called these automatic controls variety-reducers. In cybernetics terminology, variety is the range of possible outputs (or behaviour) of which a system is capable; it is evolution's way of preparing for a range of possible futures.[14] Some of the variety-reducers in *Paragraph 7*, such as the instructions 'sing any note you can hear' and 'do not sing the same note on two consecutive lines,' are specified in the score. Others, identified by Eno, arise in the course of the performance. These include the formation of new notes when two notes close to each other in pitch are sounded (beat frequency); the resonant frequency of the (usually large) room in which the piece is being performed; and the culturally determined preferences (taste) of the singers. All of these factors will tend to favour the predominance of certain notes over others, thereby helping to establish a consistent identity for the piece, within a narrow spectrum of possibilities, from one performance to the next. Eno concludes: 'The composer, instead of ignoring or subduing the variety generated in performance, has constructed the piece so that this variety is really the substance of the music.'

In Eno's view, the most elegant description of the compositional technique of experimental composers like Cardew had been provided, in a discussion of heuristics,[15] by Stafford Beer:

In Brain of the Firm *you made a statement which describes very accurately the orientation of contemporary artistic behaviour:*

'*Instead of trying to organize it in full detail, you organize it only somewhat; you then ride on the dynamics of the system in the direction you want to go'. Now, this orientation has frequently been interpreted as a tendency in the modern arts towards chaos and indeterminacy – based on the belief that if the composer deliberately withdraws from the role of controller of the process, that process will become uncontrolled. One of the lessons of cybernetics is that this does not happen. If a system is 'viable' it has, by definition, in-built and automatic controls that stabilize it; and I believe that a great deal of artistic behaviour is the attempt to create systems that are viable in this sense, and to examine, or if you like rehearse, the orientation that allows these cybernetic controls to come into play.*[16]

In *Brain of the Firm*, Beer is not concerned with experimental music, or the arts in any form. His subject is the organization of complicated management structures within commercial companies. He derives the cybernetic model of how such a system should work from the physiology of the human brain and the central nervous system. What Eno had realized, reading Beer, is that performances of *Paragraph 7*, like heuristic programming, tend towards a 'class of goals' (or range of possibilities) rather than a single goal (a perfect performance) known by the composer in advance. As such, Cardew's piece is a perfect model for the technique of adaptive behaviour found in any viable system; whether it be organic, as in the human body, or man-made, as in a business enterprise:

…an adaptive organism is one which contains built-in mechanisms for monitoring (and adjusting) its own behaviour in relation to the alterations of its surroundings. This type of organism must be

75

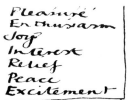

Pleasure'
Enthusiasm
Joy
Interest
Relief
Peace
Excitement

Sources
—formal intrigue
—material novelty
—outside demands
—'mood' inputs
—intellectual demands

Pressure on direction:
world views and 'relevance' barriers
uncertainty threshhold
flux duration

given intention

restrictions and freedoms of material

NOISE

'aims' comparator

zone of flux

'censorship'

transmission loss

'rewards'

return loop

visceral   intellectual

capable of operating from a different type of instruction, since the real coordinates of the surroundings are either too complex to specify, or are changing so unpredictably that no particular strategy (or specific plan for a particular future) is useful... An organism operating in this way must have something more than a centralized control structure. It must have a responsive network of subsystems capable of autonomous behaviour, and it must regard the irregularities of the environment as a set of opportunities, around which it will shape and adjust its own identity.[17]

THE ARTIST AS GUERRILLA

In his essay on 'Variety in the Arts', Eno contrasts the adaptive behaviour exhibited by a performance of *Paragraph 7* with the rigid organization of an orchestra. He is careful to note that few, if any, pieces of experimental and classical music will fall completely into either of these two hypothetical extremes. But on a continuum of possible orientations, he argues, works will tend towards one extreme or the other.

The structure of a traditional orchestra is hierarchical, like a pyramid, and the behaviour of each member is constrained by his rank within this hierarchy. The conductor at the top of the pyramid has the most responsibility; then, with progressively fewer freedoms, come the soloists, the leader of the orchestra, the section principals, the section subprincipals, and finally the rank and file members. For the duration of a typical performance the function of each of these members is to transmit the precise intentions of the composer's original score. To increase the reliability of the musicians as transmitters, their natural variety is subdued as much as possible by their professional training. They are not required to make even the smallest innovations:

This type of organization regards the environment (and its variety) as a set of emergencies and seeks to neutralize or disregard this variety. An observer is encouraged (both by his knowledge of the ranking system and by differing degrees of freedom accorded to the various parts of the organization) to direct his attention at the upper echelons of the ranks. He is given an impression of a hierarchy of value. The organization has the feel of a well-functioning machine: it operates accurately and predictably for one class of tasks, but it is not adaptive. It is not self-stabilizing and does not easily assimilate change or novel environmental conditions.[18]

Elsewhere, Eno found an analogy for the differences between non-adaptive and adaptive systems – between old and new approaches to art – in the tactics of traditional and guerrilla warfare. Like orchestras (whose rigidly hierarchical organization they share) conventional armies function best on terrain that produces no surprises or irregularities. They are unable to adapt their method or operation easily to fit the demands of their surroundings, and they prefer, wherever possible, to battle it out on flat fields. Guerrilla armies, by contrast, view variations of the landscape, such as hills, forests and rivers, not as emergencies but as opportunities – for concealment, refuge and retreat. Instead of trying to change the environment to fit in with their own limitations (as, for example, the Americans did by bombing Vietnam) guerrillas adapt their military behaviour to fit the nature of the environment. Eno writes:

I think that it is not in the least coincidental that these analogies fit so neatly, and I propose that art is an analogue of new techniques of orientation. This modifies Peckham's theory because it adds to it. We now have an image of art as a mechanism that not only disorients us, but which at the same time suggests, by its own internal mechanism, a new way of dealing with the environment, of becoming reoriented.[19]

THE MODE IS THE MESSAGE

At the end of this lecture Eno speculates that works of art like *Paragraph 7* might function as 'models for new forms of social interaction' on a much larger scale. He concludes 'Generating and Organizing Variety in the Arts' on the same note of almost political speculation:

As the variety of the environment magnifies in both time and space, and as the structures that were thought to describe the operation of the world become progressively more unworkable, other concepts of organization must become current. These concepts will base themselves on the assumption of change rather than stasis, and on the assumption of probability rather than certainty. I believe that contemporary art is giving us the feel for this outlook.

Eno has often been asked by interviewers and critics what he thinks the political role of the artist should be. But he rejects with feeling the suggestion that the arts should express party political points of view. 'To require of art that it gives political direction strikes me as rather like asking Albert Einstein to tell you the four times table. Sure he can do it, but why waste his time?'[20] Eno contends that the adaptive procedure he has described at such length in his essays, interviews and letters, does not prescribe a particular political outlook – though it may well give rise to a particular situation. The trouble with existing political systems, he argues, is that they disregard the problems of adaptation, and fail to recognize that the environment will develop and change regardless of their attempts to control it. Like his mentor Stafford Beer, Eno believes that it is the structure of a system that ultimately governs its behaviour. If you want to change the behaviour of a system you must first change its structure.

Eno's analysis led him to conclude that modes of activity which involve change at a procedural and structural level, have far greater social significance than explicitly political messages. 'To attempt to invest art with a political role is a paradoxical proposition which attempts to say "I will direct my non-goal directed behaviour towards this specific end." It is a confusion of terms.'[21] Eno therefore regards the ideologically correct but musically unadventurous song lyrics produced by Cardew after he became a Maoist as having far less value than earlier pieces like *The Great Learning*. He thought that socialist musicians of the early 1970s such as Henry Cow were equally misguided in their attempt to combine musical experiment with overtly political lyrics. Later, Eno was even more critical of the 'spurious socialism' of post-new wave musicians who grafted angry slogans on to structurally conventional musical formats:

If you say you are making music that is political people assume that you are grafting on to the music a literary content, or a set of semantic values that have political insights in them. Well, there are plenty of other ways of being political. Anything that creates change, or that encourages surrender in the listener, or that encourages a questioning of codes at any level, seems to me to be a political statement. Anything that suggests different forms of personal relationships is a political statement.[22]

Sensitive to more recent accusations that the Ambient records of the 1980s lack bite, Eno holds firmly to his belief in the ultimately political nature of his work:

To me, my decision to work in the way I do has political resonances. The decision to stop seeing yourself as the centre of the world, to see yourself as part of the greater flow of things, as having limited options and responsibility for your actions – the converse of the 'me' generation, 'do your own thing' idea – that is political theory; and it's what the music grows from.[23]

17 *Eno,* 'Generating and Organizing Variety in the Arts'.
18 *Ibid.*
19 *Eno, text for a lecture to Trent Polytechnic, 1974.*
20 *Eno, private papers, undated.*
21 *Ibid.*
22 *Interview by Tony Barrell, Radio Station JJJ, Australian Broadcasting Commission, 21 January 1978.*
23 *Interview by Mick Brown,* **The Guardian,** *1 May 1982.*

6 7-sided dice with the following values:
1 2 3 3 4 5 6.

work out the probabilities (and plot on graph)
for the outcomes 6 - 36.

with 2 dice : outcome 2 =

$3 = \begin{cases} 1:2 \\ 2:1 \end{cases}$ $4 = \begin{cases} 3-1 \\ 2-2 \\ 1-3 \end{cases}$ $5 = \begin{cases} 1:4 \\ 2:3 \\ 3:2 \\ 4:1 \end{cases}$

outcome		
2 =	12:1	36:1
3 =	9:1	18:1
4 =	4:1	12:1
5 =		9:1
6 =		7.2:1
7 =		6:1
8 =		7.2:1
9 =	1	9:1
10 =	4:1	12:1
11 =	9	18:1
12 =	12:1	36:1

$6 = \begin{cases} 1:5 \\ 2:4 \\ 3:3 \\ 4:2 \\ 1:5 \end{cases}$ $7 = \begin{cases} 1:6 \\ 2:5 \\ 3:4 \\ 4:3 \\ 5:2 \\ 6:1 \end{cases}$

1:1	2:1	3:1	4:1	5:1	6:1
1:2	2:2	3:2	4:2	5:2	6:2
1:3	2:3	3:3	4:3	5:3	6:3
1:4	2:4	3:4	4:4	5:4	6:4
1:5	2:5	3:5	4:5	5:5	6:5
1:6	2:6	3:6	4:6	5:6	6:6

36^5 7^6

7^2 7^3 7^4 7^5 7^6
7 49 343 2401 16807 117649

$6\,\underline{117649}$
$196\,011.5$

$\frac{1}{2}\cdot\frac{2}{3}\cdot\frac{3}{4}\cdot\frac{4}{5}\cdot\frac{5}{6}$

$\frac{27}{4}$ $\frac{27}{5}$ $\frac{27}{3}$ $\frac{27}{7}$
108   135   81   189

$27\,\underline{117649}$
4357.4

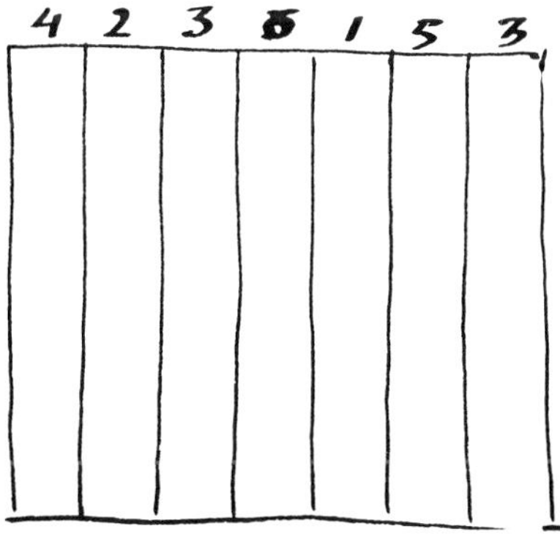

| 4 | 2 | 3 | 6 | 1 | 5 | 3 |

probability of getting / requisites

6 = 117649 : 1
7 = 196011 : 1 ←
8 = 43574 : 1

1	1	1	1	1	1
2	1				
1	2				
1		2			
1			2		
1					

9 can be made as follows

1 + 1 + 1 + 1 + 1 + 4
1 · 1 · 1 · 1 · 2 · 3
1 · 1 · 1 · 2 · 2 · 2

3 — — — — 6

-

76 ways of getting 9

2	2				
2	1	2			
2	1		2		
2	1			2	
2	1				2
1	2	2			
1	2		2		
1	2			2	
1	2				2
1		2	2		
1		2		2	
1		2			2
1			2	2	
1			2		2
1				2	2

15

· FLEX
- CARPET TACKS (BAYONET 1")
- BULBS / STAPLES

6	29
7	30
8	31
9	32
10	33
11	34
12	35
13	36

All the clouds turn to words
All the words float in sequence
No one knows what they mean
Everyone just ignores them.

Refrain *(sung simultaneously with above verse)*

Mau Mau starter ching ching da da
Daughter daughter dumpling data
Pack and pick the ping pong starter
Carter Carter go get Carter
Perigeeeeeeeee
Open stick and delphic doldrums
Open click and quantum data.

78   Sky Saw

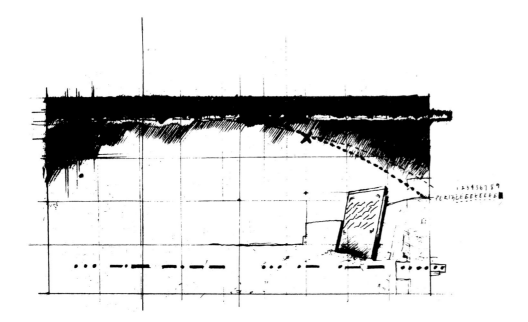

The photographic plate box was a gift from a painter-friend, Ian Walton. I had kept it for a few years waiting to find a suitable use for it. 'Sky Saw' for some inexplicable reason(s) seemed to be the exciting vehicle for the plate box, containing as it does a number of unrelated random images, enabling me to produce contrasting images on the six available surfaces. Using the first 'top' verse as a guide, I chose to illustrate the second 'lower' verse which is sung simultaneously with the first verse, thus becoming almost completely obscured.

1   · — — — —

The first image, on the front of the box, concerns the 'Mau Mau starter', being Jomo Kenyatta and evidence of the atrocities committed under his rule.

2   · · — — —

The second image shows a young girl in a darkened clinical area, presumably going through some form of medical check-up.

3   · · · — —

For the third I was initially tempted to make some satirical comment about ex-President Richard Nixon's visit to China and the subsequent press coverage (overcoverage) of himself and Chairman Mao indulging in 'Ping-Pong Diplomacy'. But I bored very quickly and eventually searched out an action photo of a table-tennis player; mainly to indulge my liking for movement against static backdrops.

4   · · · · —

The fourth image, based on the line 'Carter Carter go get Carter' reminded me of the film *Get Carter* starring Michael Caine. But I couldn't remember much about the film, only tiny mosaic-like fragments. So my image is no more than a vague impression of the sense of the film.

5   · · · · ·

Perigee
…is the point where an orbit is closest to the earth.

6   — · · · ·

Open stick and delphic doldrums
Open click and quantum data
…is resolved in the form of an aeroplane engine undergoing wind tunnel tests which paradoxically indicates the opposite of doldrums; the engine is still/secure/static and yet at the same time is operable/in motion/going…

The small beetle in the lower right hand corner is a click beetle, which, when on its back, has the ability to leap in the air with a click, and land on its feet.

The title of the song is hidden in the images thus corresponding to the lines in the first verse:

All the words float in sequence
No one knows what they mean

R.M.

. . . various views

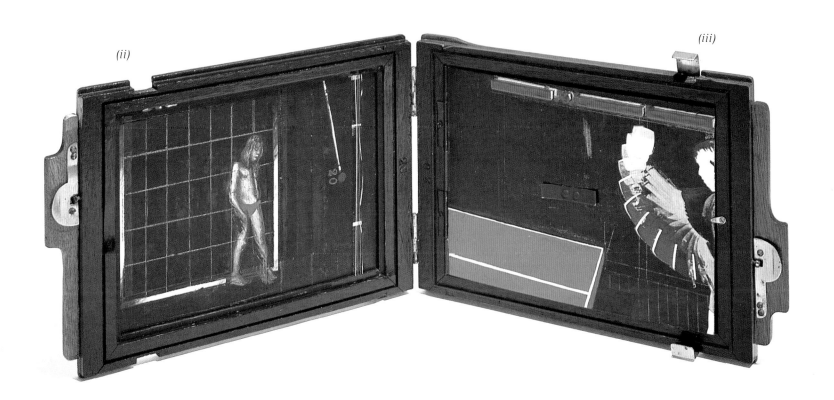

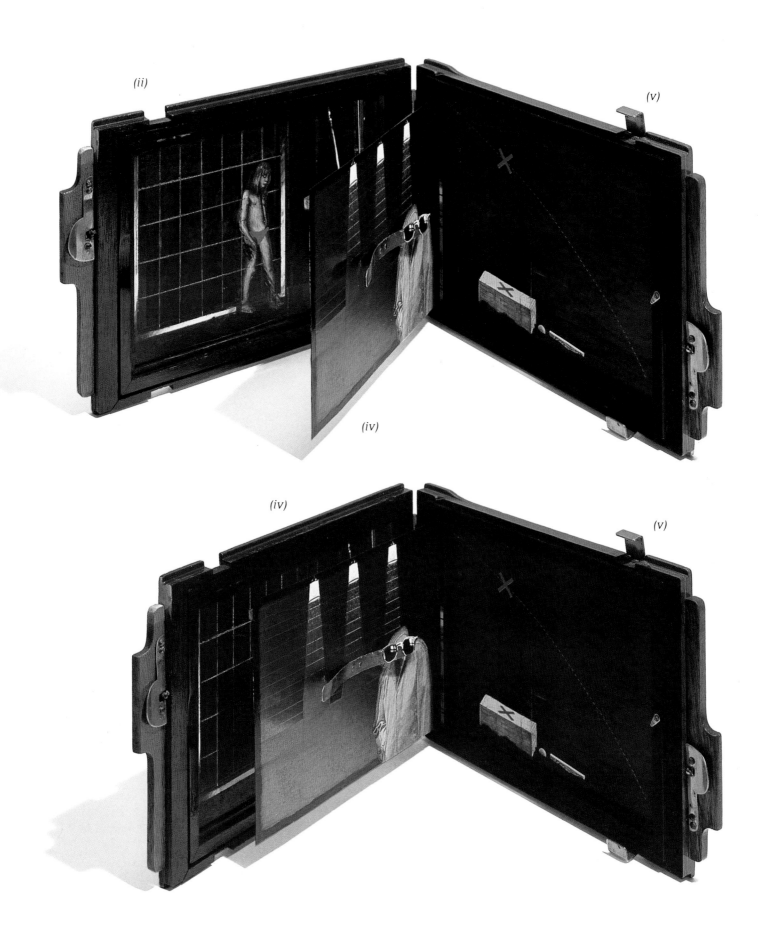

(ii)　(v)　(iv)　(iv)　(v)

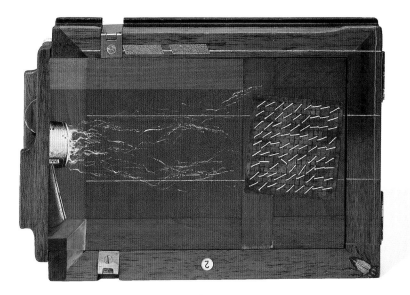

Brown eyes and I were tired
We had walked and we had scrambled
Through the moors and through the briars
Through the endless blue meanders.

In the blue August Moon
In the cool August Moon

Over the nights and through the fires
We went surging down the wires
Through the towns and on the highways
Through the storms in all their thundering.

In the blue August Moon
In the cool August Moon

Then we rested in a desert
Where the bones were white as teeth sir
And we saw St Elmo's fire
Splitting ions in the ether.

In the blue August Moon
In the cool August Moon

In the blue August Moon
In the cool August Moon.

6.—SINUOUS LIGHTNING, WITH RAMIFICATIONS.
From a Photo. by Rev. G. Bastout, Saint-Palais-Sur-Mer (Charente-Inférieure), France.

82   St Elmo's Fire

(a)

cause ⟶

Exhaustive searches for pictorial reference for the phenomenon of St Elmo's Fire proved fruitless; Meterological Office, Royal Aeronautical Society, Farnborough, etc. were all tried without luck. I had to rely on interpretations of descriptions given to me by people who had witnessed it in various circumstances; up a mountain in a storm, with the lightning licking up ropes and around pins; sweeping around propellors and along the barrels on guns in bombers during the Second World War.

With this admittedly limited and confused knowledge, I began work on aluminium cooking foil – covering it with six layers of enamel paints, primary colours, through to black; each application being scrubbed around a pre-determined rectangle, this being the area of action, where St Elmo's Fire was to be. Coloured exploding 'shrapnel' – ions – were added later.

The desert area is scattered with pieces of furniture – travellers for the use of.

'effect' as a piece is executed on a cut-up and re-assembled cardboard envelope. It shows the mesmeric effect of St Elmo's Fire on 'Brown eyes and I.'

(Brown eyes rests on a convenient bench.)

I liked the idea of there being furniture available for use in the desert; it reminded me of the incongruity of massive furniture showrooms that one comes across in desolate areas of France. The lurex thread and white gouache 'zig-zag' at the left is an interpretation of the path of electricity as seen on an electrical generator in the Science Museum, South Kensington, London. This machine is activated for the benefit of observers at 2.00 p.m. every day. Eno based Fripp's guitar solo on the action of this generator.

The capstan on the plinth at the bottom right is a symbol of St Erasmus or St Elmo, who died in 303AD. A legend claims that he was put to death by having his intestines wound out of his body on a windlass; therefore, because of the resemblance of the windlass and a capstan, Erasmus/Elmo became the patron saint of sailors. The term 'St Elmo's Fire' given to the electrical discharges sometimes seen at the mastheads of ships, derives from the belief that it was a sign of his protection.

R.M.

83

(b)

effect ⟶

I'll find a place somewhere in the <u>corner</u>
I'm gonna waste the rest of my days
Just watching patiently from the <u>window</u>
Just waiting seasons change, some day
Oh, oh, my dreams will pull you through that garden gate.

I want to be the wandering sailor
We're <u>silhouettes</u> by the light of the <u>moon</u>
I sit playing <u>solitaire</u> by the <u>window</u>
Just waiting seasons change, ah, ah
You'll see, one day, these dreams will pull you <u>through my door</u>
And I'll come running to tie your shoe
I'll come running to tie your shoe
I'll come running to tie your shoe.

84 I'll Come Running (To Tie Your Shoe)

(dedicated to Ritva Saarikko's shoes and Ian Macdonald's polish)

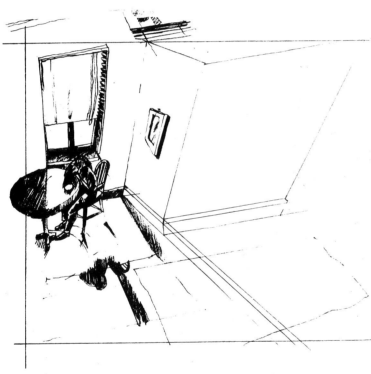

As the song is dedicated to Ritva Saarikko's shoes, I asked her what colour and style of shoes she would like me to show; hence the bright signal red shoes, which reminded her of the story 'The Little Red Shoes' by the Brothers Grimm.

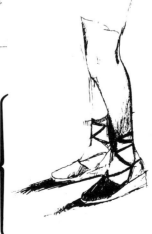

The legs are those of my wife, Ann.

The picture is constructed on a metal duplicating machine base plate, which I varnished. The window section is cut and folded card. Behind the window is a 6 inch fluorescent tube which throws a cold even light on to the seated figure. But, just in case this idea didn't work I also painted the figure with light flooding his right side. I looked at the paintings of Edward Hopper and Georges de la Tour in an attempt to learn about the balance between light and dark.

R.M.

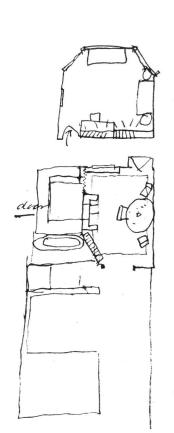

1 **The passage of time**
   Is flicking dimly up on the screen
   I can't see the lines
   I used to think I could read between
   Perhaps my brains have turned to sand.

2 **Oh me oh my**
   I think it's been an eternity
   You'd be surprised
   At my degree of uncertainty
   How can moments go so slow.

3 **Several times**
   I've seen the evening slide away
   Watching the signs
   Taking over from the fading day
   Perhaps my brains are old and scrambled.

4 **Several times**
   I've seen the evening slide away
   Watching the signs
   Taking over from the fading day
   Changing water into wine.

5 **Several times**
   I've seen the evening slide away
   Watching the signs
   Taking over from the fading day
   Putting grapes back on the vine.

(Simultaneously with the last two verses,
another voice sings another melody with different words, as follows:)

4(a) **Who would believe what a poor set of eyes can show you**
      Who would believe what an innocent voice could do
      Never a silence always a face at the door.

5(a) **Who would believe what a poor set of ears can tell you**
      Who would believe what a weak pair of hands can do
      Never a silence always a foot in the door.

(a)

86   # Golden Hours

As with 'Some Of Them Are Old'', I regard this song to be about the precious and rare periods of privacy. Thus, the first picture is vast and empty, indicating an area where one can be free to think, relax and move in whatever way one chooses, without intrusion.

The BBC test card girl at the bottom right is the same as she has been since she first appeared, only her face has aged. It is an 'icon' that is so constant, permanent and commonplace, if a change was made in the test card I suspect it would take a while before a viewer recognized a difference. This image refers to the lines:

The passage of time
Is flicking dimly up on the screen

The neon sign shown through the window (left) shows water changing into wine, again a reference to subtle change.

Over the hinged leaf of paper (left), a door is shown, complete with the security locks, chain locks, spy hole and scuff marks synonymous with American apartments, the threat of intrusion and violence being an ever present concern.

This thinking is continued in the image through the window. A doorway of an apartment block is open, light from inside floods the street, illuminating a trail of blood that travels in the cracked pavement to the gutter. It shows the result of an incident that occurred to an artist/friend of mine, Sue Coe. She and a friend were entering the lobby of her apartment building at about 4.00 a.m. one day in the summer of 1978. As they unlocked the two outer doors to gain entry to the apartments they were viciously attacked by

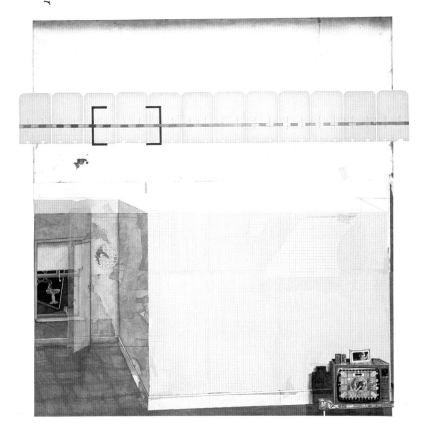

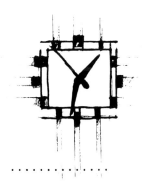

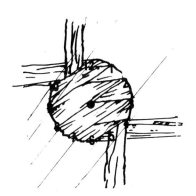

four youths, one brandishing a knife which was used on Sue's friend. She was slashed about the face. Both were beaten up badly and were lucky to be saved by a group of off-duty New York firemen who, on seeing the attack, rushed over the street and fought the youths. Whilst the fighting was going on one of the attackers had reached Sue's apartment and ripped the place up, and dropped her TV and video recorder down three flights of stairs. One of the firemen received bad cuts to his face, whilst all the youths but one

escaped. When Ann and I visited Sue the next day to see how she was the blood was still thick in the cracks in the pavement and was still smeared on the lobby walls and up the stairs.

Despite all the locks used in American apartments it seemed to me that as long as the savage fear still pervades the society no manner of security locks, etc. will stop the murders, muggings, rapes, etc. Fear breeds fear.

R.M.

The second piece developed over a long spell and was consequently produced much later than my first interpretation. It deals with the preciousness of one's favourite, dearest friends, relationships and objects and their inherent fragility especially when threatened. The base board of the piece is a patchwork of gold leaf squares some of which have been left exposed while the majority have been sprayed with two metallic gold car sprays. The moulded picture framing has been painted in signal red enamel and was then wrapped in half-inch wide gauze bandaging.

I asked an illustrator/friend of mine, Robert Mason, to contribute an element for the picture. The idea being that whatever he chose to do would dictate my responses to the piece and my mode of working. He responded perfectly, by presenting me with such a strong and uniquely personal solution, that I was immediately stopped in my tracks. It evokes some of his personal dilemmas of the past, related to the song. Initially I felt apprehensive about utilizing the 'heart'. Nevertheless, having set the experiment in operation, I was determined to carry it through to a conclusion, for better or for worse. The 'heart' proved to be a catalyst, for it directed my thoughts in even more extreme ideas of preciousness. I decided to use one of Eno's notebooks (these contain everything from musical notation, lecture notes, shopping lists, pet theories, etc.) Like the treasures of the Egyptian Kings, entombed in the centre of pyramids, the notebook was made almost inaccessible by being set in resin, which slightly occludes the writing. Rob's 'heart' is also set in resin, as is the 3-D picture of a blinking eye.

The 'blinking eye' suggests one's first secret desires and widely extravagant imaginings of close encounters with the opposite sex; the apparent importance of it all, the curiousity and fears bred by ignorance and second-hand tales and lies. Then…the actual encounter; clumsy fumblings with unfamiliar hooks and straps, buttons and elastic; unexpected tree roots/stones/light switches/etc…and an incomplete knowledge of the procedure required to affect the act. This moment is a universal experience, common to all teenagers, and yet each encounter is a private cherished memory that whether a failure or success can be remembered with a grin of idiot glee.

The small green/blue and white squares show examples of the 'Ames Chair Demonstrations'. Adelbert Ames Jnr, using his experience as an artist, made *trompe l'oeil* models (peep shows) to study man's perception of what is reality and what is illusion. Using three peep-holes one can look with one eye at each of the three objects displayed in the distance; each view gives the impression of one and the same object (in this case a chair). But the impression is shattered when the chair is viewed from an alternative angle. One finds that one is a distorted rhomboid, one a series of extended wires in front of a backdrop on which is painted what was at first believed to be the seat of the chair; only one is a chair, the two others clever illusions. (See *Art and Illusion* by E. H. Gombrich) *

R.M.

88

* *E.H. Gombrich*, **Art and Illusion** *(Phaidon Paperback, fifth edition, 1977, Phaidon Press Ltd, St Ebbe's Street, Oxford. First published 1960).*

(b)

Never a silence always a face at the door

*The arms of the clock and the spectrum colours that partially circle
the diameter of the clock from 12 to 4 o'clock, refers to my private
and precious moments, the early morning hours through which I
can work undisturbed...*

R.M.

Rosalie
I've been waiting all evening
Possibly years I don't know
Counting the passing hours
Everything merges with the night.

I stand on the beach
Giving out descriptions
Different for everyone I see
Since I just can't remember
Longer than last September.

Santiago
Under the volcano
Floats like a cushion on the sea
Yet I can never sleep here
Everything ponders in the night.

Rosalie
We've been talking all summer
Picking the straw from our clothes
See how the breeze has softened
Everything pauses in the night.

90 Everything Merges With The Night

The lyrics and music of this piece are in the same vein as the song, 'On Some Faraway Beach'. The similarity in mood is not the reason why the pictures for both songs are on either side of a rectified tea tray. (See 'On Some Faraway Beach'.)

The softness and lilting quality of the song is reflected in the 'pretty postcard' visual solution that I produced. As I decided from the outset each song would be approached as I felt it deserved to be treated, each on its merits. Paradoxically, despite not particularly liking literal, pretty pictures I enjoyed the process of painting a near traditional picture.

The narrator is standing in the shallow water dispensing written descriptions of wildly differing girls in a vain attempt to locate one particular girl, Rosalie.

The montage in the left-hand section, depicting three different girls; one being the star of bondage model photos, Betty Page, another is a slightly supreme blonde exposing an obvious asset...; the last girl is oriental, possibly Japanese or Korean. These three represent a few possible realizations of the narrator's written descriptions.

R.M.

I stand on the beach
Giving out descriptions

Taking our time before it's through
Passing our days in old shoes
Sister – think I'm returning to Peru
Wish that I never came here
They can't pronounce my name here
Everyone asks me 'Where's Peru?'

In Peru we've lengthened the day
In Peru we've strengthened the dollar
There are mountains piercing our skies
And the ocean at our shores
I will save up all of my wages
Even retail crummy cosmetics
I will work my passage in stages
As the winter slips away.

Miles of golden beaches
Excellent wines and features
Mister – take a week off in Gay Peru
Penitent monks to stare at
Colonial dons in old straw hats
Everyone's there in old Peru
Oo-poo-Peru.

92 Big Day

ITINERARY

London

Southampton

Tangier

Salvador

Rio de Janeiro

Buenos Aires

Tierra del Fuego

Valparaiso

LIMA

As with most of my pictures, the heterogeneous nature of the piece creates a mesh of lateral meanings that, when seen as a whole, illustrate my interpretation both logically and emotionally. For this reason it is difficult to explain honestly why or how most pictures evolve as they do, this one is one of those....

Knowing Eno, I felt that 'Excellent wines and features' probably referred to lovely ladies. I could be wrong though. The 13-hour Geek time clock refers to a group of artist acquaintances of mine, who all share similar beliefs about art and our work – a spirit. We all tend to approach our work in an oblique manner. A magazine called *Geek* which we published in 1977 is partial evidence of this spirit. The fact that the clock provides an extra hour does not specifically refer to time but is a kind of metaphor to describe the belief we have in our work without pandering to the dictates of others. The bird flying at the top of the picture is a Brown Pelican which is a regular resident of the Peruvian coastline, feeding off shoals of anchovy that live off the plankton in the cold waters of the Humboldt Current.

The male figure (narrator) who is skidding in through the door at left, is carrying a much travelled suitcase containing 'crummy cosmetics' and a personal survival kit.

R.M.

Excellent wines and features ••••••••••

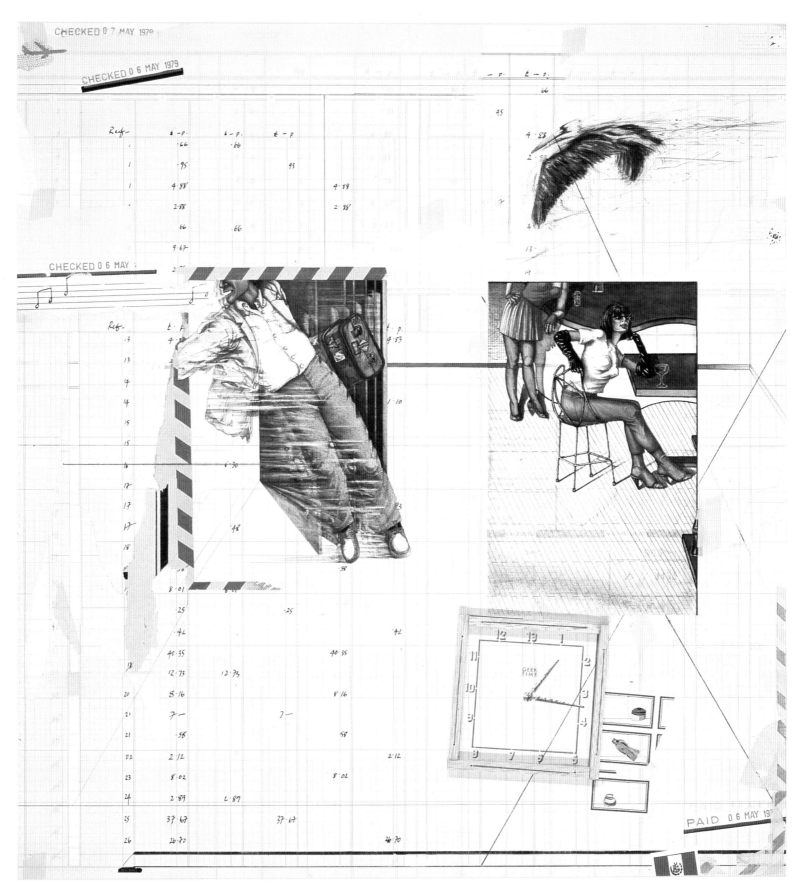

All the peasants in the squares
At their tables and their chairs
Set to salvage certain numbers
From the wonder of the Tundra
And the muses in the gloom
Counting needles in their rooms
On the carpet in the corner
In a kind of secret slumber
While the in formation rain
Slashed the dirty window pane to the square.

Smoky broads and smoky windows in the square
Come come charmer come on over for the day
Disappearing cocoa forests flash and die
Fortunes crumble all demolished in the bay.

Over forty pointed people
In the perfect pointed steeple
Looked to see the lucky number
Yes the wonder of the Tundra
Had come up to fame and fortune
Singing his tune, my tune, your tune
Wooing daughters of the gifted
On the carpets of the courtrooms
While the tickets were expensive
The show was quite relentless in the square.

Smoky broads and smoky windows in the square
Come come charmer come on over for the day
Disappearing cocoa forests flash and die
Fortunes crumble all demolished in the bay.

Dalai Llama lama puss puss
Stella maris missa nobis
Miss a dinner Miss Shapiro
Shampoos pot-pot pinkies pampered
Movement hampered like at Christmas
Ha-ha isn't life a circus
Round in circles like the Archers
Always stiff or always starchy
Yes it's happening and it's fattening
And it's all that we can get into the show.

Smoky broads and smoky windows in the square
Come come charmer come on over for the day
Disappearing cocoa forests flash and die
Fortunes crumble all demolished in the bay.

> The Muses:
> Clio—history
> Euterpe—lyric poetry
> Thalia—comedy
> Melpomene—tragedy
> Terpischore—dance and song
> Polyhymnia—religious or sublime hymns
> Urania—astronomy
> Cassiope—epic poetry

The lyric chosen as a title for this image reminded me of a piece of bondage slang – 'turkey-trussed', which is pretty self-explanatory. The turkey is traditional Christmas fare and the following lyrics also refer to traditions of England:

Round in circles like the Archers
Always stiff or always starchy
Yes it's happening and it's fattening . . .

The image is an invention of a situation which attempts to parody many of our respected traditions and values which publicly appear to be 'right and proper' but which also conceal bizarre rituals and practices. The central figure, wearing the required formal evening dress, is surrounded by the accoutrements of the 'lounge lizard'; the drink; the cigarette; the cuff links; the mirror; the prompt card (presumably a crutch to remind him of the conversational snippets needed to partake in trivial exchanges at gatherings of other 'lounge lizards'); the chandelier; the carefully sculptured trousers and jacket creases; the modern textiles, etc. His padded jacket shows a dotted line indicating the actual size of his torso – another snipe at the hypocrisy as practised by these creatures. The legend 'lips saying ''oo''' above the lounge lizard's head serves to emphasize his need to elaborate and affect his speech. This piece of text came from an old book of ventriloquism, which I think was a humourous coincidence. The broken text at the base of the image is from a 1950's Pepsi advertisement and was found and added to the finished main picture simply as a further ridiculous emphatic device.

I was curious to attempt to merge the two behavioural extremes which are suggested by my interpretation of the lyrics. The 'lounge lizard' who is apparently 'correct', controls and observes the bound men ('woos the daughters of the gifted . . .') as if they too are required possessions necessary for all 'trim, sociable moderns'; without them in attendance he would be lacking. Their movements are 'hampered like at Christmas' not because they are full of turkey, roast potatoes, Christmas pudding and the rest but because the lizard has turkey-trussed them. His life is a 'circus/Round in circles like the Archers/Always stiff or always starchy'. The whole scene depicts a sparse and tacky courtroom, carpeted in areas; another stage set view. At left and right are two strips of mirror tiles (more essentials for the 'come come charmer . . .' with five tiles occluded by monochrome (limited views) of female forms. The central male figure epitomizes those whose identity is defined by their similiarity to others; they are merely comparable.

94   Miss Shapiro

This song was the last work in a certain era of my life (in fact, since I was knocked down by a taxi on the way home from the studio after recording it, it was nearly my last work . . .) It was a period of confusion and hysteria and glee – I didn't know what I was doing, and I was working non-stop on all sorts of different things; it was a messy time.

I like the third verse. It was one of the times that I touched pure glossolalia – speaking in tongues. I suppose it came out of a movement in poetry that impressed me – Gerard Manley Hopkins, Belloc's 'Tarantella' and Schwitters' phonetic work – where the rhythmic and phonetic value of language overwhelms its semantic value.

They don't write songs like this anymore.

B.E.

R.M.

Today's trim, sociable moderns are giving a new light look, a fresh elegance and grace to themselves and all their possessions. Join this happy new crowd. Look smart. Stay young and fair and debonair. Be sociable.

Movement hampered like at Christmas

THE HIDDEN INTENTION

Rock music in the early 1970s was a time of dues-paying, lick-playing guitar and keyboard virtuosi. When Eno joined Roxy Music in 1971, as a resident technical expert with a Revox tape recorder in tow, he could not read or write a note of music. He was unable to play a single musical instrument and declared that he had left it too late to learn. The primitive VCS 3 synthesizer which he went on to operate for the band did not even have a keyboard. Like some crazed telephonist at his own private switchboard, Eno would plug connector pins into matrix sockets, and twiddle knobs on the console to bend and warp the contours of sound coming from Andy Mackay's saxophone and Phil Manzanera's guitar. No one, especially not Eno, knew quite how these 'treatments' would turn out.

Today, Eno is no longer the 'non-musician' he was as a novice. He is still unable to read and write music, but he has learned to play a number of instruments passably well – guitar, bass, percussion, and a

erase, Eno's trial and error approach to composition would be unthinkable. Without the recording studio, Eno probably would not be a composer at all.

In recent years, Eno has often compared the way that he works to the process of painting. He seems to see himself nowadays not so much as a non-musician, as a 'painter of sound':

When you work on to tape as I do, it means that music has become physical material; a substance which is malleable, mutable, cuttable and reversible. Tape puts music in a spatial dimension. I can have a direct, empirical relationship with the sound itself. I relate to music the way a painter relates to a painting.[1]

Making *On Land*, Eno pushed the analogy between painting and recording even further. He wanted, he said, to retain in his work the same sense of its own past history that he had found in the paintings

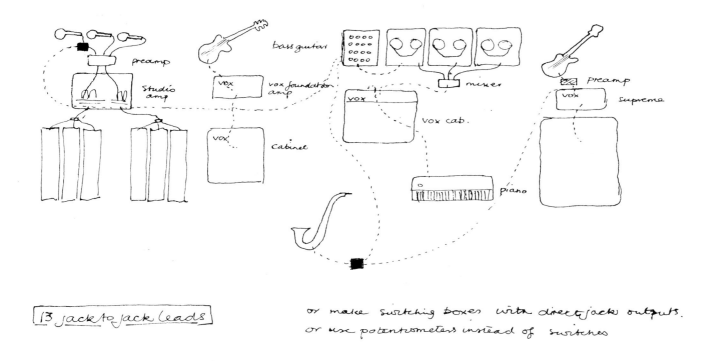

range of keyboards. This is not where his real strength as a musician lies, though. Eno's best-loved instrument, the one he can play to perfection, is the recording studio. To Eno, the studio is not just a passive transmitter of predetermined sounds, but an active tool in the compositional process. Working with tapes, Eno assembles his music by manipulating and treating raw sound, rather than by notating on paper, like conventional composers, the tunes that he hears in his head. Without the tape machine's power to record, recall, overdub and

of his friend Michael Chandler. In a painting, no brushstroke is entirely retractable; even if it is painted over and hidden it must leave a trace – and history is the gradual accumulation of such traces.[2] To this end, Eno made himself two working rules. Anything that was recorded on tape must appear in the final mix, transformed or reduced perhaps, but not destroyed; and anything that he rejected from one piece must be fed into another. 'This technique,' he concludes, 'is like composting: converting what would otherwise have been waste into nourishment.'[3]

1 *Interview by Michael Zwerin,* International Herald Tribune, *14 September 1983.*
2 *The highly-worked, many-layered surfaces of Russell Mills's pictures also have this sense of hidden history.*
3 *Eno, press statement for* Ambient 4 : On Land, *1982.*

THE RELUCTANT GURU

As Eno's own mastery of studio craft has grown, so the idea of the non-musician has become increasingly commonplace and unremarkable. Pre-punk performers of the mid-1970s, such as the American poet turned singer Patti Smith, extolled the triumph of feeling over technical ability. The punk movement itself was founded on the democratic idea that anyone, given a guitar, a couple of chords and the enthusiasm, could play music. When cheaper synthesizers like the Wasp became available at the end of the 1970s, a new wave of young hopefuls flocked to form groups and cut their own sounds. Ice-cold electronic records like 'TVOD' by the Normal; 'Being Boiled' by the Human League; and 'United' by Throbbing Gristle (all from 1978) offered a blueprint for new-age synthesizer music. When groups like these were asked to name influences, Eno, the original 'synthesizer guru', was usually well to the fore. Richard H. Kirk of Cabaret Voltaire:

I wouldn't say it was the way that Eno approached sound that influenced me so much, it was more the fact that here was someone who was making music but actually making the point that he was not a musician. At that time most people thought that if you were going to make music you had to learn to play an instrument. Here was someone who was saying that anyone could do it; just give it a go![4]

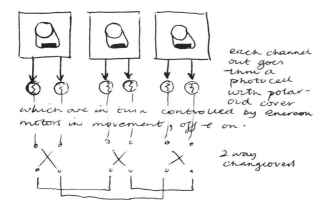

Unfortunately, in the rush to do-it-yourself, the conceptual demands that non-musicianship should place on the performer were frequently overlooked and forgotten. All too often, the results of the new synthesizer bands' efforts, particularly when they were trying for chart hits, were shallow in content, and – despite plenty of studio attention – thin in sound. By 1982, the year of *On Land*, Eno was sick of the trend he had unwittingly helped to inspire:

My main criticism of most recent records is that they use the studio in precisely the way I used to advocate. The material is made in the studio. The problem is that it's dead at every stage. It's dead at inception [and] it's dead at execution.[5]

The truth is that Eno was never quite as committed to the synthesizer as his reputation might seem to suggest. Eno has always been at ease with technology, but he does not have an engineer's interest in the synthesizer for its own sake. 'You can either take the attitude that it has a function and you can learn how to use it, or you can take the attitude that it's just a black box that you can manipulate any way that you want,' he says.[6] Eno understood from the outset that the new wonder machines, by doing all the work, could lead to complacency on the part of the musician. 'I find its simplicity – or rather the simplicity of the programming – rather frightening. You just select something, a loose idea, and let it run. I'm only too aware of how easy it is to seduce the public with synthesizers.'[7] To stop himself from opting for tried and tested solutions, Eno made a rule never to write down any of the settings he discovered, no matter how beautiful the sounds that they generated. Each time he came to the synthesizer he was forced to experiment afresh. To increase their unpredictability still further, Eno allowed his synthesizers to fall into disrepair. Just as he had once collaged together the individual noises of his broken-down tape recorders, Eno now cultivated the idiosyncratic sounds of his malfunctioning machines. He was always careful, though, to use his synthesizer effects sparingly. Where groups like Kraftwerk and the original Human League used nothing but machine-made sound, right down to their precision-tooled percussion tracks, Eno mixed a wide range of conventional instruments into his music. On *Taking Tiger Mountain (by Strategy)*, his second solo album, most of the music is generated by the classic rock line-up of guitar, bass, and drums. Synthesizers, where they are used at all, are employed to treat and distort these instruments, rather than as primary sources of sound.

THE ART OF COLLABORATION

Eno has always resisted the illusion that the answer to a musical problem lies inside the machine waiting to be discovered. The answer, he stresses, always comes from somewhere in the musician himself; the instrument is just a way of externalizing it. Far more important than his use of the synthesizer to the music of Eno's early albums were the strategies or 'processes' that he developed for working in the studio. Indeed, the sensitivity and sophistication of these techniques is what distinguishes his work from most of the other artists working in this area. Eno believed that technical skills, though useful, are not essential, but that a discriminating judgement is crucial. The trick is to accept the constraints imposed by your limitations and turn them to your own advantage. Eno's shortcomings as an instrumentalist were his strength as an experimental musician because they forced him to discover other, non-traditional ways of generating music.

These procedures, which are inseparable from Eno's ideas about the adaptive function of art, were refined and applied with increasing self-consciousness from one album to the next. Arguably, they reached a peak on *Another Green World*, regarded by many, including this writer, as Eno's masterpiece from this period. On *Before and After Science*, the album which followed, the same techniques failed to generate such satisfactory results.

Eno himself identified four separate though overlapping processes by which his music was produced: social, personal, technological, and compositional. These processes varied in degree and importance from track to track and album to album, but what they all shared was Eno's determination not to choose the safe route to a known goal:

What I'm interested in is creating the kind of situation, or at least setting in motion procedures, which have no specific aim, and which end up in places you couldn't predict, so that you have to improvise a new set of principles as you go along.[8]

When Eno spoke of social processes for the production of music, he was referring to the extensive collaborations with other musicians that have characterized his career. During the 1970s Eno worked, sometimes as producer, sometimes as 'ideas man', with rock performers as various as Roxy Music, Robert Fripp, Robert Wyatt, John Cale, Phil Manzanera, Quiet Sun, 801, Ultravox, Devo, Cluster, the No New York groups, David Bowie, and Talking Heads:

When you work with somebody else, you expose yourself to an interesting risk: the risk of being sidetracked, of being taken where you hadn't intended to go. This is the central issue of collaboration for me. I work with people who I believe are likely to engender a set of conditions that will create this tangent effect, that will take me into new territory.[9]

4 *Quoted in M. Fish and D. Hallbery,* Cabaret Voltaire: The Art of the Sixth Sense *(Serious Art Forms, London, 1985).*

5 *Interview by Richard Grabel,* New Musical Express, *24 April 1982.*

6 *Interview by Lester Bangs,* Musician, Player & Listener, *No. 21, November 1979.*

7 *Interview by Angus Mackinnon,* New Musical Express, *12 July 1975.*

8 *Interview by Allan Jones,* Melody Maker, *29 November 1975.*

9 *Eno, private papers, 4 October 1977.*

Since the rise of the modern rock group in the early 1960s many musicians have preferred to stay, and play, only with the members of their own band. As they become increasingly familiar with the styles of their fellow musicians the original 'chemistry' of the group's sound hardens into formula. Eno would have none of this. In his view, one task of the early Roxy Music was to resist this hardening of the musical arteries. For a time the Roxy Music experiment was brilliantly successful. The tension between the clashing styles of Ferry, Eno, Mackay, Manzanera, Thompson and Simpson produced a bizarre hybrid rock, part backward-looking, part futuristic, that was completely new. But the period of high experiment was not to last. When the Roxy Music sound started to become stylized in 1973, Eno left the group.

On *Here Come the Warm Jets*, his first solo album, Eno pushed his ideas about collaboration a stage further. Rather than form another group with a fixed and ultimately predictable line-up, Eno invited a wide range of musicians to record with him. He selected them on the assumption that they would not normally have worked together, and because their styles were, in theory at least, incompatible. 'Driving Me Backwards', for example, featured in addition to Eno: Robert Fripp from King Crimson on guitar (art-rock); Paul Rudolph from the Pink Fairies and John Wetton from King Crimson on basses (hard and art-rock); and Simon King from Hawkwind on percussion (space-rock). The approach was dialectical. When it worked, the clash of identities and styles produced a synthesis that none of the musicians could have predicted. Eno's role in this process was that of co-ordinator. He furnished, as he put it, 'the central issue' around which all the other musicians revolved. The players were encouraged to influence the direction of each track, but the controlling hand, from the original idea and lyrics for each song, through to the final mixes, was Eno's.

Taking Tiger Mountain does not employ this procedure to anything like the same degree. Phil Manzanera, Freddie Smith, and Brian Turrington of the Winkies formed the nucleus of a band that stayed the same from track to track. But on *Another Green World* social processes were once again high on Eno's agenda. In addition to Robert Fripp, Paul Rudolph and Brian Turrington, Eno was joined by Phil Collins of Genesis and the jazz-rock band Brand X; Percy Jones of Brand X; Rod Melvin of pub-rockers Kilburn and the High-Roads; and John Cale, formerly of the Velvet Underground. This time Eno imposed even greater demands on the flexibility and intelligence of the musicians by entering the studio with nothing written or prepared. He wanted to apply Stafford Beer's dictum about the organization of systems to the musical process: 'Instead of trying to organize it in full detail, you organize it only somewhat; you then ride on the dynamics of the system in the direction you want to go':

The specific purpose of the experiment was to put together this group which would work together in a way which would be impossible to predict. I fed in enough information to get something to happen and the chemical equation of the interaction between the various styles of the musicians involved – who were intelligent enough not to retreat from a situation which was musically strange – took us somewhere that we would have been unable to design.[10] We were working with no preconceived attitude other than that of conscious experimentation. And if something failed, we tried again. So many musicians are so frightened by the possibility of failure that they restrict their format to one that is almost bound to achieve something which can be predicted in advance. That's not what I call success.[11]

To begin with the failure rate was high. It was several days, and as many as thirty-five dispiriting false starts, before the method began to yield more than banal results. As before, Eno retained complete control over the musical material that was generated by his guests. Everything then depended on the taste, economy and precision with which these random results were edited together and developed.

To produce a particular effect, or class of effects, Eno would sometimes issue the musicians with simple verbal instructions. On one occasion, timing with a stop watch, he asked them to play for exactly ninety seconds, leaving more spaces in the piece than they made noises. The 'Wimshurst guitar' which Robert Fripp is credited with on 'St Elmo's Fire', one of the faster numbers, was the result of a similar directive. Eno had already established the song's backing track on his own using a combination of organ, piano, bass pedals, guitars, and synthetic percussion. Now he wanted a melodic counterpoint. So he asked Fripp to improvise a guitar run that would be as fast and unpredictable as the erratic electrical charge that flows between the two poles of a Wimshurst high-voltage generator. The resulting solo, like 'a sledge shooting over snow' as Eno once described it, is a brilliant exercise in controlled rapture.

ONE HUNDRED WORTHWHILE DILEMMAS

Probably the most famous of all the techniques that Eno used to prompt intuition and to escape from blind alleys in the studio were the *Oblique Strategies* cards that he produced with Peter Schmidt. It was these cards, which functioned as a kind of private oracle, that Eno had in mind when he spoke of 'personal' processes for generating music.

Like many of Eno's procedures, the idea for the cards had its origins in his experiences of recording with Roxy Music. Working in the studio, Eno had often noticed how the presssure not to waste time and money meant that interesting ideas and sounds that arose by chance were constantly passed over and lost for ever. Sometimes the musicians were so caught up in the task at hand that these special moments went by entirely unnoticed. To combat this tendency, Eno began to compile lists of reminders designed to open his eyes to the aleatory occurrences of the recording process. By the time of *Taking Tiger Mountain* he had transcribed sixty-four or so of the messages – some technical, some conceptual, some just plain cryptic – on to a deck of small cards. Whenever he was unable to decide what to do next during recording, he would pick one of the cards from the deck at random. Whatever the card said he would try to apply to his problem.

Soon after this, Eno discovered that Peter Schmidt, his artist friend, had produced a similar set of observations to aid his work as a painter. The two decided to combine their cards, produce some new ones that did not arise specifically from their work, and publish the pack as a boxed set. The first version of *Oblique Strategies*, with the subtitle 'Over one hundred worthwhile dilemmas', appeared in 1975.[12] The function of these dilemmas, explains Eno, was 'simply to bring the consciousness one has as a listener to one's consciousness as a composer – to deal with things in a much more *studied* way.[13] Perhaps the best known of the cards is the first one that Eno ever formulated: 'Honour thy error as a hidden intention.' Its classic injunction to keep a watchful eye on the secret workings of chance could stand as an epitaph to Eno's entire career. Many of the other cards also take the form of prescriptions designed to open up the range of creative possibilities: 'Discover the recipes you are using and abandon them'; 'Change nothing and continue with immaculate consistency'; 'Repetition is a form of change'; 'Make a sudden, destructive, unpredictable action; Incorporate'; 'Don't be afraid of things because they're easy to do'; 'Remove specifics and convert to ambiguities'; 'Emphasize the flaws'. The implications of some of the cards are rather more mysterious: 'Ghost echoes'; '(Organic) machinery'; 'Water'; 'Twist the spine'. There is even an Oblique Strategy to negate all the others in the pack: 'Discard an axiom' it suggests.

The first album on which *Oblique Strategies* were used extensively and credited was *Another Green World*. In the same year, 1975, the cards were also used in the recording of three other albums

10 *Also important in this respect was the contribution of Rhett Davies, Eno's engineer from* Taking Tiger Mountain *onwards, and subsequently his co-producer. Unlike many studio professionals, Davies was always prepared to experiment.*

11 *Interview by Allan Jones,* Melody Maker, *29 November 1975.*

12 *So far* Oblique Strategies *has been published, privately, on three occasions. The first printing was in 1975 (500 copies); the second, with slight revisions, was in 1978 (2,500 copies); and the third, with further revisions, was in 1979 (2,500 copies). A statement from Eno and Schmidt inside each of the editions reads: 'These cards evolved from our separate observations of the principles underlying what we were doing. Sometimes they were recognized in retrospect (intellect catching up with intuition), sometimes they were identified as they were happening, sometimes they were formulated. They can be used as a pack (a set of possibilities being continuously reviewed in the mind) or by drawing a single card from the shuffled pack when a dilemma occurs in a working situation. In this case the card is trusted even if its appropriateness is quite unclear. They are not final, as new ideas will present themselves, and others will become self-evident'.*

13 *Interview by Ian MacDonald,* New Musical Express, *26 November 1977.*

Exercises:

1   From all possible sets of instruments (as detailed) random sets are chosen and each section of one of the songs is played by one of these sets.

2   A completely sung piece (or all whistles, or all percussion).

3   Each player mentally invents a phrase, all begin together and continue playing: the mixer fades them in one by one.

4   Use the instruments to produce noises in ways other than those normally used.

5   Feed all instruments thru the synthesizer—unfeed them one by one.

6   Record a bass line. Record a guitar solo to that bass-line on another piece of tape. Record another guitar solo to that bass line etc. Play all back simultaneously with bass line.

7   All instruments play on a long delay echo.

14 *Interview by the author, London, 26 July 1984.*

on which Eno collaborated: *Lucky Lief and the Longships* by Robert Calvert; *Mainstream* by Quiet Sun (with Phil Manzanera); and *Ruth is Stranger than Richard* by Robert Wyatt. Bill MacCormick, bass player with Matching Mole, Quiet Sun, and 801, describes the key role the cards played in the recording of *Mainstream*:

Oblique Strategies was uncanny in a number of areas. We tried not to use it too often for fear of destroying the feeling about it. But on occasions we would get to a complete and utter blockage and wouldn't know what to do. Then someone would say, 'Look, I think it's time for the Strategies.' The box would emerge and the card drawn would be uncannily accurate as to what was needed, or what was going wrong. We got to the stage of trusting it implicitly. Even on occasions when the card would have been open, in other circumstances, to a number of interpretations, it seemed that everybody reached the same conclusion about it. It did have, I think, a very crucial effect in certain areas.[14]

MacCormick recalls an argument in the studio during the mixing of *Ruth is Stranger than Richard*. Robert Wyatt, at the mixing desk, was becoming increasingly harassed by the noisy demands of the other musicians. Finally, someone suggested that they should consult *Oblique Strategies*, and Alfie, Wyatt's wife, pulled out a card at random. It read simply: 'Tape your mouth'. Everybody immediately stopped talking and the problem was quickly resolved.

Plan for a piece:

. . . . record many layers of faded-up piano chords against a count. ~~At some point~~ The piece is divided into n sections and at each division the chord changes. The faded-up chords are all inversions of one another. The chord changes are very delicate except for one which is quite distinct

on top of this: string parts — incomplete melodies particularly across the junction

use this as a bass line for a number of repeating parts which cross the FACE chord. use voices for the parts.

after a mix I said to Rhett 'I bet you'll find that the moog is twice as loud as it should be' He replied "it should be twice as loud as it should be"

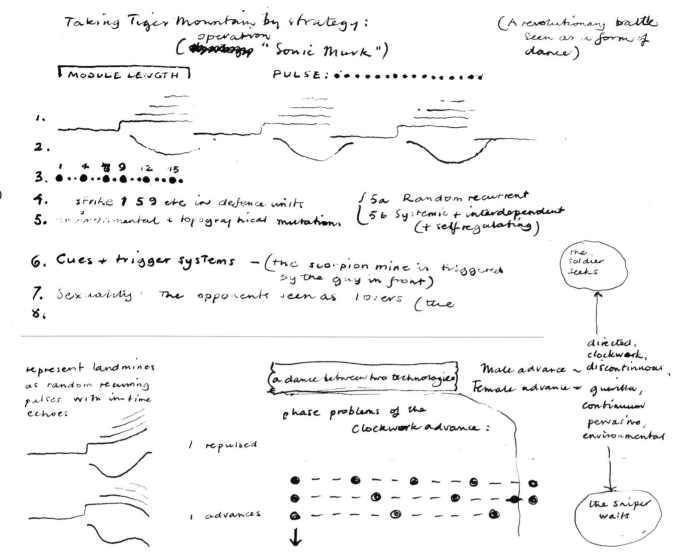

THE STUDIO AS AN INSTRUMENT

Eno's studio techniques have always entailed a high degree of wastage. In 1974 he estimated that as much as 85 per cent of the material that he had on tape would never see the light of day. Many of the tapes were filed away for future reference, and over the years an enormous body of unreleased material has amassed. Eno has always acknowledged that his view of such material is prone to change with the passage of time – that initially unpromising ideas, approached from a new angle at a later date, can yield unexpected discoveries. Many of the songs on *Taking Tiger Mountain*, for instance, were edited together, with the help of Phil Manzanera, from existing fragments of music in Eno's tape library. Another of Eno's techniques, used in the recording of *Before and After Science* and earlier, was to select a spool of unlabelled tape from his library, and record it on the same tape as the piece of music he was already working on. When he played back the composite tape much of it would sound garbled, but at some points the two pieces of music might coincide in a way that suggested a new direction. This would then be pursued, and the unwanted parts of the original tape – perhaps as much as 70 per cent – would be edited out.

In the studio, Eno would often begin an instrumental by experimenting playfully with a piece of equipment. He likened this process of technological tinkering to 'revving up'; it was a way of warming up the creative motor. Sometimes accidental discoveries with a new piece of equipment, in the course of one of these sessions, would prompt a musical idea. The choppy organ riff that underpins 'Golden Hours' on *Another Green World* resulted from Eno's experiments with a Farfisa organ that he had just hired. This was improvisation of a kind, but always with the aim of arriving somewhere eventually, even if there was no way of predicting the destination in advance. Improvisation as an end in itself, as in free jazz, has never appealed to Eno. He has always wanted to build a framework around chaos: to contain and control it. Robert Fripp's searing guitar work in 'Baby's on Fire' derives much of its aesthetic power from being heard in high relief against the closed structure of the song. Isolated on its own, or set against another equally chaotic instrumental, the tension would be gone. In 'The Great Pretender', Eno produces a comparable disorientation by the opposite means. One by one the instruments are introduced to form a dense and impenetrable wall of sound: synthetic percussion, piano, 'snake' guitar, voice, metallic percussion, fuzz guitar, and finally, heavy fuzz guitar. When the guitar theme abruptly cuts out – at the exact moment that the voice, underscored by menacing electronics, returns – it is like a void opening up in the heart of the song. Then, restoring a kind of perverse equilibrium of noise, the relentless layering begins once again.

Like 'Golden Hours', 'Baby's on Fire', and 'The Great Pretender', much of Eno's work is characterized by extreme simplicity, both of means and effect. From *Here Come the Warm Jets* onwards, he showed a taste for absolutely stable and unvarying rhythm tracks that would come to characterize his music. Against stable grids like those in 'Needles in the Camel's Eye' and 'St Elmo's Fire', Eno would set the melodic 'information' of the song:

I enjoy working with simple structures... because they are transparent – comparable perhaps to the grid on a piece of graph paper which serves as the 'container'/reference point/system for the important information – the graph line itself. For my purposes, to use complex time signatures and complex structures would serve only to conceal or obscure (which I believe is often precisely the motivation for its usage), just as a graph drawn on a network of wavy lines would yield little information in terms of a graph. So, although I don't deny that there are other kinds of knowledge that need those wavy lines, I regard them as antithetical to my own work.[15]

Eno's commitment to repetition (which he derived, ultimately, from his experiences performing LaMonte Young's *X for Henry Flynt*) led him to propose the continuum as the ideal structure for a rock song. Eno admired the Velvet Underground, in particular, for the feeling that their songs were excerpts from a much longer piece of music which had begun before the song had started, and which would go on long after it finished. Pointing to the smooth, minimalist music of Steve Reich and to 'field' painting, Eno argued that the continuous, even, uniform contour of much modern art was innately more democratic. This kind of structure, with its lack of pronounced highs and lows, and its willing acceptance of stasis, refuses to direct or focus the perceiver's attention. Traditional forms of art and music use focus as a way of determining which elements within the artwork should be perceived as the most important. Most of Eno's work during this period, from the longer 'systems' pieces – *Discreet Music*, *(No Pussyfooting)* and *Evening Star* – through to the shorter songs, exhibits this sense of being sliced, like a representative extract, from a much larger continuum. Some tracks, notably 'Another Green World' and 'King's Lead Hat', even emphasize this quality by fading in as they begin, as well as fading out at the end.

During the protracted composition of *Before and After Science*, Eno continued to refine his ideas about focus and hierarchy. Increasingly, he began to distinguish between two kinds of rock music. In the first, the old-fashioned kind, the ranking of the instruments is more or less fixed. As with orchestral music there is a 'hierarchy of events'. At the bottom of this hierarchy are the bass instruments and the drums; then come the rhythm guitar and the piano, which carry the chord information, but have a little more freedom; at the top are the lead guitar and the vocals, with the guitar usually subordinate to the voice, except when a solo is called for. The kind of rock which Eno preferred overturned this rigid ranking. In Eno's view, both Bo Diddley and the Who had explored this alternative approach at various times, but it was the Velvet Underground, once again, that provided the ultimate example:

The Velvet Underground... used all of their instruments in the rhythm role almost and the singing is in a deliberate monotone, which is a deliberate non-surprise, so when you listen to the music your focus is shifting all the time because there's no ranking, which doesn't only reflect the internal structure of the music, but also the structure of your attention to it. It's not the extremes of strict ranking and focus, or no ranking and disorientation that interest me, but how much of each I want. I want the thing to have a certain amount of 'perceptual drift' where the ranking is being shuffled all the time, so at times you're not sure what you're meant to be listening to.[16]

Sophisticated experiments with ranking were also being undertaken in black music. From Jamaican dub reggae and Sly and the Family Stone, Eno learned techniques that made *Before and After Science*, released in 1977, his most radical use of the recording studio as an instrument so far. Beginning from nothing, as he had done on *Another Green World*, Eno built up the songs layer by layer, then stripped them away again track by track as new possibilities became apparent, until the emerging song had undergone a complete transformation. The process was almost sculptural; it was composition by subtraction, rather than addition. In some cases, all that remained at the end of the process was the palest trace – no more than a suggestion of the frenzied remixing that had brought the song into being. In a year that saw the commercial rise of punk rock, with its scraping guitars and clanking drums, songs from *Before and After Science* like 'Julie with...' and 'By this River' were remarkable for their emptiness and serenity.

1976 and 1977 were years of transition for Eno. His experience of working with David Bowie on *Low*, particularly on the album's instrumental pieces, confirmed his conviction that rock without focus was the music of the future. In 1976, Eno released the first limited edition of *Music for Films*, his album of soundtracks for real and imaginary movies. Film music, which is composed – ostensibly at least – to accompany visual images, is inherently unfocused. Already Eno was beginning to think about the first of his Ambient records. Soon he would abandon the insistent pulse of his earlier pop albums for a music of drift and contemplation.

15 *Eno, review of* Here Come the Warm Jets, *requested by Spare Rib, 1973.*

16 *Interview by Hal Synthetic, Sounds, 26 November 1977. Interestingly, this interview formed part of an attempt by Sounds to identify Eno as a member of a so-called 'cold wave' of New Musick (sic). In an overview of the genre, David Bowie's Low is seen as a key album. Also featured are Devo (whose first album Eno later produced); Throbbing Gristle; The Residents; and Kraftwerk. Elsewhere, Eno resisted the categorization vigorously.*

It will shine and it will shudder
As I guide it with my rudder
On its metalled ways
It will cut the night before it
As it leaves the day that saw it
On its metalled ways
Nobody passes us in the deep quiet of the dark sky
Nobody sees us alone out here among the stars
In these metal ways
In these metal days.

Through a fault of our designing
We are lost among the windings
Of these metal ways
Back to silence back to minus
With the purple sky behind us
In these metal ways
Nobody hears us when we're alone in the blue future
No one receiving the radio's splintered waves
In these metal ways
In these metal days.

102   No One Receiving

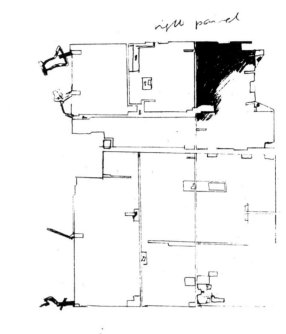

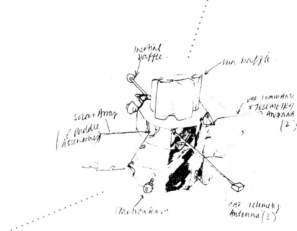

Having suffered the practice of art directors on magazines to categorize severely, I had spent my first year out of college being employed to produce illustrations that fell into the following pigeon holes: Futurology, Economics, Mathematics, Medical, Sciences, or 'Quirky'. So I approached this song with an apprehension of regression. I didn't relish tackling yet another 'Sci-Fi' biased picture.

Eventually my translation of the song became more abstract with the only reference to representational forms being the solar array panels attached to the space module, and even these, with their pattern of silver ribs and black panels are abstract in themselves.

I decided to keep everything to a minimum; whilst including all the space elements, module, splintered radio waves, galaxies (manipulated rust clusters on the metal plate) and also emphasizing the loneliness of the travel.

The line, 'On its metalled ways', is from 'Burnt Norton' by T. S. Eliot : ✳

....; while the world moves
In appetency, on its metalled ways
Of time past and time future

R.M.

✳ T.S. Eliot, **Four Quartets** (Faber and Faber, London. First published 1944).

Back to silence back to minus

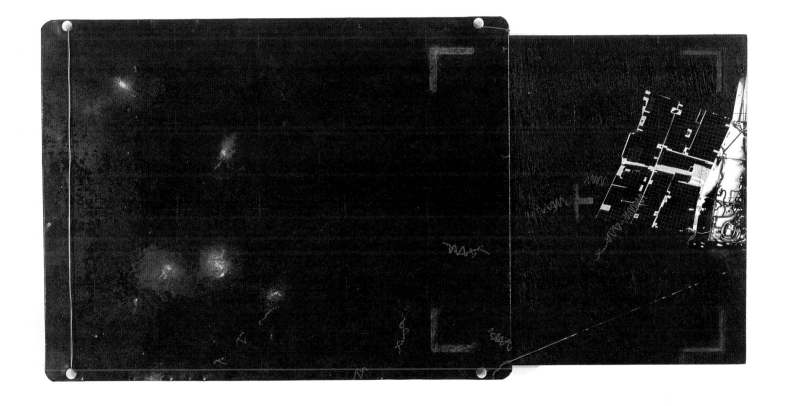

Backwater
We're sailing at the edges of time
Backwater
We're drifting at the waterline
Oh we're floating in the coastal waters
You and me and the porter's daughters
Ooh what to do not a sausage to do
And the shorter of the porter's daughters
Dips her hand in the deadly waters
Ooh what to do in a tiny canoe.

Black water
There were six of us but now we are five
We're all talking
To keep the conversation alive
There was a senator from Ecuador
Who talked about a meteor
That crashed on a hill in the South of Peru
And was found by a conquistador
Who took it to the Emperor
And he passed it on to a Turkish Guru.

His daughter
Was slated for becoming divine
He taught her
He taught her how to split and define
But if you study the logistics
And heuristics of the mystics
You will find that their minds rarely move in a line
So it's much more realistic
To abandon such ballistics
And resign to be trapped on a leaf in the vine.

104   **Backwater**

The song I found to be too busy, too confused and laboured. Only a few lines really appealed to me, primarily because of the clever rhyming. I liked the idea of producing a picture that included a figure who wasn't there, hence the ghost-white shape in the boat. This device is a favourite of colour supplements when dealing with groups of people such as terrorists, criminals, regiments, etc. where there are individuals within the group who have been killed, died naturally, or who were absent when the main photo was taken.

The plastic lifebelt, from a model shop, was added as an afterthought, possibly explaining the reason for the loss of the 'Porter's daughter'.

The green buoy to the right of the boat signifies the position of a 'wreck.'

R.M.

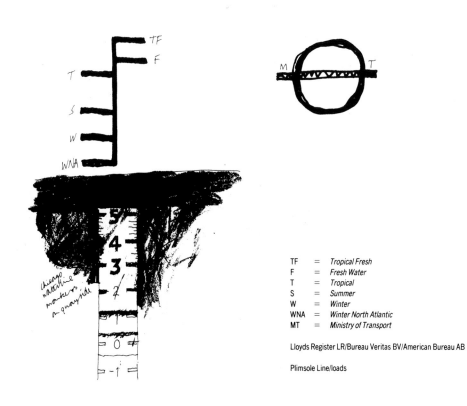

(Deck line)

TF	=	*Tropical Fresh*
F	=	*Fresh Water*
T	=	*Tropical*
S	=	*Summer*
W	=	*Winter*
WNA	=	*Winter North Atlantic*
MT	=	*Ministry of Transport*

Lloyds Register LR/Bureau Veritas BV/American Bureau AB

Plimsole Line/loads

There were six of us but now we are five

Burger cruising just above the ground ground ground
And gunner puts a burnish on his steel
Anna with her feelers moving round round round
Is sharpening her needles on the wheel.

Burger Bender bargain blender shine shine shine
And gunner burn the leader on the fuse
Bundle up the numbers counting 3 – 6 – 9
Here's Anna building webs across our shoes
Celebrate the loss of one and all all all
And separate the torso from the spine
Burger Bender bouncing like a ball ball ball
So Burger Bender bargain blender shine.

Do the Do-si-do, do the Mirror Man
Do the Boston Crab, do the Allemande.

106   Kurt's Rejoinder

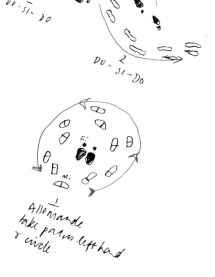

One Sunday lunchtime in 1978, I was in bed reading the papers and listening to Radio Three. The programme that I was listening to was previewing a series of German Cultural events organized by the Goethe Institute under the umbrella title of 'London – Berlin. The 70s Meet the 20s.' Among those highlighted was a 'Schwitters Evening', which included recitals of Schwitters' phonetic poems, (either recordings of Schwitters himself or a rendering by Eberhard Blum?) I was so excited that I immediately phoned Brian (Eno) with the idea that he might be interested in recording it for future use. Coincidentally he too was listening to the same programme and was already taping it. Extracts of the poems appear under the main lyrics sounding like a distant extra instrument.

The central rectangle of the three main pieces, was originally executed as a separate picture for inclusion in the Press Kit that Brian prepared to accompany Before And After Science. I found that the set of apparently arbitrary lyrics suggested a strange sensation similar to my experience when I see a painting or collage by Schwitters. A mass of disparate images, subtle colours, worn, used fragments each with their own histories. I tried to integrate this sensation with a comment on Schwitters' life.

When Schwitters first exhibited his collages of rubbish, tickets, etc. they were priced from about eight guineas up to twenty (this was in England in 1944)… none sold. In 1947, the year of his death, he was trying to sell them for £1 a piece. Now, his collages can sell for up to £39,000 – £40,000, and are increasing all the time. Pure Dada. Sad irony.

The tiny semi-Schwitters collages that move from the bottom left to the main area of the picture represent his prolific output. On entering the main picture they meet with destruction. (Hitler proclaimed that Schwitters was a degenerate artist and he was obliged to flee Germany to Norway, and when the Germans invaded Norway he moved to England.)

At the extreme top right is a semi-Schwitters collage comfortably hung on a wall above a cosy armchair and a lamp. There is a red dot under the picture to indicate that it has been sold. This is how Schwitters' work is regarded today…

The dance steps (right panel) realize the confusion of two real dance steps, the Do-si-do and the Allemande, both barn dance steps; and two imaginary dance movements, the Mirror Man and the Boston Crab, the latter being a back-breaking wrestling hold.

All other elements refer, albeit somewhat obliquely, to the lyrics · · · · · · · · · · · · · ·

R.M.

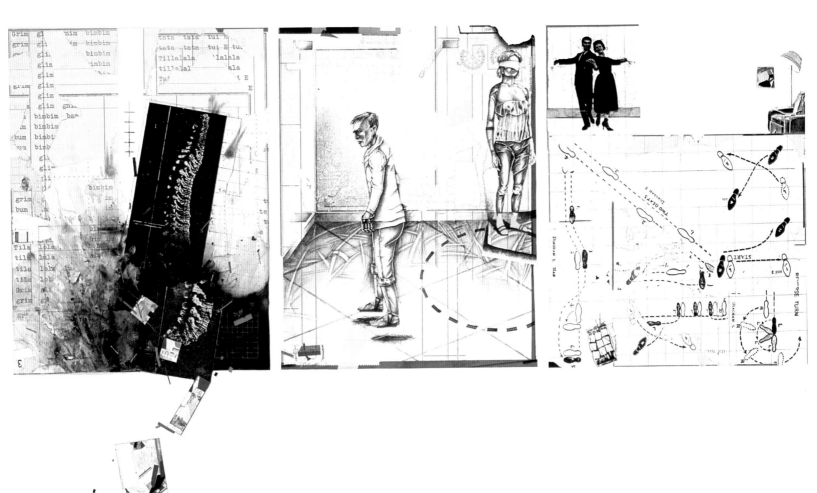

Lyrics in parentheses are sung in parallel with main lyric

Dark alley *(dark alley)* **black star**
Four turkeys in a big black car
The road is shiny *(bright shine)* **the wheels slide**
Four turkeys going for a dangerous ride
The lacquer crackles *(black tar)* **the engines roar**
A ship was turning broadside to the shore
Splish splash I was raking in the cash
The biology of purpose keeps my nose above the surface (OOH)
King's lead hat put the innocence inside her, it will come, it will come, it will surely come
King's lead hat was a mother to desire, it will come, it will come, it will surely come

In New Delhi *(smelly Delhi)* **and Hong Kong**
They all know that it won't be long
I count my fingers *(digit counter)* **as night falls**
And draw bananas on the bathroom walls
The killer cycles *(humdrum)* **the killer hertz**
The passage of my life is measured out in shirts
Time and motion *(motion carried)* **time and tide**
All I know and all I have is time and time and tide is on my side
King's lead hat was a poker in the fire, it will come, it will come, it will surely come
King's lead hat was a mother to desire, it will come, it will come, it will surely come

The weapon's ready *(ready Freddy)* **the guns purr**
The satellite distorts his voice to a slur
He gives orders *(finger pie)* **which no one hears**
The king's hat fits over their ears
He takes his modicate *(indecipherable)* **cold turpentine**
He tries to dial out 999999999
He dials reception *(moving finger)* **he's all alone**
He's just a victim of the telephone
King's lead hat made the Amazon much wider, it will come, it will come, it will surely come
King's lead hat was the poker in the fire, it will come, it will come, it will surely come
King's lead hat was a mother to desire, it will come, it will come, it will surely come
King's lead hat put the innocence inside her, it will come, it will come, it will surely come
King's lead hat was a hammer to desire, it will come, it will come, it will surely come.

108   King's Lead Hat

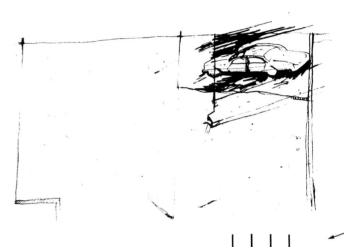

Shaking detail
Dash Gale Knot
King's lead hat.   dealt
leaking   shaking
Hang, sad
T A L K I N G H E A D S   kill
dig tale shank (dig?)
L A D I E S   T H A N K   Hank Stank
shading lake
thanks a glide
BE624 15·25 / Friday / Köln 16·35
ADTAKN

Think a sad leg / Dakes halting
Dank shit gale / TAKIS HANGED
HANKIED STAG / I STAGED HANK
His data

electric blue

The title is an anagram of Talking Heads, an American band whom Eno admires greatly; he has produced and acted as fifth member on three of their albums (see full discography on page 138). This song is his tribute to them.

Both pieces were made on a black polythene refuse bag, as supplied by the local council. In the process of making this piece, especially the larger left panel, I had trouble getting it to lie flat. This was a happy accident, for it caused creases to lead one's eye towards the speeding car, thus emphasizing the movement. The car contains the Talking Heads, contradicting the laws by driving up a one-way/no entry street.

The shrink-wrapped shirts that bridge the gap between the two panels represents Eno's solo recording ventures up to 1977. Each shirt has been designed/treated in relation to the character of each album thus:

Shirt No 1 – silver – *Here Come The Warm Jets* – recorded in Eno's Glam Rock cum transvestite period

Shirt No 2 – gradated bands of red – *Taking Tiger Mountain (By Strategy)* based on Mao Tse Tung's military opera of the same name.

Shirt No 3 – green with yellow suns – *Another Green World*, self-explanatory.

Shirt No 4 – grey pinstripe – *Discreet Music* – the shirt is smaller than the others and quieter.

Shirt No 5 – black with beam of light hitting screen – *Music For Films*

Shirt No 6 – black plus abstract flashes – *Before And After Science*

Shirt No 7 – impressionist sky with clouds – *Music For Airports*.

The shirts refer to the line:

The passage of my life is measured out in shirts

The second panel shows a figure idly drawing silver penises which look like bananas, the sort of inaccurate obscene graffiti one sees in public toilets.

R.M.

talking heads

Four turkeys in a big black car

(b)

And draw bananas on the bathroom walls

Here he comes the boy who tried to vanish to the future or past
　　　is no longer here with his sad blue eyes
Here he comes he floated away and as he rose above reason
　　　he rose above the clouds he was seven feet high
Here he comes the night is like a glove and he's floating like a dove
　　　that catches the wind in the deep blue sky
Here he comes the boy who tried to vanish to another time
　　　is no longer here with his sad blue eyes.

Here he comes here he comes
Here he comes the boy who tried to vanish to another place
　　　sees us following him all one at a time
Here he comes and we're checking out each others supplies
　　　and looking at the eyes of all the others standing in the line
Here he comes the night is like a glove and he's floating like a dove
　　　with his deep blue eyes in the deep blue sky
Here he comes the boy who tried to vanish to the future or past
　　　is no longer alone among the dragonflies
Here he comes here he comes.

　　　Who will remember him?

112　**Here He Comes**

Another 'spacey' song, with the 'outsider' being the 'star'. The

individual approaches a line of queuing people (queuing for what?

they don't know, we don't know); they are willing to follow him and

learn by imitation. . .

R.M.

I am on an open sea
Just drifting as the hours go slowly by
Julie with her open blouse
Is gazing up into the empty sky.

Now it seems to be so strange here
Now it's so blue
The still sea is darker than before . . .

No wind disturbs our coloured sail
The radio is silent, so are we
Julie's head is on her arm
Her fingers brush the surface of the sea.

Now I wonder if we'll be seen here
Or if time has left us all alone
The still sea is darker than before . . .

114   Julie With . . .

A sense of calm and innocence slowly becomes threatened, The music is deceptively charming and seductive, luring one into the song so that one easily ignores the change of mood in the lyrics.

I produced one picture in full colour, complete and bland, suggesting nothing of what might follow. Using the same picture I produced a negative print toned in a blue, leaving only a symbol of danger, the red sails. The negative picture answers the underlying foreboding of the song;

The still sea is darker than before . . .

and:

The radio is silent, so are we

and finally:

**Now I wonder if we'll be seen here
Or if time has left us all alone.
The still sea is darker than before . . .**

This interpretation also fits in with a curious assessment that Eno read, written by an American critic in one of the American music papers:

. . . Eno, the narrator is in a row boat at sea, accompanied by a young girl (perhaps 13 – 14 years old), named Julie. She is apparently a pubescent pleasure to behold. Eno intends to sexually assault Julie when they are far enough out at sea. . .

R.M.

(a)

(b)

Here we are stuck by this river
You and I underneath a sky
That's ever falling down   down   down
Ever falling down

Through the day as if on an ocean
Waiting here always failing to remember
Why we came   came   came
I wonder why we came

You talk to me as if from a distance
And I reply with impressions chosen
From another time   time   time
From another time.

116   **By This River**

Like 'Julie With...', this piece undulates seductively. I suppose that equally sinister meanings could be read into it, but I couldn't find any and am quite content to accept it on its face value. And as it is such a lyrical song, it presented me with a dilemma, considering that my instinct/sensibility tells me to back away from such blatant romanticism...

Around the time of working on this song I was re-discovering the peculiar unpredictable nature of a specific type of photo-copying paper. I was experimenting with the effects of light and heat on this paper when exposed. I had been holding sheets of it up against the bars of an electric fire; after about 30-40 seconds the paper began to develop blurred areas of sepia colour. The misty quality of the shapes suggested a hazy swamp-like wasteland or a river bank at dawn, indefinite rising mists. These results were worked into with coloured pencils.

I reached a stage when I painted and repainted the girls eyes so many times that the surface was becoming impasto in its texture, making it impossible for me to hope to achieve a decent pair of eyes. *But* thinking of the line: 'You talk to me as if from a distance' I resolved to present the girl with a pair of ridiculously thick lensed spectacles. My eye problem was solved, whilst hers was getting worse...

To apologize for my lack of reverence to the text I did eventually add a scale in foot measurement on the silver ground under the figures.

R.M.

**Spider and I sit watching the sky
On a world without sound
We knit a web to catch one tiny fly
For our world without sound
We sleep in the mornings
We dream of a ship that sails away
A thousand miles away.**

Spider And I

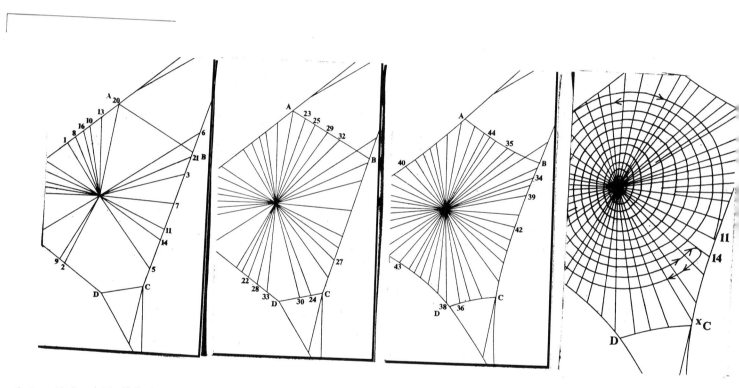

Yet another quiet, gentle piece, with almost minimal lyrics. I was
determined not to fall into the trap of making a picture of a spider
weaving its web whilst close by sits the narrator.

The background 'wallpaper' was a huge map of the world, which I
rectified with texture paste, gouache, watercolour and graphite.
There are scientific drawings at the top right, these describe step by
step the way that a garden spider goes about constructing one of
the most perfect examples of geometry in nature.

The sleeping head is my own, fixed on acetate, then laid over a
rectangle of mirror tiles, this is in turn embedded flat into a pillow.

R.M.

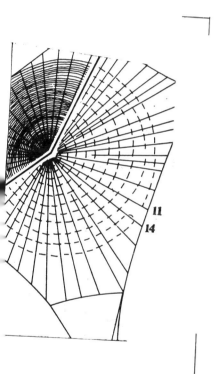

We sleep in the mornings

120

Between 1973 and 1978 Brian Eno composed and sang thirty-nine songs, but he is not, and never wanted to be, a songwriter, not in the sense in which natural 'wordsmiths' such as Bob Dylan, John Lennon, and Bryan Ferry are songwriters. With Eno the writing of lyrics has always been a by-product of his desire to sing, and the need for a vehicle for his voice, rather than an expression of an inherently literary sensibility. Even while he was still composing words, Eno always insisted that he had nothing to say, that there was no message or statement that he wanted to express in songs through the medium of language. When it came to words, he said, he felt far more strongly about the intellectual side of himself that was expressed in essays and lectures.

As a corollary of this, Eno has always argued that far too much attention is paid to rock lyrics – both his own and those of other artists. Reviewers and critics, who are often from literary rather than musical backgrounds, have tended to interpret the words as though they were poetry and contained the real message of the song. The music, meanwhile, goes largely unanalysed. For Eno the truth of the matter is the other way round: 'For me it's nearly always the music that does the talking – the words (with a few exceptions) are at best vague clues, appendages'.[1] Most of the time, he said, he didn't even hear the lyrics of a song:

... I listen to songs millions of times without ever bothering to hear the lyrics, or, if this is unavoidable, without bothering to understand them. As far as I'm concerned any other set of words would generally serve as well. The other facet of this is that my interpretations (if I finally make them) of other people's lyrics are completely strange and rarely agree with the accepted interpretation.[2]

Eno's growing uncertainty about the role of words in his songs led him finally to abandon (public) lyric writing in 1978.[3] The repudiation of lyrics went hand in hand with a move towards very much gentler pieces of 'ambient' instrumental music. Many of the reviewers who supported the innovations of Eno's earlier work have found this change of course hard to accept, seeing it almost as a denial of his true calling as a songwriter. But the facts must speak for themselves. In the cover notes for a 1981 US promotional album containing ten of his songs, Eno points out that of the nearly 600 minutes of music he had committed to record up to that time only 155 minutes consisted of songs with lyrics. 'This collection is therefore by no means a cross section,' he writes, 'it is an edge of my work that others tend to regard as the centre'.[4] Five years on, the ratio is weighted even more heavily in favour of instrumentals.

MOOD GENERATORS

It is ironic that such an offhand attitude towards lyrics should have resulted in such a compelling collection of songs. Since the work of Bob Dylan inspired the Beatles to introduce serious themes and imagery into the traditionally trivial world of the pop song, writers of rock lyrics have been lining up with the poets rather than the songsmiths. 1967 was, in many respects, a turning point. That year, for the first time, the Beatles printed their lyrics on the sleeve of *Sgt. Pepper's Lonely Hearts Club Band*. Their fans were thereby encouraged not just to listen to the lyrics as songs, but to read the words as literature. Small wonder that this bid for literary credibility was swiftly taken up by other members of the serious rock community. Seeing your lyrics in cold print was like a hallmark of quality.

To be found in a capsule
To be capped by a dentist
To get dents from a poker
To be poked by a hooker
To be hooked by a harpoon
To be harped by an angel
With my name in gold letters
written out in a halo
and my bones in glass boxes
in remote country churches
~~and in old lady's tumblers~~
Yes To have my own Sunday
And a place on the altar.
Till the bishop discovers
I was hooked on a poker
I was not such a good-un
There's a fly in the ointment

1 *Letter from Eno to Russell Mills, 1977.*
2 *Ibid.*
3 *This was the year that* **After the Heat** *was released. Since then Eno has co-written lyrics with David Byrne for two songs on* **Remain in Light** *by Talking Heads (1980): 'Cross-eyed and Painless' and 'Born under Punches (The Heat Goes On)'.*
4 Music for Airplay, *US promotional record, 1981.*

Unlike many of his contemporaries Eno has never regarded himself as a poet. 'I have no pretensions to poetry at all,' he said in 1974, following the release of *Here Come the Warm Jets*.[5] With the exception of 'Miss Shapiro' and 'Big Day' on Phil Manzanera's *Diamond Head* album, none of Eno's lyrics were ever printed on the album covers. Eno wanted his words to remain mysterious, to function as mood generators with no life independent of their musical setting. The voice was just another element in the mix of instruments that made up the finished song. It was therefore no more relevant to print the lyrics than it was 'to score the top line that the guitar is playing'.[6] To illustrate the kind of effect he wanted to achieve in his own lyrics Eno pointed to 'What Goes On' by the Velvet Underground, and 'Little Wing' by Jimi Hendrix. In each case the words are vague and mysterious. Both songs appear to be saying something, but the meaning is impossible to pin down – they have a definite, even intense feeling without making a particular statement. Significantly, Lou Reed, writer and singer of 'What Goes On', also declined to print the words to his songs. Like Eno, he believed that lyrics should not be read as poetry.

Eno's comparison between his own lyrics and those of the Velvet Underground is a telling one. Although Eno's early songs don't explore the urban scene with the same documentary relish as those of the New York band, Eno does share their taste for the perverse. The sadistic imagery of songs like 'Baby's on Fire', 'Third Uncle' and 'The Great Pretender', combined with Eno's sneering vocal delivery and delirious instrumental attack, place the songs in a direct line of descent from such Velvet Underground classics as 'Venus in Furs' and 'Heroin'. Their unwholesome emotions and macabre scenarios are a thousand miles from the sugary sentiment and toytown surrealism of the English psychedelic underground of the late 1960s. Songs like these seemed, at the time, to function as teasing verbal equivalents of Eno's sexually ambiguous image. The effect of calculated decadence was reinforced by Eno's outrageous stage clothes and use of make-up,[7] and by camp visual props like the pornographic picture playing cards used on the covers of both *(No Pussyfooting)* and *Here Come the Warm Jets* – from Eno's own collection of fifty or so packs. The title of *Warm Jets* itself turned out to be to a punning reference to pissing, while the jokey lyrics of 'Seven Deadly Finns' conceal a glossary of prostitute slang. Whatever the psychological origins of the image projected by his lyrics and behaviour, Eno exploited its effect quite deliberately. Discussing his appearance during this period he writes:

In terms of my own music the following qualities seem important since they endorse the kinds of feelings I try to inject into the music: sexy/insane/grotesque/sinister/beautiful/passionate/incessant/ aesperate/angular/reptilian. Obviously there are internal contradictions in this set of qualities, but for me this increases rather than depletes the effectiveness. I suppose I am most interested in my own madness – which is the contradiction between the part of me that seeks to analyse and rationalize (as in this letter) and the other, probably more exploratory, part that wants to smash things up and throw them together in a different pattern.[8]

Musically, Eno's four rock albums divide into two phases – one ending with *Taking Tiger Mountain* and the next starting with *Another Green World* – and the same is broadly true of his concerns in the lyrics. If the enduring image of the first two albums, 'Seven Deadly Finns', and Eno and the Winkies' cover version of 'Fever'[9] is fire – an emblem of extreme, even destructive, passion; of love reduced to ashes – that of the last, *Before and After Science*, is water. It is as if the deadly passions of the earlier albums are extinguished – cancelled out – by the cool, calmative liquids of the later songs. Beneath the empty, deep blue skies that dominate the imaginary landscapes of *Before and After Science* a series of figures drift slowly by on rivers and oceans that seem to go on for ever. The prevailing mood, brittle with menace in many of the early songs, is now one of nostalgia and yearning, of pleasure in melancholy. Where fire does recur after *Taking Tiger Mountain*, in 'St Elmo's Fire' on *Another Green World*, it is beatific rather than minatory; identified, in an electrifying couplet, with the redemptive powers of the landscape itself: 'And we saw St Elmo's Fire/Splitting ions in the ether'.

There is a shift of interest, too, away from the gallery of larger-than-life characters who populate the early songs: Baby, Luana, the Paw Paw Negro Blowtorch, the Great Pretender, Blank Frank, the Fat Lady of Limbourg, the Seven Deadly Finns. The inhabitants of the later songs are much paler figures, even in their names: 'brown eyes', Rosalie, Spider, Julie, 'the boy who tried to vanish to another time'. Sometimes, as in 'I'll Come Running to Tie Your Shoe' and 'By this River', the subject of the song, the 'you' that the singer addresses, is never even named. No longer are the songs' characters the object of detached and voyeuristic interest – like exotic specimens trapped under glass. Increasingly, they tend to be the figurative (at times, perhaps, literal?) objects of the singer's longing and affection. As the lyrics become simpler in their construction, and more direct in their statements, so the sentimentality first glimpsed in 'Cindy Tells Me' and 'Some of them Are Old', becomes more and more pronounced in songs like 'Everything Merges with the Night' and 'Here He Comes'. As in the later Velvet Underground of 'Candy Says' and 'Pale Blue Eyes' (listed by Eno in 1977 as one of his favourite songs) Eno has his sweeter side.

THE AUTOMATIC MUSE

The unconventional techniques used by Eno to generate his lyrics were an early source of press and public interest in his work. Although he claimed that some of his lyrics were written by conventional means, Eno always concentrated on the less familiar techniques in his explanations, because he believed them to be more interesting. Chief of these techniques was improvisation to pre-recorded backing tapes, a procedure he had first employed in 1969 when he was for a short time a singer with an improvisatory rock group called Maxwell Demon.[10]

Sometimes Eno based a set of lyrics on an idea or a title that existed before any music had been produced. *Taking Tiger Mountain by Strategy*, the Chinese revolutionary opera title which he 'found' on a visit to San Francisco, inspired an entire album. Both the lyrics and the music that Eno went on to create, were an attempt to embody the contrasting images of medieval rustic simplicity and contemporary urban complexity suggested by the title. During the recording of *Taking Tiger Mountain*, and on the later albums, Eno explored a technique for generating lyrics which he had first employed on 'Baby's on Fire'. Typically, he would begin work on a backing track with no thought of how the lyrics might turn out; and often with no plans to turn the piece into a song at all. As the instrumental took shape, the mood of the music sometimes suggested the need for a voice. But there was no way this change of direction could be predicted in advance. On *Another Green World* only five of the fourteen tracks crossed the line into songhood.

Baby's on fire .
and all the instruments agree that
The temperature's higher
But any idiot can see that

Dejected young call girls
with double mirrors in the windows
They go whichever way the wind
blows

5 Interview by Chrissie Hynde, New Musical Express, 2 February 1974.

6 Interview by Allan Jones, Melody Maker, 26 October 1974.

7 Eno was not, of course, alone in cultivating this kind of image. David Bowie and Marc Bolan, in particular, were also testing the limits of glamorous androgyny during this period. Glitter or 'glam' rock quickly came to be the prevailing sartorial style.

8 Letter from Eno to the Museum of Art, Lucerne, 1974.

9 Davenport and Cooley's 'Fever', as performed by Eno and the Winkies on a John Peel radio session in early 1974, ends with the lines: 'Fever/I'm on fire/But what a lovely way to burn'. Note also the words to an early version of 'I'll Come Running' included in the same session: 'I'll find a place somewhere on the carpet/I'm gonna waste the rest of my days/Do all the dreadful things you might ask me/Condemned to life as an ashtray'

10 Maxwell's Demon was an imaginary being posited by the nineteenth century physicist James Clerk Maxwell. The demon's task was to reverse the process of entropy within a cloud of gas by sorting through its disorganized molecules. Eno formed Maxwell Demon with the guitarist Anthony Grafton. Only one recording by the group is known to exist, a song called 'Ellis B. Compton Blues', made on 4-track tape, 25 December 1968.

Once he had decided to transform an instrumental track into a song, Eno would take a rough mix of the music home with him. The next step was to improvise vocals over the backing track. Eno would begin by singing abstract sounds rather than specific words. Once a phonetic and rhythmic framework had been established, he would improvise lyrics to fit the metre, by shouting and singing whatever flashed into his head as he stood at the microphone. As many as fifteen or more different versions of the song might be produced in this way, each one recorded for reference. Finally, the different options for each part of the song – line, verse and chorus – were compiled in the form of a chart. Only when Eno began the conscious process of editing this spontaneously generated material did he discover what the song was 'about'. As the manifest content of the song became clearer he would fill in the blanks that remained in the verse structure. Sometimes new lines that had arisen in the course of the improvisation would seem particularly significant and the song would change course again. Earlier lines that no longer seemed to fit would then be discarded. Like Eno's other studio techniques the method was empirical. The process of addition and subtraction continued until the result seemed to balance – until Eno felt intuitively that the song had reached 'the point where it doesn't go anywhere else':

'Baby's on Fire' was written this way, you know. 'Baby's on Fire' was just a line that came out while I was doing this process and... I thought instantly of spontaneous human combustion, which was something I'd been reading about at the time. I just imagined this little scenario involving this kid, and the various other characters who'd come up in the course of my shouting into the microphone, and I imagined this situation of a baby bursting into flames, and somebody dousing the flames by throwing her into the river – which I thought was very funny at the time. It was vaguely to do with the aphorism about throwing out the baby with the bathwater, but the connection wasn't quite clear...[11]

Eno identified this process as a form of automatic writing – though automatic speaking would perhaps be closer to the truth. Automatism was pioneered as an artistic tool by André Breton and Philippe Soupault in *Les Champs Magnétiques*, a collection of automatic transcripts which lays claim to being the first official surrealist text.[12] As Breton made clear in the first *Surrealist Manifesto* of 1924, automatism was the very crux of the surrealist project. In the words of his famous definition, surrealism itself was:

Pure psychic automatism, by which it is intended to express, verbally, in writing, or by other means, the real functioning of thought. The dictation of thought, in the absence of all control exercised by reason, and outside all aesthetic or moral preoccupations.[13]

For surrealists like Breton and Soupault, psychic automatism was a way of freeing thought from the chains of academic logic and bourgeois morality. They believed that by removing conscious intervention on the part of the writer or artist, automatism allowed the unconscious mind to broadcast its enigmatic messages unfettered. To the surrealists these messages possessed both meaning and beauty; they were poetic and, at their best, convulsive revelations of secret desire. For Eno, the automatic process by which his lyrics came into being was a source of both mystery and excitement:

I liked the idea of making myself into a channel for whatever it is to transmit ideas and images through. So my lyrics are receivers, rather than transmitters, of meaning – very vague and ambiguous, but just about evocative enough to stimulate some sort of interpretation process to take place.[14]

In 'The Belldog', one of the most overtly poetic songs he has written – despite his repeated rejection of the title 'poet' – Eno offers a powerful image for this process of unconscious reception: 'I held the levers that guided the signals to the radio/But the words I receive,

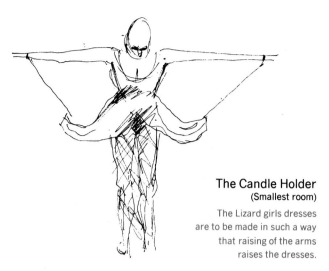

The Candle Holder
(Smallest room)

The Lizard girls dresses
are to be made in such a way
that raising of the arms
raises the dresses.

random code, broken fragments from before'.

Where Eno, along with other more recent exponents of the technique, parts company with orthodox surrealism, is in the degree to which he shaped, by conscious thought, the raw material of his unconscious mind. 'The Belldog', which was rewritten many times before Eno was happy with it, is only the most striking example of this tendency. There are many others, as the endless reworking of lyrics in the notebooks reveal. The surrealists, by contrast, were much more inclined to preserve the purity of the original transcript. In *Les Champs Magnétiques*, Breton and Soupault made a rule not to alter or improve any of the material that they transcribed at high speed in the course of their automatic sessions. There was no attempt to rehabilitate or embellish the messages of the unconscious by the application of conventional literary technique. They were valued absolutely as ends in themselves.

Two other devices employed by Eno link his work to the surrealist tradition. The first is his use of mischievous black humour, especially on the first two albums. Violent humour has always been an important weapon in the surrealist arsenal of shock tactics, a way of mocking bourgeois assumptions about taste and morality.[15] Songs like 'The Paw Paw Negro Blowtorch'('He'll set the sheets on fire/Mmm, quite a burning lover'); 'Dead Finks Don't Talk' ('Oh you headless chicken/Can those poor teeth take so much kicking'); and 'The Great Pretender' ('All those tawdry late night weepies/I could make you weep more cheaply') embody a cruel, amoral wit, made all the more disturbing by the way Eno's mood swings from playfulness to menace and back again. Some of these dark jests survive the journey from disc to page, but it is on record, in the ironic inflections and deadpan intonations of performance, that Eno's humour cuts deepest. Listen to the small cast of voices (each one by Eno) in 'Dead Finks Don't Talk'; or the call of the 'girlie' chorus (with Robert Wyatt) in 'The True Wheel' – 'Looking for a certain ratio'; and Eno's gleefully idiotic response; 'Someone said they saw it parking in a car lot'.

Like the surrealists, Eno was fascinated by his own dreams as a source of bizarre and irrational imagery. During the period of his early solo records he regularly recorded the contents of his dreams in his notebooks. Luana, the sinister mistress of reptiles from 'Driving Me Backwards', first appeared in a dream:

Luana's eyes [are] like butterfly wings on [a] cold white face. She wears a surgeon's mask. One of the Lizard Girls is bound naked and gagged, face down on the operating table. One of the rhythm guitarists is stretching her arms. Luana the surgeon lifts the whip (the bamboo whip). The first six blows occur at regular school intervals. The pace quickens for the final eleven. The dream [is] subtitled 'The Punishment of the Lizard Girls'. The remaining Lizard Girls wail at each blow.[16]

11 *Interview by Tom Carson,* New York Rocker, *No. 13, July/August 1978.*

12 *André Breton and Philippe Soupault,* The Magnetic Fields *(trans. David Gascoyne, Atlas Press, London, 1985).*

13 *Quoted in Franklin Rosemont,* André Breton and the First Principles of Surrealism *(Pluto Press, London, 1978).*

14 *Interview by Ian MacDonald,* New Musical Express, *26 November 1977.*

15 *André Breton published a surrealist* Anthologie de l'humour noir *in the 1940s.*

16 *Dream notation from one of Eno's notebooks, spring 1973. The dream formed the basis of an unrealized theatrical project, to be called 'Luana and the Lizard Girls', which Eno planned for a short period following his departure from Roxy Music.*

Most of the day we were fixing machinery
In the dark shed that the seasons ignore
I had control of electricity (in the barn)
And the ~~girl/dressed in green~~ on the steps behind the door

Alibi please? out here in the scenery
All the dark clouds cluster over the shore
In ~~a~~ ~~present~~ and the sense of my role
certain moment I lose control of recent history
And the sea/washes in ~~across~~ over the floor
never still (evergreen)
What did I say or what did I fail to do?
Alibi please give me reasons galore

In the hall/in the present moment/I find a strange kind of intensity
In the ~~barn~~/with the girl/on the steps/behind the door
I'm blind to danger and

In the barn/with the girl/dressed in green/on the steps
behind the door.

(left margin, vertical) I held the pole and my finger here control it electricity

THE BELLDOG

....

BURNING AIRLINES GIVE YOU SO MUCH MORE

flow
blow
go
know
crow   Stain

I shall put it in my pocket
I shall get it all

I guessed where she'd got the cash / fare

only time can tell

(2)
So I took stock undid the lock
and sat down in a chair
I saw how she'd got the cash the
room was nearly bare
maybe she will do a bit of spying
ch: with micro cameras hidden in her hair
> I'll light a lonely candle in ~~your room~~ the hall
her
watch the shadows dancing on the wall

knows there was no answer to it all

(1)

but even though she stripped my room and
stole ~~the~~ stereo things
~~I hope she won't forget me~~ my favourite ~~books~~
I'll ~~think of~~ ~~that wine tea she made~~
~~each time the little rings~~
I'm jump to see if she's returned each time
the doorbell rings

When I got back home I found a message on the door
Sweet ^ Regina's gone to China crosslegged on the floor
Of a Turkish jet that's ~~smoothly~~ flying
Turkish airlines give you so much more

On at least two occasions Eno used lyrics he had 'heard' in dreams for songs. All of the words of 'On Some Faraway Beach', a kind of *memento mori*, are said by Eno to have occurred in a dream. In 'The True Wheel' only the words of the chorus have oneiric origins ('We are the 801/We are the central shaft') but the circumstances and imagery of the dream, described in Eno's notes to Russell Mills, have been used as the basis for one of his most enigmatic texts, The remainder of the lyrics were 'written' by vocal improvisation and slotted into a pre-determined framework, as in 'Baby's on Fire' and other tracks. According to Eno, 'Julie with…' also derives in part from an image he had seen in a dream (and in part from the painting *Houseboat Days* by the artist Ron Kitaj).

124

THE LANGUAGE BARRIER

From the first album onwards, 'Baby's on Fire' included, phonetic considerations played a key role in shaping Eno's lyrics. Quite apart from their literal meanings, Eno has always been intrigued by words as shapes made out of sound – as another component in the musical sculpture. Many of the early songs, after all, were fashioned from phonetic babble and moved only by degrees towards 'meaning'. The puns, the wordplay, the famous anagrams, are all part of an abstract, sensual involvement with the malleable stuff of language which goes all the way back to Eno's childhood. Attending church every Sunday as a child, Eno was entranced by the mysterious rhythmic Latin of the Catholic mass. 'Tarantella', Hilaire Belloc's exercise in musical metre, which Eno learned at school, also made a deep impression on him:

Do you remember an Inn,
Miranda?
Do you remember an Inn?
And the tedding and the spreading
Of the straw for a bedding,
And the fleas that tease in the High Pyrenees,
And the wine that tasted of the tar?[17]

In June 1965, during his first year at Ipswich Art School, Eno attended the massive festival of poetry, organized by Allen Ginsberg and others, at London's Albert Hall. There, he heard examples of modern phonetic poetry that would have a lasting influence on his approach to the melding of words and music. Back at Ipswich, he discovered the abstract sound poems of Kurt Schwitters, Hugo Ball and other Dadaists, and began, along with his fellow students, to produce phonetic experiments of his own. These usually took the form of live performances of carefully scripted poems set against a prepared bed of voices recorded on the art school's tape recorder.

Parallel with Eno's move in his later songs towards simpler, more sentimental lyrics is a shift away from meaning into an even more explicitly phonetic use of language. In this respect, 'Sky Saw' on *Another Green World* is almost a manifesto. The intelligible part of the lyric – 'All the clouds turn to words/All the words float in sequence' – is counterpointed and undermined by alliterative nonsense: 'Mau Mau starter ching ching da da/Daughter daughter dumpling data'. Since everyone just ignores the words anyway, says Eno, it makes no difference if they are meaningless. Eno pursued this logic in 'Miss Shapiro' ('Dalai Llama lama puss puss/Stella maris missa nobis') and in 'Kurt's Rejoinder', which features – to make the connection with

17 *Hilaire Belloc,* **Complete Verse** *(revised edition, Duckworth, London, 1970).*

BEFORE AND AFTER SCIENCE

IN A SEED BEREFT OF CANCER
Cretins feared boneface
* Fade, O brief Cretan scene
Beret finder faces ocean
OF FATE BRED NEAR SCIENCE

INNATE FORCES FEED BRACE

FACTION - BASED
REFERENCE
END DEFECATES FINER CRAB

I AN EFFECT ON
SACRED BEER

A BIN OF ACCENTED
REEFERS

ANOTHER GREEN WORLD

O LEWD NORTHERN RAGE
(A LEWD NORTHERN OGRE)
ENO – THE WORLD RANGER
THE LOW DRONE RANGER
"A WET GREENHORN, LORD"

're, her own
dog rental'

Enthrone world rage
ENLARGED TORN WHORE

RON – THE WRONG LEADER

LEARN TO
GROW, RED HEN

Another
northern
terror
wrong

Dadaist sound and nonsense poetry explicit – a found vocal fragment from Kurt Schwitters' *Ursonate*.[18] The wordplay in these songs, the assonance, alliteration, and chiming internal rhymes also recall an earlier pop model: the 'Expert texpert choking smokers' of Lennon's 'I am the Walrus'. In 'Tzima N'arki', one of Eno's last songs, he went one step further and dispensed with the English language entirely. A tape run backwards translates the vocal, sections of it lifted from Eno's own 'King's Lead Hat', into exotic gibberish. Deprived of the possibility of meaning, the words are restored to their primary condition: as sounds. Once again the Beatles had provided a precedent for the technique. 'Tomorrow Never Knows' on *Revolver* makes dramatic use of similar tape effects applied to instruments rather than voices.[19]

In rejecting not just meaning but language itself, Eno had possibly been influenced by his work with David Bowie on *Low* (1977). Certainly, he spoke with admiration of the freedom with which Bowie had discarded lyrical narrative on the second side of the album in favour of a purely expressionist vocal technique. 'It's something that I've always wanted to do', Eno said, 'but have never convincingly been able to'.[20] On 1978's *Music for Airports*, Eno attempted something comparable, by replacing his own voice with the wordless choral singing of Christa Fast, Christine Gomez, and Inge Zeininger. On '2/1' and '1/2', the three vocalists help to evoke an enclosed, architectonic space strikingly similar in feeling to Bowie's 'Warszawa' (for which Eno had provided all of the music, and Bowie the vocals). Although they are lighter in mood than 'Warszawa,' the pieces share the same sense of religious observance.

The Plateaux of Mirror, which Eno recorded with Harold Budd in 1980, makes sparing use of similar vocal effects, but Eno has not, so far, developed this approach. As the 1970s drew to a close, he was moving, with a mounting sense of purpose, in the direction of an entirely non-vocal music. Film soundtracks, in which the music provides a passive setting for the voices of the actors, offered an attractive alternative to the personal expression demanded by the song format. Ambient music was another way of escaping from the limits of language.

For a while, though, Eno continued to explore ways of combining words and music, using tapes of found vocals in place of his own voice. There were plenty of examples in Eno's experience to guide him. As long ago as 1952, his early mentor John Cage had incorporated bursts of spoken and musical sound generated by twelve radios in his *Imaginary Landscape No. 4*. *It's Gonna Rain* by Steve Reich and *Jesus' Blood Never Failed Me Yet* by Gavin Bryars had both been built up from tapes of found vocals. During the recording of *Before and After Science*, Holger Czukay of Can had brought his short wave radios into the studio, and these were used in some of the pieces not finally released on the record. 'Kurt's Rejoinder', on the same album, was Eno's first sustained attempt to employ found vocals, but 'RAF' (Red Army Faction) on side two of the 'King's Lead Hat' single is a much more thorough exploration of the technique. Recorded with Judy Nylon and Pat Palladin of Snatch, 'RAF' features a pre-recorded telephone message made by the Cologne police to solicit information about terrorist groups, cut in with spoken overdubs by Nylon and Palladin.

Inspired by the success of this project, and increasingly interested in the musical qualities of speech, Eno went on to record *My Life in the Bush of Ghosts* with David Byrne of Talking Heads. This was an entire album of songs incorporating voices taken from radio phone-ins and other records. 'The decision to use voices in this way', Eno and Byrne explained in a joint statement, 'arose from a disenchantment with conventional song formats and from an excitement generated both by the intrinsic qualities of the voices and by the peculiar new meanings that resulted from placing them in unfamiliar musical contexts.'[21] Since 1981, Eno has abandoned the human voice entirely, preferring to concentrate in his solo albums (as well as many of his collaborations) on wholly instrumental work. A body of unreleased songs is said to exist, but he seems in no hurry to break his long silence.

18 *Some doubt surrounds the identity of the performer of the Ursonate on 'Kurt's Rejoinder'. Russell Mills believes him to be Eberhard Blum, an accomplished Schwitters interpreter, but Eno attributes the performance to Schwitters himself (see Mills's notes on the song). A recording of Schwitters reciting a shortened version of the work in 1943 does exist. A limited edition of one hundred long playing discs of this recording was pressed by P. Granville of the Lords Gallery, London in 1958. Eno subsequently incorporated an abstract poem by Hugo Ball, the Zurich Dadaist, into 'I Zimbra' on Talking Heads'* Fear of Music *(1979).*

19 *Eno (with 801) performs a version of 'Tomorrow Never Knows' on* 801 Live *(1976).*

20 *Interview by Miles,* New Musical Express, *27 November 1976.*

21 *Eno and David Byrne, US press statement for* My Life in the Bush of Ghosts, *1981.*

→ Latent Songs   Nov 10 76

- who is it you talk to
- herr Kapitan Black
- Everybody took it
- The last 600
- Tamberlaine
- Days Nights Wheels
- But not in a shoe
- Oh them leaves
- Why go on
- When you came down
- Judy was a desperate child
- mystified by the door
+ - I just don't go anywhere 7/2/5/0
- who put Johnny in the Tyne
+ - If I was a doo doo doo 7/0/7/0
- gazebos
+ - Ellery Please 5/2/5/2/5#/5½
- In the garden
- I have to work so hard
- matchstick people
- Rope
- Father Johnson
- Erin
- In all this time
- Beautiful Melody
- Somebody called me
- Rope and string will never bind me
- I'd like to get a ticket
- My brains
- Seven hours ago
- Belize
- My last brush with time
- who do you want as a monitor
- Labour truly lost
- me, I'm quietly erased
- Living in the woods
- La Zonga
- Man making measurements

I was just a broken head
I stole the world that others punctured
Now I stumble through the garbage
Slide and tumble, slide and stumble
Beak and claw, remorse reminder
Slide and tumble, slide and stumble
Back and forth and back to nothing
Keep them tidy, keep them humble.

Chop and change to cut the corners
Sharp as razors shiny razors
Stranded on a world that's dying
Never moving, hardly trying.

I was just a broken head
I stole the world that others plundered
Now I stumble through the garbage
Slide and tumble, slide and stumble.

126   Broken Head

I'm not sure where the phrase 'Broken Head' came from, except that it came
from some obscure corner of my own Broken Head. Whether or not it was
thus self-referential is a question best left to art-historians and academics. I
do recall at some time being aware that the lyric could be autobiographical,
but that wasn't its conscious source. I guess the image is something like:
'victor of a useless world'. The stumbling through the garbage suggests a
desperate chaotic search for something other than garbage… I don't know.

B.E.

bandage par
expression study

Using only the image of the head, I concentrated on the
visualization of the confusion, pain, and frustration of the individual
under stress. In a sense it is autobiographical, for at the time of
working on this picture I was undergoing a period of self-doubt with
regard to the direction that my work was taking.

The heads are partly *(mostly)* self-portraits.

R.M.

early starter
dead and dirty
oil on sunday
flotsam jetsam
exit the corner

all and sundry
back to nothing
slight reversal
no rehearsal
easy starter
noo etcetera
stick and stubborn
sharp and shining
part and parcel
cold and stumble
falling over
now move forwards
now move backwards
son and daughter
clean and simple
frozen moment
think of nothing
nothing doing
kiss the carpet
kiss the culprit

Most of the day
We were at the machinery
In the dark sheds
That the seasons ignore
I held the levers that guided the signals to the radio
But the words I receive, random code, broken fragments from before.

Out in the trees
My reason deserting me
All the dark stars
Cluster over the bay.

Then in a certain moment
I lose control and at last I am part of the machinery.

(The belldog) Where are you?
And the light disappears
As the world makes its circle through the sky.

128   The Belldog

Apart from the fact that this piece was recorded in Germany, with the musicians Dieter Moebius and Hans-Joachim Roedelius of the groups Cluster/Harmonia, it is the strongest reminder of my time spent in Germany, and this is a good reason for feeling very close to this piece. It is also a very successful marriage of music and lyrics.

While I was working on this picture I was also reading *The Haunted Screen* by Lotte H. Eisner,∗ an appreciative study of expressionism in the German cinema and the influence of Max Reinhardt. It provided a text which could almost be considered as a guide for the treatment of my interpretation:

The German Soul instinctively prefers twilight to daylight. In *The Decline of the West* Oswald Spengler exalts the mist, the enigmatic chiaroscuro, the 'Kolossal' and infinite solitude. The unlimited spaces cherished by the 'Faustian Soul' of Northern Man are never clear and limpid but swathed in gloom; the Germanic Valhalla, symbol of a frightful solitude, is a *grisaille* ruled by unsociable heroes and hostile gods.

Spengler asserts that solitaries are the only men to know the 'cosmic experience', they alone are capable of experiencing the inexpressible isolation and nostalgia of the forest.

Spengler's 'Faustian Soul', enamoured of this gloom, has a predilection for the colour brown – Rembrandt's atelier brown: this brown, a protestant colour missing from the rainbow, is consequently the 'most unreal of all colours', it is the colour of the soul, it becomes the symbol of the transcendental, the infinite and the 'spatial'. The adoration of brown and its tints and, inevitably, of shadow goes back to the famous book by Julius Langbehn, *Rembrandt als Erzieher*, published in 1890, which argues that

Rembrandt represents the authentic Aryan with the instinct for chiaroscuro characteristic of the Low German. Consequently, like the Germans, Rembrandt, the master of melancholy and the 'bilious black', is, according to Langbehn, always in quest of the 'dark side of existence, the twilight hour when the dark seems darker and the light lighter'.

I felt that, whilst acknowledging the theory about the colour brown, the song was predominantly blue: electric blues, metallic blues, the gunmetal blue of the shed, the blue of the night sky and the blue/black of the infinite beyond.

The music is 'large', filling every space; whilst the narrator is 'small' within the framework, and for this reason I attempted to emphasize the relationship between the individual and his environment. In this the two 'engineers' become almost lost in the confusion of machines and instruments at the base of the great hangar. They are either awaiting the arrival of something (the belldog?) or are witnessing its departure out of the picture area.

The first definite piece in the picture was the central horizontal panel/beam; once this had been established a light grid was mapped out. Subsequent layers of paper and Xeroxes provided several exciting areas which were manipulated before a further layer was applied. This mode continued until the basis for the picture 'felt' right. Certain points were then either consolidated or removed, all with the relation of the figures being carefully considered. The machinery grew out from the picture, with pieces being added until I felt satisfied.

_____ *The whole mood is based/inspired by the workers and the powerhouse of Fritz Lang's film* Metropolis.

R.M.

∗ Lotte H. Eisner, **The Haunted Screen** (Thames and Hudson, London, 1969; first published in France as L'Ecran Démoniaque, Le Terrain Vague, 14 Rue de Vermeuil, Paris VII, 1952).

On board ship, time is measured in four-hour 'watches', counted from noon to noon. The second four-hour period is divided into two halves each called a 'dog watch'.

Noon _____4 p.m. _____afternoon watch
4 _____6 p.m. _____1st Dogwatch
6 _____8 p.m. _____2nd Dogwatch (last Dogwatch)
8 _____midnight _____1st watch
midnight ____4 a.m. _____middle watch
4 _____8 a.m. _____morning watch
8 _____12 noon _____Forenoon watch

A bell is rung every half-hour, the number of strokes showing the number of half hours of watch or dog watch that have expired.
1.30 a.m. is middle watch: 3 bells.

Belldog—Chinese—as a guardian of the night hours, the dog becomes yin and symbolises destruction, catastrophe, and is connected with meteors and eclipses —when the dog goes mad and bites the sun or moon.

to bell the cat:
to take the leading part in any
hazardous movement,
from the ancient fable of
the mice who proposed to hang
a warning bell round the
cat's neck.

'The Belldog' has an interesting history. The body of the song was begun nearly four to five years ago, and used to begin: 'Most of the day we were fixing machinery in the dark sheds, etc.' But these lyrics were written for another song, so they get re-written quite a lot. 'The Belldog' comes from a strange incident in New York, just after I moved there last year. I was walking through Washington Square Park, towards the 'Arc de Triomphe' style monument there. There was a little group of people under the arch, and the full moon stood low on the horizon, visible through the top of the arch. As I got closer I saw what it was that had attracted their attention. A very grubby man of indeterminable age was playing an out-of-tune upright piano on wheels; his touch was that of a plummy night club pianist, but the chords he used were completely strange. Over this sequence of soft discords he sang again and again, in a trembling voice:

'The belldog, where are you?'

I have no idea what he meant by the belldog. For me it was (and is) an unidentified mythical character from some unfamiliar mythology. I was thinking vaguely of the bells on a ship (although I'd never heard of 'dogbells' or 'dog-watches'), in fact; but only in the sense that such use of bells (and also their use in churches) is to summon attention or to announce the beginning of something. So the vague feeling I have about the belldog is that he is a herald; of what is not clear. Whatever it is, in the song he has either not yet appeared or has gone away: it says 'The belldog, where are you?'

I like the lyrics of this song quite a lot. I worked very hard on them and actually erased two earlier versions (one of which had already reached a final mix) in order to change in one case a line and in the other a few words. Prior to that I wrote the song at least six times, and each time I re-sang it I kept altering words. To be quite honest, I can't remember now what the final words were; I mean I can remember a set of words, but I'm not sure that they are not an earlier incarnation. One thing I know is that there is a sublime conjunction of music and lyric at the end of the line, 'my reason deserting me...' and similarly at the end of the verse, 'as the world makes its circle through the sky.' The first one is, for me, an almost perfect musical translation of a literal idea. I was so interested in that moment in the piece that I thought of making a new piece that would be, as it were, a microscopic

examination of those few seconds, zooming in to enlarge them such that texture becomes form, and form becomes geography. Maybe that isn't very clear. The thought arises from an analogy I have been using recently where I see the particular form of a piece of music as being dictated by structural constraints beneath it, just as the particular form of a landscape is dictated by geographical and geological events. Thus the analogy is as follows:

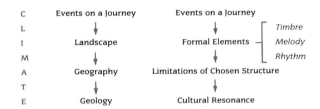

C	Events on a Journey	Events on a Journey	
L	↓	↓	Timbre
I	Landscape	Formal Elements	Melody
M	↓	↓	Rhythm
A	Geography	Limitations of Chosen Structure	
T	↓	↓	
E	Geology	Cultural Resonance	

Where each level is a subset of the one below. 'Cultural Resonance' is a term I use to connote the 'unquestioned' aspects of the work: 'the things that nobody has ever had the idea of not doing'. So what I mean by putting it under a microscope is the same as regarding the landscape as a geology, then the details of landscape as geography and so on. It is a way of saying that all these levels are recursive and that what appears to be the macrocosmic is in fact embedded within a larger system, and what appears to the microcosmic in turn encloses smaller systems. The image of dissolution into recurssion is suggested by the lyrics:

Then in a certain moment
I lose control and at last I am part of the machinery.

(The belldog) Where are you?
And the light disappears
As the world makes its circle through the sky.

The song has a type of zoom lens on it. It starts in a shed (which I imagined as a big hanger, its ceiling in darkness), then it moves out into 'the trees' and finally it watches the world spinning through space. It's a song of surrender to something, but with this anxiety based on the belldog's non-appearance; a surrender with risk.

B.E.

king's lead hat was the poker in the fire it will come, it will surely come
king's lead hat made the Amazon much wider, it will come, it will surely come

if God had listened to my story
none of this would ever have happened
if God had listened to my story
none of this would ever had occurred.

you gave me precious information
on that imaginary morning
i wrote it down in desperation
and gave out the notice to be served.

if God had listened to my story
none of this would ever have happened
if God had listened to my story
none of this would ever had occurred.

you gave me precious information
on that imaginary morning
i wrote it down in desperation
and gave out the notice to be served.

king's lead hat put the innocence inside her it will come, it will surely come
king's lead hat was a hammer to desire it will come, it will surely come.

if God had listened to my story
none of this would ever have happened
if God had listened to my story
none of this would ever had occurred.

you gave me precious information
on that imaginary morning
i wrote it down in desperation
and gave out the notice to be served.

132   Tzima N'Arki

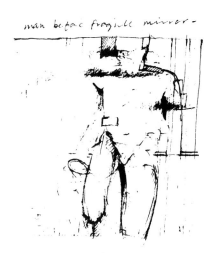

man before fragile mirror –

† *'Ping' and 'Enough' by Samuel Beckett from* Six Residua *(John Calder Publishers, London, 1978; 'Ping' originally published by Les Editions de Minuit, Paris, as 'Bing', 1966; 'Enough' originally published by Les Editions de Minuit, Paris, as 'Assez', 1966).*

This picture is probably the least reverential to the song of the whole set but, partly for this reason, I feel that it is one of the most successful.

The music, being tribal in rhythm, jerky and discordant, and the lyrics in reverse, give the impression that it is the music of a lost race. Once turned around the lyrics prove to be made up of two separate units; the chorus lines from 'King's Lead Hat' are dropped on either side of two paragraphs that are precise, quiet and ambiguous. As a whole it provides little in the way of an immediate, accessible image, being more to do with emotions than events.

Initially I visualized a grey monochrome picture of three walls of a small square room occupied only by a slumped figure at a simple wooden table, his only possessions being a few sheets of paper, and a fountain pen (preferably italic). It reminded me of Samuel, Beckett's precise, stark imagery. Two of his texts, 'Enough' and 'Ping' † were the strongest parallels that came to mind. Both evoke strange images of the existence within enclosed spaces, reactions to heat, light and other sensory stimuli, providing a static vision. So I returned to the stories and re-read them very carefully. Apart from the definite structural constraints of Beckett's environments, rooms, two clear images haunted me, one from each story. The first, from 'Enough', concerned an old man who was bent almost double:

In order from time to time to enjoy the sky he resorted to a little round mirror. Having misted it with his breath and polished it on his calf he looked in it for the constellations. I have it he exclaimed referring to the Lyre or the Swan. And often he added that the sky seemed much the same.

The second from 'Ping':

All known white bare white body fixed one yard legs joined like sewn. Light heat white floor one square yard never seen. White walls one yard by two white ceiling one square yard never seen. Bare white body fixing only the eyes just…

and

Eyes alone uncover given blue light blue almost white

In my mind the two figures became one; a lone figure using a mirror to see beyond the confines of his enclosed space: I felt that this merger should appear somewhere within the final image.

Feeling guilty and a little confused for not relating more truthfully to the lyrics, I consulted the *Oblique Strategies*. I drew the card with the instruction, 'Go slowly all the way round the outside'. After a little while I began constructing a 'border' of indeterminate length which through my intuition eventually defined a rough area to enclose the eventual piece. It was like an empty picture frame at this point.

Soon after this stage had been reached I had to phone Eno's Management Company regarding something or other, and spoke to Anthea Norman-Taylor, my link so to speak. During the course of our conversation she asked how work on the pictures for the book were progressing. I explained the problem of translating 'Tzima N'Arki' and asked her what she made of it. As she had only heard it with the lyrics in reverse she had an impression derived from the complete sound. Anthea said it made her think of some lush tropical island, palm trees, blue skies, exotic animals, etc. I could only see this in as far as the music suggests a primitive dance, ritualistic, but when related to the lyrics it made little impression on me. But with Anthea's image in mind I produced a tiny painting of palm trees set against a pink evening sky. Still confused I again consulted the *Oblique Strategies*, this time I got 'Use an unacceptable colour'. No trouble there, *GREEN*, as with Mondrian. Thus the window frame that encloses the palm trees is green. This was then added to the previously devised border, giving me an intrusion into the picture area, making it much easier to continue. With the imagery from Beckett, the progress hereon was quite fast and natural.

Another piece of self-indulgent side-stepping came about when pondering about the line, 'On that imaginary morning'. For some inexplicable reason I thought of the use of blocks of dry ice in films to create the illusion of hazy swamps, swirling mists in horror film graveyards, etc. I thought that these blocks of dry ice would be a useful addition to a household. When one wanted to escape the reality of everyday problems and everyday objects, without actually having to travel great distances to do so, one could simply put a record of very calmative music on, activate the dry ice and sit back lost in one's own imagination. Hence the clouds of white smoke emanating from the boxes along the walls behind the box.

The 'You' in the song has been answered with the dotted outline of a Bull Terrier, my favourite dog.

R.M.

You gave me precious information

This piece does not refer to a song, although Luana does make an appearance in 'Driving Me Backwards'; it was based on a scene from an open-ended dream that Eno remembered. The dream involved the leader of a female band who was whipping the other members of the band with a bamboo. While the speed of the whip strokes increases the other members of the band wait their turn and howl a chorus.

R.M.

CATALOGUE OF WORKS

Measurements are in centimetres, height before width before depth.

HERE COME THE WARM JETS (EG)
Eno
1973

NEEDLES IN THE CAMEL'S EYE
1978
65×57×3.75
Watercolour, gouache, enamel paints, lacquer, shoe dye, varnish, blood, pencil, inks, Xeroxes, printed papers, gauze, balsa, needles, mirrors, adhesive tapes, decisive incisions, on paper, aluminium foil and wood.

PAW PAW NEGRO BLOWTORCH
1978
51.5×52×2
Watercolour, gouache, enamel paints, pencil, inks, etching varnish, Xeroxes, printed papers, polythene, chain, wire, score lines, staples, fabric, burning, graph paper, decisive incisions, paper, adhesive tapes, on wood block.

BABY'S ON FIRE
1978
30.5×49
Watercolour, gouache, pencil, inks, etching varnish, Xeroxes, printed papers, sewn threads, etching points, decisive incisions, adhesive tapes, on paper.

CINDY TELLS ME
... the rich girls are weeping
1977
31×24
Watercolour, gouache, pencil, graphite, inks, Xeroxes, printed papers, rubber stamp, cigarette paper, sewn thread, decisive incisions, adhesive tapes, on paper.

DRIVING ME BACKWARDS
Meet my relations
All of them
Grinning like facepacks
1977
(a)
16×11×2
Watercolour, gouache, pencil, inks, printed papers, adhesive tapes, on wood block.
(b)
12×8.5×2
Watercolour, gouache, pencil, inks, printed papers, adhesive tapes, on wood block.
(c)
22.5×32.5×0.5
Watercolour, gouache, pencil, inks, crayons, printed papers, scored lines, varnish, adhesive tapes, on slate and wood.
(d)
17.5×25.5
Watercolour, gouache, pencil, inks, Xeroxes, printed papers, adhesive tapes, on paper.
(e)
26×32
Watercolour, gouache, pencil, inks, printed papers, Xeroxes, adhesive tapes, on paper.

ON SOME FARAWAY BEACH
1978
34×53.5×2.5
Watercolour, gouache, enamel paints, aluminium paint, acrylics, pencil, inks, crayons, varnish, adhesive tapes, Letraset, on rectified wooden tea tray.

BLANK FRANK
...is the siren, he's the air-raid, he's the crater
He's the menu on the table, he's the knife and he's the waiter
1977
60.5×43
Watercolour, gouache, pencil, inks, crayons, varnish, Xeroxes, printed papers, burning, tracing paper, sewn thread, decisive incisions, adhesive tapes, on paper.

DEAD FINKS DON'T TALK
They thrive on disasters
They all look so harmless
1977
37.5×30.5
Watercolour, gouache, pencil, inks, Xeroxes, printed papers, weaved papers, etched points, sewn thread, decisive incisions, adhesive tapes, on paper.

SOME OF THEM ARE OLD
1978
(a)
25×24
Watercolour, gouache, pencil, inks, Xeroxes, printed papers, graphite, varnish, scored lines, decisive incisions, adhesive tapes, on book cover and paper.
(b)
19.5×14×12.5
Artificial eyes, satin pillow, jar, papers, elastic bands, scissors, earth, threads, nails, ticket, balsa, tooth of comb, enamel paints, on box.
(ci)
15×18.5
(cii)
29×21
(ciii)
14×20.5
All: Magazine photographs, rectified with watercolour, pencil, inks, blood, varnish, Xeroxes, adhesive tapes and Letraset.

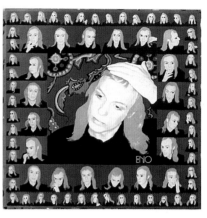

SEVEN DEADLY FINNS (EG)
Eno
1974

SEVEN DEADLY FINNS
1978
(a) The French Girls
33.5×38.75
Watercolour, pencil, pen and ink, shoe polish, Xeroxes, tracing paper, adhesive tapes, on paper.

(b) The Seven Deadly Finns
53.25×72.5
Watercolour, gouache, gold ink, pencil, inks, Xeroxes, printed papers, postage stamp, tracing paper, adhesive tapes, Letraset, on Japanese rag paper.

TAKING TIGER MOUNTAIN (BY STRATEGY) (EG)
Eno
1974

BURNING AIRLINES GIVE YOU SO MUCH MORE
The painted sage sits just as though he's flying
1978
81.25×62
Watercolour, gouache, enamel paints, pencil, graphite, inks, etching varnish, printed papers, envelope, postcards, postage stamp, adhesive plaster, adhesive label, burning, shattered windscreen fragments, brass hinges, decisive incisions, adhesive tapes, on Japanese rag paper.

BACK IN JUDY'S JUNGLE
The Squadron assembled what senses they had
1979
50.75×62.75
Watercolour, pencil, inks, varnish, Xeroxes, printed papers, Letraset, netting, on Japanese rag paper.

THE FAT LADY OF LIMBOURG
Looked at the samples that we sent
1979
49.5×69.5
Watercolour, gouache, enamel paints, pencil, crayons, graphite, inks, Xeroxes, printed papers, staples, decisive incisions, adhesive tapes, on paper.

MOTHER WHALE EYELESS
Heroes are born
But heroes die.
1979
45.75×61
Watercolour, gouache, pencil, inks, varnish, Xeroxes, printed papers, blood, staples, Emergency War Edition Diary cover (1914-18), sewn threads, adhesive tapes, on etched papers.
Poppy supplied by the British Legion Poppy Factory, Richmond Surrey. White feather contributed by Terry Dowling, Newcastle.

THE GREAT PRETENDER
1977
(a)
30.5×45.5×2
Watercolour, gouache, pencil, inks, Xeroxes, printed papers, tracing paper, incised lines, nail, adhesive tapes, on wood block.

(b) Furniture to get it right on
35.5×30.5
Watercolour, gouache, pencil, inks, sewn threads, adhesive tapes, on paper.

(c) She was moved by his wheels
She was just up from Wales
29.5×29.75
Watercolour, gouache, pencil, inks, Xeroxes, printed papers, tracing paper, sewn thread, adhesive tapes, on paper.

THIRD UNCLE
1977
(a)
28×42.75×2.5
Watercolour, gouache, pencil, inks, varnish, Xeroxes, printed papers, burning, Letraset, adhesive tapes, on cardboard and rectified wooden notice board.

(b) Does it fit me
Or you?
It looks tight on you
31.75×45
Watercolour, gold ink, pencil, graphite, inks, Xeroxes, printed papers, burning, sewn thread, decisive incisions, adhesive tapes, on paper.

THIRD UNCLE (*Arena* version)
There are scenes
There are blues
1980
37×53×2
Watercolour, gouache, enamel paints, graphite, pencil, inks, crayons, silver foil, Xeroxes, etching residue, printed papers, staples, sewn cotton threads, wire, Bostik, Zap glue, Seccotine, Britfix, burning, small wooden drawer frame, balsa wood, adhesive tapes, on paper and card.

PUT A STRAW UNDER BABY
...they all live in Jesus
It's a family affair.
1977
26×37
Watercolour, pencil, inks, Xeroxes, printed papers, photograph, sewn thread, adhesive tapes, on stamp album paper.

THE TRUE WHEEL
1978
(a)
50.75 × 53.25
(b)
50.75 × 53.25
(c)
50.75 × 53.25
All: Watercolour, gouache, enamel paints, gold ink, pencil, graphite, inks, crayons, silver foil, Xeroxes, printed papers, etched points, sewing pattern papers, wire, decisive incisions, adhesive tapes, on paper.

CHINA MY CHINA
1979
(a)
49.5 × 49.5
Watercolour, gouache, enamel paint, pencil, inks, biro, Xeroxes, printed papers, computer cards, tissues, toilet paper, lurex thread, on Japanese rag paper.

(b) These poor girls are such fun
They know what God gave them their fingers for
47.5 × 40.5 × 32.5
Xeroxes, carbon paper, lacquered balsa, emulsion paints, shoe dye, mannequin's gloved hands, cotton gloves, fabric, graphite, burning, wired security glass, set in lacquered and enamelled wooden box.
Sleeves on hands made by Ann Mills.

TAKING TIGER MOUNTAIN
1978
45 × 59 × 15
Watercolour, gouache, enamel paints, varnish, pencil, inks, Xeroxes, printed papers, luminous stars, magnet, hook, threads, adhesive tapes, shallow wooden tray hinged on to picture face, paper mounted on wood.

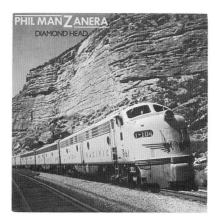

ANOTHER GREEN WORLD (EG)
Eno
1975

SKY SAW
1979
15 × 59 × 2
Photographic plate box made of wood and metal, with brass clasps and hinges, providing six working surfaces. Planes of the box are moveable and can be dismantled. Watercolour, gouache, acrylics, enamel paints, pencil, inks, varnish, Xeroxes, printed papers, silver foil, balsa wood, cotton and lurex threads, blood, burning, scored lines, adhesive tapes, Letraset.

ST ELMO'S FIRE
1979
(a) cause
45.75 × 45.75
Enamel paints, acrylics, Xeroxes, printed papers, matchbox strike, etching points, staples, threads, adhesive tapes, on paper and aluminium foil.

(b) effect
40 × 48.25
Watercolour, gouache, acrylics, pencil, graphite, inks, crayons, Xeroxes, printed papers, matchbox strike, etching points, lurex threads, adhesive tapes, on paper.

I'LL COME RUNNING (TO TIE YOUR SHOE)
1978
26.75 × 44 × 5
Watercolour, gouache, enamel paints, pencil, inks, varnish, frottage, Xeroxes, shoe polish, etched points, fluorescent light, cardboard, paper, adhesive tapes, on metal and wood.

GOLDEN HOURS
1979
(a) Several times
I've seen the evening slide away
63.5 × 63.5
Watercolour, gouache, fluorescent paints, pencil, graphite, inks, etching varnish, gold ink, scored lines, printed paper, sewn threads, adhesive tapes, decisive incisions, vertical hinged leaf, on paper.

(b) Never a silence always a face at the door
40.5 × 81.25 × 5.5
Watercolour, gold leaf, metallic spray, enamel paints, emulsion, gauze, bandaging, perspex, resin, Xeroxes, clock mechanism, threads, rubber stamp, Eno's notebook, on wood.
The angular heart was executed and contributed by Robert Mason.
The winking eye was unwittingly contributed by Holly Metz (USA).
Assistance with resin work from David Leverett.

EVERYTHING MERGES WITH THE NIGHT
I stand on the beach
Giving out descriptions
1978
34 × 53.5 × 2.5
Watercolour, gouache, acrylics, enamel paints, pencil, graphite, inks, Xeroxes, printed papers, Letraset, adhesive tapes, on wooden tea tray.

DIAMOND HEAD (EG)
Phil Manzanera
1975

BIG DAY
Excellent wines and features
1979
45 × 41.5
Watercolour, gouache, pencil, inks, Xeroxes, printed papers, balsa wood, thread, rubber stamp, adhesive tapes, decisive incisions, on paper.

MISS SHAPIRO
Movement hampered like at Christmas
1979
46.5 × 59
Watercolour, gouache, gold ink, pencil, graphite, crayons, inks, Xeroxes, printed papers, photographs, threads, mirror tiles, decisive incisions, adhesive tapes, on paper.

BEFORE AND AFTER SCIENCE (EG)
Brian Eno
1977

NO ONE RECEIVING
Back to silence back to minus
1978
32.5 × 64.75 × 2.5
Watercolour, gouache, enamel paints, emulsion, varnish, pencil, inks, crayons, etching points, silver foil, printed papers, thread, lurex threads, wire, on metal plate and wood.

BACKWATER
There were six of us but now we are five
1979
31 × 48.25
Watercolour, gouache, enamel paints, pencil, Xeroxes, printed papers, plastic lifebelt, adhesive tapes, on paper.

KURT'S REJOINDER
1977-79
50.75 × 50.75
Watercolour, pencil, graphite, crayons, inks, Xeroxes, printed papers, etching varnish, typing, burning, staples, Bostik, Araldite, Copydex, Evostik, Seccotine, Gloy, Fastik, decisive incisions, adhesive tapes, on paper.

KING'S LEAD HAT
1979
(a) Four turkeys in a big black car
55.75 × 50.75

(b) And draw bananas on the bathroom walls
28 × 48.25
Both: Watercolour, gouache, enamel paints, varnish, pencil, inks, Xeroxes, printed papers, cellophane, tracing paper, adhesive tapes, on paper and polythene.

HERE HE COMES
1979
47 × 68.5
Watercolour, gouache, enamel paints, inks, graphite, crayons, photo dyes, etching points, silver foil, Xeroxes, printed papers, decisive incisions, adhesive tapes, on paper.

JULIE WITH . . .
1979
(a)
42 × 21
Watercolour, gouache, photo dyes, varnish, pencil, inks, printed papers, thread, on paper.

(b)
42 × 21
Negative photograph of (a), toned with photo dyes, colour Xerox.

BY THIS RIVER
1979
42 × 50.75
Watercolour, gouache, enamel paints, pencil, crayons, inks, Xeroxes, aluminium foil, adhesive tapes, on paper.

SPIDER AND I
We sleep in the mornings
1979
76.25 × 61
Watercolour, gouache, graphite, Xeroxes, printed papers, map of the world (adjusted), texture paste, balsa wood, mirror tiles, on paper with pillow attached.

AFTER THE HEAT (SKY)
Eno/Moebius/Roedelius
1978

BROKEN HEAD
1979
41 × 64.75
Watercolour, gouache, pencil, graphite, Xeroxes, photographs, photo dyes, Letraset, decisive incisions, adhesive tapes, on paper.

THE BELLDOG
...random code...
1979
42.5 × 38
Watercolour, gouache, pencil, graphite, crayons, Xeroxes, printed papers, photographs, scored lines, electric valves, staples, decisive incisions, adhesive tapes, on paper.

TZIMA N'ARKI
You gave me precious information
1979
42.5 × 40.5
Watercolour, gouache, pencil, graphite, crayons, Xeroxes, printed papers, photograph, staples, burning, rust, Letraset, adhesive tapes, on paper.

LUANA – CHEMICAL CHOICES
1977
36.3 × 47.3
Watercolour, gouache, pencil, graphite, crayons, Xeroxes, etching papers, photograph, staples, burning, rust, Letraset, adhesive tapes, on paper.

BIOGRAPHICAL NOTES – BRIAN ENO

1948 Brian Peter George St. John le Baptiste de la Salle Eno
Born 15 May, Woodbridge, Suffolk, England

education

1953 – 64 Nuns and brothers of de la Salle order, Ipswich
1964 – 66 Ipswich Art School, Foundation studies
1966 – 69 Winchester Art School, Diploma in Fine Art

The discography that follows aims to cover all UK record releases featuring Eno and, where records were only issued abroad, selected foreign releases. There are two exceptions to this rule.
(1) Compilation albums by Eno's collaborators featuring otherwise available material have not been included.
(2) With the exception of Roxy Music, singles have been restricted to those under Eno's own name.

Note: from 1969 – 76 EG Records released material on the Island label, and from 1977 on Polydor. The Editions EG label, for selected EG recordings, was launched in 1979.

solo albums

1973	*Here Come The Warm Jets* (EG)
1974	*Taking Tiger Mountain (by Strategy)* (EG)
1975	*Another Green World* (EG)
	Discreet Music (Obscure/Editions EG)
1976	*Music For Films* (limited edition of 500 copies) (EG)
1977	*Before And After Science* (EG)
1978	*Music For Films* (Editions EG)
	Ambient 1: Music For Airports (Editions EG)
1982	*Ambient 4: On Land* (Editions EG)
1983	*Apollo: Atmospheres And Soundtracks* With Daniel Lanois and Roger Eno (EG)
	Working Backwards 1983-1973 (10 album boxed set)
	Music For Films Volume 2 (*Working Backwards* boxed set only) (Editions EG)
1985	*Thursday Afternoon* (compact disc) (EG)

singles

1972	*Virginia Plain* Roxy Music (EG)
1973	*Pyjamarama* Roxy Music (EG)
1974	*Seven Deadly Finns* (EG)
1975	*The Lion Sleeps Tonight (Wimoweh)* (EG)
1977	*King's Lead Hat/RAF* Brian Eno/Snatch (EG)
1981	*The Jezebel Spirit* Brian Eno/David Byrne (EG)
1983	*Rarities* (EP: *Working Backwards* boxed set only) (Editions EG)

album productions and co-productions

1973	*Portsmouth Sinfonia Plays The Popular Classics* Portsmouth Sinfonia (Transatlantic)
1974	*Hallelujah* Portsmouth Sinfonia (Transatlantic)
	Fear John Cale (Island)
1975	*The Sinking of The Titanic* Gavin Bryars (Obscure/Editions EG)
	Ensemble Pieces Christopher Hobbs/John Adams/Gavin Bryars (Obscure/Editions EG)
	New And Rediscovered Musical Instruments David Toop/Max Eastley (Obscure/Editions EG)
	Lucky Lief And The Longships Robert Calvert (United Artists)
1976	*Voices And Instruments* Jan Steele/John Cage (Obscure/Editions EG)
	Decay Music Michael Nyman (Obscure/Editions EG)
	Music From The Penguin Cafe Penguin Cafe Orchestra (Obscure/Editions EG)
1977	*Ultravox!* Ultravox (Island)
1978	*More Songs About Buildings And Food* Talking Heads (Sire)
	Q: Are We Not Men? A: We Are Devo! Devo (Virgin)
	No New York Contortions/Teenage Jesus and the Jerks/Mars/DNA (Antilles)
	Machine Music John White/Gavin Bryars (Obscure/Editions EG)
	Irma – An Opera Tom Phillips/Gavin Bryars/Fred Orton (Obscure/Editions EG)
	The Pavilion Of Dreams Harold Budd (Obscure/Editions EG)

1979	*Fear Of Music* Talking Heads (Sire)
1980	*Ambient 3: Day Of Radiance* Laraaji (Editions EG)
	Remain In Light Talking Heads (Sire)
1981	*The Pace Setters* Edikanfo (Editions EG)
1984	*The Unforgettable Fire* U2 (Island)

primary collaborations

1972	*Roxy Music* Roxy Music (EG)
1973	*For Your Pleasure* Roxy Music (EG)
	(No Pussyfooting) Fripp/Eno* (Editions EG)
1974	*June 1, 1974* Kevin Ayres/John Cale/Eno/Nico (Island)
1975	*Evening Star* Fripp/Eno* (Editions EG)
1976	*801 Live* 801* (EG)
1977	*Cluster & Eno* Cluster/Eno (Sky)
	Low David Bowie (RCA)
	Heroes David Bowie (RCA)
1978	*After the Heat* Eno/Moebius/Roedelius* (Sky)
1979	*Lodger* David Bowie (RCA)
1980	*Ambient 2: The Plateaux Of Mirror* Harold Budd/Brian Eno* (Editions EG)
	Fourth World Vol. 1: Possible Musics Jon Hassell/Brian Eno* (Editions EG)
1981	*My Life In The Bush Of Ghosts* Brian Eno/David Byrne* (EG)
1984	*The Pearl* Harold Budd/Brian Eno with Daniel Lanois* (Editions EG)
1985	*Hybrid* Michael Brook with Brian Eno and Daniel Lanois (Editions EG)
	Voices Roger Eno with Brian Eno and Daniel Lanois (Editions EG)
	(Eno also produced or co-produced on these collaborations.)*

secondary collaborations

1971	*The Great Learning* Cornelius Cardew/Scratch Orchestra (Deutsche Grammophon)
1973	*Matching Mole's Little Red Record* Matching Mole (CBS)
1974	*Captain Lockheed and the Starfighters* Robert Calvert (United Artists)
	The End Nico (Island)
	Lady June's Linguistic Leprosy Lady June (Caroline)
	The Lamb Lies Down On Broadway Genesis (Charisma)
1975	*Diamond Head* Phil Manzanera (EG)
	Mainstream Quiet Sun (Editions EG)
	Slow Dazzle John Cale (Island)
	Helen Of Troy John Cale (Island)
	Ruth Is Stranger Than Richard Robert Wyatt (Virgin)
	Peter And The Wolf Various artists (RSO)
1977	*Listen Now!* Phil Manzanera/801 (EG)
	Rain Dances Camel (Nova)
1978	*Jubilee* Film soundtrack: various artists (EG)
1979	*Exposure* Robert Fripp (EG)
	In A Land Of Clear Colors (limited edition of 1000 copies with book) Robert Sheckley (Galeria el Mensajero, Ibiza)
1981	*Dream Theory In Malaya: Fourth World Vol. 2* Jon Hassell (Editions EG)
	Songs From 'The Catherine Wheel' David Byrne (Sire)
1982	*One Down* Material (Elektra/Celluloid)
1984	*Caribbean Sunset* John Cale (Island/Ze)
	Dune Film soundtrack: various artists (Polydor)
1985	*Africana* Theresa de Sio (Polydor)

selected commissions to score music

1975	*The Devil's Men:* Frixos Constantine (UK: film)
1976	*Sparrowfall:* Alan Drury (UK: play)
	Sebastiane: Derek Jarman (UK: film)
1977	*Science Report: 'Alternative 3':* Anglia (UK: TV)
1978	*Jubilee:* Derek Jarman (UK: film)
1982	Silk Cut: Collett, Dickinson, Pearce (UK: commercial)
	Apollo: Al Reinert (USA: film)
1984	*Great River Journeys of the World: 'The Nile'* BBC2 (UK: TV)
	Dune: 'Prophecy theme' David Lynch (USA: film)
1985	*Creation of the Universe* theme: PBS (USA: TV)

selected uses of *Music For Films*
and other compositions

1976	*Heritage Of Islam:* Central Office of Information (UK: film)
1978	*Hazel:* Thames (UK: TV)
1979	*The Hard Way:* Stuart Urban (UK: film)
	The Greeks: BBC2 (UK: TV)
1980	Spray 'n' Fry: Wasey, Campbell·Ewald (UK: commercial)
	The Falls: Peter Greenaway (UK: film)
	The Shock Of The New: BBC2 (UK: TV)
	Riding The Summer Sun: BBC2 (UK: TV)
	Opel cars: The Rally Club (UK: commercial)
	The Sunken Tomb Of Truk Lagoon: Chris Goosen (UK: film)
	Good For Business: BBC2 (UK: TV)
1981	*Arena* theme: BBC2 (UK: TV)
	Warming, warning: Thames (UK: TV)
	The Money Programme: BBC2 (UK: TV)
1982	Seiko men's watches: ADI/NHK (Japan: commercial)
	Les Maitres Du Temps: Patrice Fichet (France: film)
	The Underground Elgar: Yorkshire (UK: TV)
	World In Action: 'The Sinai Desert' Granada (UK: TV)
	Horizon: 'Rape Seed Oil' BBC2 (UK: TV)
	Same As It Ever Was: Albert Falzon (Australia: film)
	American Football theme: Channel 4 (UK: TV)
	Remembrance: Channel 4 (UK: TV)
	Day Two: Pilobolus (USA: dance company)
	Joy: Serge Bergon (France: film)
	We Learn To Ski: Channel 4 (UK: TV)
1983	*The Longest War:* 'The Middle East' Thames (UK: TV)
	Hans van Sweeden: Louis van Gasteren (Holland: film)
1984	*The Road To Timbuktu:* Albert Falzon (Australia: film)
	Astronomer's Gallery: London Planetarium (UK: exhibition)
	Omnibus: 'Muzak' BBC2 (UK: TV)
1985	*Before The Jungle Gods:* Albert Falzon (Australia: film)
	Zanussi electrical products: Wight, Collins, Rutherford, Scott (UK: commercial)

video works

1979	*Two Fifth Avenue* (for three or four video monitors)	1
1980	*White Fence* (for three or four monitors)	2
	North From Broome (for one monitor)	3
1981	*Mistaken Memories Of Mediaeval Manhattan* (for one monitor)	4
1983	*Video sculptures*	5
1984	*Video paintings*	6
	Thursday Afternoon (seven video paintings for one monitor) (released by Sony)	7

(*First prize best non-narrative video, Video Culture Canada, 1984.)

audio-visual installations

1979	July	Kitchen Center, New York, USA—**1**
1980	February	Paul Ide Gallery, Brussels, Belgium—**1**
	May	Hallwals, Buffalo, New York, USA—**1**
	June	La Guardia Airport, New York, USA—**1**
	July	Walker Art Center, Minneapolis, USA—**1**
	August	New Gallery of Contemporary Art, Cleveland, USA—**1**
		Contemporary Arts Museum, Houston, Texas, USA—**1**
	Aug./Sept.	ARC, Toronto, Canada—**2, 4** (early version)
	September	Grand Central Station, New York, USA—**2**
1981	June	*Aluminium Nights,* Bonds, New York, USA—**2**
	July	University Art Museum, Berkeley, California, USA—**3, 4**
		Harpo's Bazaar, Bologna, Italy—**4**
	July/Aug.	The New Museum, New York, USA—**4**
	Aug./Sept.	St Louis Arts Museum, St Louis, USA—**1**
	November	The Art Gallery, Toronto, Canada—**4**
1982	February	Vancouver Art Gallery, Vancouver, Canada—**4**
	Feb./March	Espace Lyonnais d'Art Contemporain, Lyon, France—**4**
	April/May	Biennale of Sydney, Australia—**4**

	May/June	Stedelijk Museum, Amsterdam, Holland—**4**
	June	Almeida Theatre, London, England—**4**
	July	ICA, London, England—**4**
1983	January	Museum of Modern Art, Oxford, England—**4**
		Concord Gallery, New York, USA—**4**
	April	Galleria del Cavallino, Venice, Italy—**4**
	May	Festival of Vienna, Vienna, Austria—**4**
	July/Aug.	La Foret Museum, Akasaka, Tokyo, Japan (large installation with thirty-six monitors)
	September	Centre National d'Art et de Culture Georges Pompidou, Paris, France—**4**
	December	ICA, Boston, USA—**5**
1984	January	Der Hang zum Gesamtkunstwerk, Festival, Institute Unzeit, West Berlin, Germany—**4**
1984	February	Tegel Airport, Berlin, Germany (audio only)
	March	Maison d'Accueil, Lille, France—**4**
	May	Maison de la Culture, Grenoble, France—**4**
	Sept./Oct.	*The Luminous Image,* Stedelijk Museum, Amsterdam, Holland—**5, 6**
		Crystals, Church of S. Carpoforo, Milan, Italy—**5**
	October	Video Culture Canada, Toronto, Canada—**7**
	December	Century 66, Toronto, Canada—**7**
1985	January	2nd International Contemporary Art Fair, Olympia, London, England—**5, 6**
	February	Museo del Risorgimento, Rome, Italy—**5**
		Another Room, Frankfurter Musikmesse, Kongresshalle, Frankfurt, Germany—**4, 7**
	June	Galleria del Cavallino, Venice, Italy—**6**
	October	1st Frankfurt Public Design Fair, Frankfurt, Germany (audio only)
	November	Kulturhuset, Stockholm, Sweden—**4, 5, 6**
		Art Fair, Zwirner Gallerie, Cologne, Germany—**5, 6, 7**
1986	January	Barbican Art Centre, London, England—**5, 6**

publications

1968	*Music For Non-Musicians* (25 copies of privately printed pamphlet)
1975	*Oblique Strategies* (limited edition of 500 copies: revised and reissued in 1978 and 1979) with Peter Schmidt
1976	'Generating and Organizing Variety in the Arts' *Studio International* November/December

Brian Eno – Photograph by Ray Stevenson

BIOGRAPHICAL NOTES – RUSSELL MILLS

1952 Born 22 November, Ripon, Yorkshire, England.

education

1962–70 Royal Alexandra & Albert School, Surrey, England.
1970–71 Canterbury College of Art, Kent: Foundation Studies.
1971–74 Maidstone College of Art, Kent: Graphic Design/Illustration
Dip. AD (1st Class Hons.)
1974–77 Royal College of Art, London: Illustration MA (1st Class Hons.)

awards

1976 Royal College of Art Travelling Scholarship: Berlin.
1977 Berger Award (for RCA Degree Show)
1983 International Editorial Design Three: Award of Excellence for Total Design of
'International Resource Management' publications
1984 Designers & Art Directors Association Silver Award – for Most Outstanding
Complete Magazine for 'International Resource Management' publications.

teaching/lecturing

1977 Maidstone College of Art: Illustration
Watford School of Art: Foundation Studies
East Ham College of Technology: Graphics
1977–80 Presented Annual Seminars for Syracuse University Arts Department Exchange
Students: ICA London
1978 Royal College of Art: Illustration
Watford School of Art: Foundation Studies
1979 National College of Art & Design: Fine Art
Brighton Polytechnic: Postgraduate Printmaking
Brighton Polytechnic: Graphics
1980 Chelsea School of Art: Postgraduate Printmaking
Chelsea School of Art: Graphics
Birmingham Polytechnic: Graphics
Lanchester Polytechnic: Graphics
1981 Royal College of Art: Illustration
Liverpool Polytechnic: Sculpture
Liverpool Polytechnic: Illustration
Birmingham Polytechnic: Postgraduate Graphics
School of Visual Arts, New York: Illustration
Parsons School of Design, New York: Illustration
Pratt Institute, New York: Illustration
Corsham School of Art: Illustration
1982 Lanchester Polytechnic: Illustration
Kingston Polytechnic: Illustration
Royal College of Art: Illustration
Chelsea School of Art: Postgraduate Printmaking
Lancashire (Preston) Polytechnic: Graphics
St. Martin's School of Art: Illustration
1983 Architectural Association: Special Projects
National College of Art & Design, Dublin: Illustration
Royal College of Art: Illustration
1984 Royal College of Art: Illustration
Leeds Polytechnic: Illustration/Printmaking
Lancashire (Preston) Polytechnic: Graphics
Lancashire (Preston) Polytechnic: Fine Art
1985 Chelsea School of Art: Illustration
Leeds Polytechnic: Illustration/Printmaking
Leeds Polytechnic: Fine Art
Liverpool Polytechnic: Illustration
Lancashire (Preston) Polytechnic: Graphics
Bournemouth College of Art & Design: Photography/Audio-Visual
National College of Art & Design Dublin: Illustration
1986 Chelsea School of Art: course advisor, illustration

exhibitions

1975 *Royal College of Art: Illustration:* Kettles Yard Gallery, Cambridge
Dog Show: Royal College of Art
1976 *Air Show:* Royal College of Art
Folio Society Illustration Awards: Royal College of Art
Association of Illustrators: Reed House, Piccadilly
European Illustration: Design Centre, London & Touring
1977 *SWALK/KLAWS:* Illustrators Gallery, London
Association of Illustrators: Reed House, Piccadilly
European Illustration: ICA London & Touring
Degree Shows: Royal College of Art
Geek Work No 1: Air Gallery, London
Geek Work No 2: Greenwich Theatre Art Gallery, London
1978 *Contemporary British Illustrators:* Belgrave Gallery, London
Artworks & Bookworks: Geek Magazine: Touring, USA: Canada: Australia:
Europe
Association of Illustrators: Reed House, London
European Illustration: Centre National d'Art et de Culture Georges Pompidou,
Paris: touring in Europe
Cover Art: Illustrators Gallery, London
1979 *Five English Artists:* Galerie Mokum, Amsterdam
Artificial Light: Newcastle-Upon-Tyne Polytechnic Art Gallery
Images To Order: Scottish & Welsh Arts Councils Touring Show
International Competition of Young Painters: Sofia, Bulgaria
Shoes: Neal Street Gallery, London
Association of Illustrators: Mall Galleries, London
European Illustration: Somerset House Gallery, London
Group Show: Curwen Gallery, London
1980 *FINE LINES* (one person exhibition): Thumb Gallery, London
Into Print: Royal College of Art, London
Creative Handbook Diary Art: Creative Handbook, London
Art à la Carte: Thumb Gallery, London
100 × 100 × 100: Gallerit, Stockholm, Sweden
Association of Illustrators: Mall Galleries, London
European Illustration: Hobhouse Court Gallery, London: touring
1981 *Art in Advertising:* Sainsbury Centre for the Visual Arts, University of East Anglia
Summer Reflections: Thumb Gallery, London
Gallery Artists: Moira Kelly Gallery, London
Association of Illustrators: Seven Dials Gallery, London
European Illustration: National Theatre, London: touring
*A Weekly Look Behind the Scenes (25th Anniversary of New Scientist
Magazine):* Neal Street Gallery, London
Culture Shock: Midland Group Gallery, Nottingham
100 × 100 × 100: Gallerit, Stockholm, Sweden
MZUI: Waterloo Gallery, London (recording installation)
1982 *Interiors:* Curwen Gallery, London
Gallery Artists: Moira Kelly Gallery, London
Personal View: Thumb Gallery, London
Hayward Annual 1982/British Drawing: Hayward Gallery, London
Xerographers Summer Show: Xerographers Gallery, London
European Illustration: National Theatre, London: touring
Sainsbury's Images for Today: Graves Art Gallery, Sheffield: touring
MU:ZE:UM/Traces: Museum of Modern Art, Oxford (Audio-Visual installation)
1983 *. . . returns an echo: (one person exhibition):* Curwen Gallery, London
. . . returns an echo: Abbot Hall Art Gallery, Kendal, Cumbria
. . . returns an echo: Lancashire (Preston) Polytechnic
Personal Choice: AOI Gallery, London
Collage: Curwen Gallery, London
Britain Salutes New York: Brooklyn Museum of Modern Art, New York
European Illustration: National Theatre, London
The Music Show: Thumb Gallery, London
1984 *Group Show:* Curwen Gallery, London
Association of Illustrators: Five Dials Gallery, London
European Illustration: 1974–84 Tour: Cooper-Hewitt Museum & tour
The Box Train: Touring Show
Ten Years On: Thumb Gallery (10th Anniversary), London
Group Show: Roughs Gallery, London
On the Small Side: Curwen Gallery, London
D & AD Awards, London
1985 *2nd International Contemporary Art Fair:* Olympia, London

Association of Illustrators: Five Dials Gallery, London
Out of Line: ICA London
British Illustration from Caxton to Chlöe: British Council Show of British Illustration: Royal College of Art: touring world-wide
Exhibition for *Ambit* magazine at Royal Festival Hall, London
1986   *Ciphers (one person show):* Curwen Gallery, London (March)

work in Public Collections
Victoria & Albert Museum
Kent County Council

work in private collections
England, Holland, Germany, Belgium, Switzerland, Israel, USA, Canada, France, Australia, Japan, Cyprus, Yugoslavia

published/commissioned works

1976   The Luftschiffer Park Piece: Limited Edition Book 150 copies
1977   Evening Breakers: Limited Edition Book 250 copies
1977   Geek: Limited Edition Book 500 copies
        (All the above published by the Illustration Department, Royal College of Art, London)

Ambit; AOI Newsletter; Architect's Journal; ARK; Aurum Press; *Bananas; Beat The Drum; Bopeye; Boston Globe* (USA); Boudisque Records (Holland); British Council; *Building;* Butler Cornfeld Dedman Design; *Campaign;* CAP Communications; Cherry Red Records; *City Limits; Classical Music:* Collins/Fontana Publishing; Cooper-Thirkell Design; *Corporating Computing;* Creative Handbook Diary; *Creative Review; Design;* Dolon Press; EG Management; *EG Newsletter* (USA); *Engineering; Enovations;* Ericsson (Sweden); *Esquire* (USA); European Illustration; *Exhibitor;* Faber and Faber Publishers; *The Face; Film Form; Fool's Mate* (Japan); Gallaghers/Benson and Hedges; *Game;* Hamish Hamilton Publishers; *Harpers and Queen;* HSAG Design; *Illustration* (Japan); *Illustrators; Inklings* (Royal College of Art); International Resource Management; *Karm* (Sweden); *Knave;* Logica; *Mainstream* (Japan); *Melody Maker;* Michael Peters Design; *Mindscapes* (USA); *Ms London;* Moira Kelly Gallery, London; Museum of Modern Art, Oxford; *New Musical Express; New Scientist; New Society; New Style; Now!; Observer;* Opal Ltd.; Oxford University Press; *Radio Times;* Redwood Publishing; Reuters; *Rolling Stone* (USA); *Saturday Night Magazine* (Canada); Spy Records (USA); *Sunday Express; Sunday Times; Tension* (Australia); *Three; Time Out; Touch;* Virgin Books; Virgin Records; *Viz; Vogue; Vox* (Ireland); *Weekend* (Canada); *Zoom*

TV and radio

1977   London Weekend TV programme concerning contemporary illustration
1980   Capital Radio: interviews with Sarah Ward: preview of *FINE LINES* exhibition
        Double Vision. BBC2 Arena Arts programme
1980–85 Radio Station JJJ, Australian Broadcasting Commission; series of satellite link interviews
1983   Saturday Live; BBC Radio One; interview/review of *... returns an echo* exhibition

miscellaneous commissioned projects

1978   Produced 3-screen 9-projector audio-visual presentation for Design & Art Directors Association Lectures
1979   Designed European Illustration Exhibition, display sculpture and publicity; Somerset House, London

recordings/performances/audio-visual installations

1980   *Kluba Cupol:* 12 inch record with Bruce Gilbert and Graham Lewis
        Kluba Cupol: performance: Notre Dame Hall, London. (played synthesizer: designed stage set-cum-visual score)
1981   *3R4:* LP with Bruce Gilbert and Graham Lewis
        DOME: series of LPs with Bruce Gilbert and Graham Lewis
        MZUI: recording installation: Waterloo Gallery, London
1982   *MZUI:* LP released of recordings from above
        Sydney Biennale: live mix to air via satellite link
1982–83 *MU:ZE:UM/Traces:* Museum of Modern Art, Oxford (Audio-Visual installation)

1984   *Domend,* Le Havre, France: audio-visual performance with Graham Lewis and Chris Evans
1985   *Only Connect:* Museum of Modern Art, Oxford: Sound performance with Shinro Ohtake: 'Live Ones' week
        (All above activities made or collaborated with Bruce Gilbert and Graham Lewis)

audio-visual/video installations for Brian Eno

1982   ICA, London
        Museum of Modern Art, Oxford
1983   Galleria del Cavallino, Venice, Italy
        Festival of Vienna, Austria
        Centre National d'Art et de Culture Georges Pompidou, Paris, France
        Riverside: BBC TV London
1984   Institute Unzeit – Der Hang Zum Gesamtkunstwerk Festival, West Berlin, Germany
1985   Frankfurter Musikmesse, Frankfurt, Germany

Russell Mills – Photograph by David Buckland

ACKNOWLEDGEMENTS

142

✚ Rick Poynor studied the history of art at Manchester University. He writes for a monthly computer magazine, and is working on a biography of Brian Eno.

✚ Malcolm Garrett studied typography, and graphic design at Reading University, and Manchester Polytechnic. In 1978 he founded the Assorted iMaGes design stronghold, which even now maintains its timeless pursuit of the 'desirable object'.

The authors and publishers are deeply grateful to the following people for their various contributions and support throughout the evolution and preparation of this book:

✚ Anthea Norman-Taylor at Opal Ltd. who has constantly provided encouragement, calm and assistance in supplying essential information and textual material.
✚ Pete Townshend, who, as commissioning editor at Faber and Faber Ltd, created the space for this book, and who has sympathetically guided its progress throughout.
✚ Graeme Bartlett, Bruce Elder and Arnold Frollowes at Radio Station JJJ, Sydney, Australia; for their continuing interest, support and for their inspired programmes and interviews, extracts of which appear within.
✚ Ann Mills who has lived closer to this project than anyone apart from the authors themselves and who has patiently tolerated the long hours and sometimes chaotic studio conditions caused in the making of the images.
✚ Clare Beck (former Director of Thumb Gallery, London) and all at Thumb who first exhibited the work and who have continued to support the development of Mills's work.
✚ Mike Clark who kindly and unwittingly supplied the title 'More Dark than Shark'.
✚ Jane Poynor and Hilary Young for hours of discussion, and their careful scrutiny of the five commentaries.
✚ Bill MacCormick for his reminiscences about an exciting time in rock music.
✚ Tutors and students (past and present) of the Illustration Department of the Royal College of Art, London, for their spirit.
✚ Jane Hindley and all at the Curwen Gallery, London, who now exhibit the work of Mills.
✚ Thanks also to the numerous people who have constantly encouraged, offered advice and support in the process of compiling this book.

Silent Union
...Alert...
Sounding Device(s)
Taking Bearings
...Escalator...
Remote Control
Shared Visions
Actum Ne Agas (Latin: Do Not What is Already Done)
Diamonds Cut Diamonds
Pale & Spectre ... ('...Youth' – Keats of his T.B.)
Smoke Screen
Eight Nought One
801 File
Immaculate Conception
Strange Craft
Silent Future
Accumulated Wisdoms
Pooled Potential
Pooled Perspectives
Hammer To Desire (from 'Kings Lead Hat')
Running Order
Curious Visions
Strange Visions
Alternative Visions
Invented Visions
Beyond Visions
Immaculate Visions
Parallel Visions
Illuminated Visions
Mysterious Visions
Essential Visions
Dual Visions
Duplex Visions
Chance Visions
Secret Forces
Future Incidents
...Destiny...
Trigger Of Destiny
Cerebral Triggers
Future $\frac{\text{Codes}}{\text{Ciphers}}$
Tangents In Tandem
Tandem Tangents
Tandem Fragments/Splinters/Shrapnel
Occupy The Headquarters (First) (from 'Chinese Art Of Love')
Surprise Attack
Solutions/Dissolutions
Solving Dissolves
The Biology Of Purpose (from 'King's Lead Hat')
Splitting Ions (In The Ether) (from 'St Elmo's Fire')
Open Stick & Delphic Doldrums (from 'Sky Saw')
Forcing The Lines (To The Snow) (from 'Taking Tiger Mountain' (By Strategy))
Brain In The Table (from 'Put A Straw Under Baby')
Heart In The Chair (from 'Put A Straw Under Baby')
In/Advance Of The Past
Advance Past
Advance
We/Break Cover
Break Cover
After You (a study in the decline of manners)
Tactical Manoeuvres
Beyond Defined Perimeters
Beyond Perimeters
Scorched Earth
Hit & Run
Wired For Sound
Perpetual Motion
Lyrical Miracle
Light Active
Indefinite Divisibility (title of paintings by Yves Tanguy 1942)
The Silent Zone
Aeriel
Shrapnel
Allied Powers
Eons
Eno's Eons
Western Promise
Book Of Wonders
The Eighth Wonder
Heaven's Door
Dividing Lines
Fine Lines
Random Moves
Random Order
Alternative Practices
Duplex...
...Duplicity
Double Vision
Double Alteration
Inventing Situations (from 'Found a Job' by Talking Heads)
Binocular
Chance Variations
Reflex Time

Rebus
Prism
Maze
Golden Sections
The Order
Exploring...
Bones Of Ice
Dark Tangents
Dark Door(s)
Arcane Benefits Of Creed (anag. of 'Before & After Science')
Strange Journeys
Fragments Of A Fiction
Trance Mutations
The Low Drone Ranger
Steel Ciphers
Dark Ciphers
Time Ciphers
$\left.\begin{array}{l}\text{Tentative}\\ \text{Bold}\end{array}\right\}$ Movements In An $\frac{\text{Uncertain}}{\text{Unknown}}$ Landscape
Tactics Of Trance
Trance Behaviours
Tentative Movements/Manoeuvres/Moments/Memories/Futures
Fragments Of $\left\{\begin{array}{l}\text{A Hidden}\\ \text{An Undiscovered}\end{array}\right\}$ Fiction/Future
Repercussions Of An Undiscovered Proposition
Anticipated $\frac{\text{Presents}}{\text{Presence}}$ Of A Future
Various $\frac{\text{Presents}}{\text{Presence}}$ From A Future
$\frac{\text{Probable}}{\text{Dark}}$ Incidents From An Uncertain Future
Uncertain Futures Last $\frac{\text{Hard}}{\text{Sharp}}$ Shadows
$\left.\begin{array}{l}\text{Fragments}\\ \text{Splinters}\\ \text{Shards}\end{array}\right\}$ $\begin{array}{l}\text{From}\\ \text{Of}\end{array}\}$ A (Broken) Future
No Man's Trance
No Man's Dream
Tactical Trances
Trance Tactics
Dead Reckoning
Celestial Navigation
Per Ardua Ad Astra
Sound & Vision (From 'Low' By David Bowie)
...Parallels...
Two Brains
...Inventory...
Index...
Vehicles Of Vision
Visual Evidence
Random Activity
...Cycles...
Persuasion In The Air
Essential Stimuli
Future Perfect
Young Contemporaries
...Harmony...   ...Harmonies...   ...Harmonious...
Electric Nerves
Ions Of Eno
Eno's Ions
Lines Of Force
Without Parallel
Steered From Afar
Illuminated Discords
Horizontal Retort
Back Number(s)
...Relay...
...Beam...
...Contact...
Cheer In Whispers – (from 'Chamber of Horrors' film screenplay by Stephen Kandel)
Whispered Cheers
Minds Eye
Eyes Mind
Stranger Than Systems
...Soundings...
Stereoscopic Visions
Distant Visions
Rare Visions
Alluring Visions
The Acoustics Of Vision
Infinite Vision
...Net...
...Network...
More Dark Than Shark (by Michael Clark)
Strange Familiar Strange
Strangely Familiar
Exotic Visions
Seen Sound
Sound Seen
Sound Sense
Curious Acoustics
According To Another

Curious Displays
Curious Explorations
Curious Codes
Curious Articulations
Curious Calibrations
Disappearing Acts
...Escapes...
Curious Anticipations
Ten Thousand Things
Lucent Soundings
Lucent Visions
Rubic Visions   Rubric Visions
Shipshape Mishape
Shipshape Mishapes
Shipshape Mistakes
Shipshape Mishaps, Perhaps
Fringe/Of Memory Tinged
...Limitrophe
Curious Luminous
Luminous Visions
Strange Attractors
Delectable Displays
Gleam Of The Fabulous (from 'Fireside' by Seamus Heaney)
Lucent Semaphores
Smithereen Semaphores/Codes/Ciphers
Lost Through Practice
Imagic Soundings
Of Detours & Delays
Deeper Still
Technician(s) Of Ecstacy
Arch Of Sky
Extreme Mediums   Normal Surprises   Complementary Contrasts
Constant changes

Anagrams Of The Names Brian Eno/Russell T. Mills

In A Lens Rome Still Blurs
Aliens Blurt Morse
I Smell Oval Rib Tunnels
More Blurs In A Still Lens
Alien Morse Blurs (T)
Aliens Blur Morse (T)
Morse Blurs Alien (T)
Still Morsels In A Blur (EN)
Still Omen, Blurlers Rain
Still Omen, Rainless Blur
Sell Roman Rebus In Lilt
On Rimless Bull Entrails
N, Lilts All In Rebus Morse
Rebus 'N', Lilts All In Morse
Still Rebus 'N', All In Morse
Dan Rust. Million Sellers
Ban Millions: Rust Seller
Lesson 'R': Till Submarine 'L' ...
Unlimitless Ball Snorer
I Sit Sullen, Born Smaller
Small, Sullen Iron Tribes
RR ...Boil All Sluts In Semen
Troubles In Small Liners
Small Roubles, Tin Liners
Tin Roubles, Small Liners
Liners In Small Troubles
'L' Brilliant Moss Unreals
Bus Rant! Million Sellers
Less Blur On A Still Miner